DANCING
WITH DAHLIA

By the Author

Dancing Toward Stardust

Dancing With Dahlia

Visit us at www.boldstrokesbooks.com

DANCING WITH DAHLIA

by

Julia Underwood

2024

CREDITS
EDITOR: RUTH STERNGLANTZ
PRODUCTION DESIGN: STACIA SEAMAN
COVER DESIGN BY TAMMY SEIDICK

Acknowledgments

First, I owe a huge thank you to Rad and the rest of the BSB family for their continued support. Sandy Lowe is always there with help and advice. My editor, Ruth Sternglantz, has done her best to make me a better writer, and always with patience and humor. And then there are so many other people behind the scenes who have helped bring this book to completion with clear and timely publication guidance, cover choices, deadlines, production design, eBook design—the list is long.

I can't thank my friend and first reader, P, enough for taking the time to read the draft manuscript and offer invaluable comments and suggestions. There are supportive family members who have endured my neglect, and also my right-hand pup with his designated seat next to the delete button. And without all of the amazing authors who dedicate their time and skills to writing inspiring sapphic romance novels, I would never have been motivated to begin writing my own.

To you, the readers, I offer my deepest gratitude—I hope your expectations are rewarded. To those who have taken the time to leave thoughtful reviews—your feedback is deeply appreciated. To those who wrote to tell me how much my first book had moved and connected with them—it makes every hour at the keyboard worthwhile. Thank you so much. And for everyone taking the journey of two hearts… happy ending, always.

To all the animal rescue groups in the world
who bring a little light into so many lives.
To all the rescued animals,
who when celebrated with love, pass that light along.

CHAPTER ONE

It was late, and the low lighting wasn't an accident—it was orchestrated for the ambiance and mystique it created. Dal knew that. She'd been here before, although maybe not on this stool, or nursing a vodka tonic, or even at this address. Because at forty-one, Dal was no virgin to hookups.

Taking a sip from the glass in front of her, she considered why she was here on this Friday night, at this bar. There was the easy answer, and then there was a different developing need, deeper than flesh, that was beginning to make the easy answer not so easy anymore. Dal continued to nurse her drink and contemplate her options.

That was before the nice looking woman with the advertised ample cleavage paused on Dal during her not-so-subtle reconnaissance of the crowd, then attempted a nonchalant approach. Dal didn't hold it against her. She knew those exact moves.

"Looking for something, sugar?" this potential bed partner asked with a suggestive dance of her eyebrows. "Because maybe I've got it," she finished with a drawl, handing the next move to Dal.

Dal suspected they had both come for that easy answer. But damn if the *sugar* didn't obliterate the ambiance and mystique that might still have escorted her past the dawning unwelcome clarity that she was in the wrong place tonight. *Sugar* slammed Dal right back into her challenging childhood—and the loving little dog named Sugar. The canine who had been the sweet spot in a youth of bitter rebuke.

Once past Sugar's memory, Dal thought about the question: *Looking for something?* Dal had plenty of money, adequate status and power, and a self-imposed pledge that precluded allowing herself to be monetarily dependent on anyone, without control of her life, or vulnerable to heartbreak ever again. At least as much as she had a choice in it. Those few individuals currently embedded in her heart were all she wanted. So, there was the answer—the one that brought Dal to a place like this so she didn't have to compromise that pledge. The one word that was likely the response the woman was waiting for, although dressed up in a bit of small talk, faked interest, and flirtation. Sex.

Dal looked into the woman's hungry eyes and responded with a one-word answer. "No."

Then Dal pushed the rest of her drink away, slipped off the barstool, and headed out the door to home. To a therapeutic shower where she could answer the question for herself. To wake up in the morning to a life that she had defined, that needed to be enough—defined by her young daughter, the older woman who had essentially become a mother to her, the lucrative company she had built, and the nonprofit that helped fill her soul. To a Saturday morning jog at Lake Merritt with her rescue mutt, Einstein.

Piper had just been about to kiss the beautiful woman she'd been flirting with when suddenly she was dodging drone fire on a battlefield. She sat up in bed, heart pounding and hyperventilating. "It was only a dream," she whispered to the alarmed cat who had been sleeping at the foot of her bed. "Don't tell me because I already know—as much as I love you, I need to be sharing a bed with someone besides my favorite feline." As her breathing leveled out, Piper realized the sound of the rocket barrage had not let up. Well, she was awake now, even if she'd planned to sleep late on this Saturday morning. She crawled out from under the covers with a good idea of who was behind the persistent bombardment.

"I know you're a little lion, but I'd run if I was you." Caught between fight or flight, Sunny took her advice and headed to the kitchen to recheck his empty food bowl.

Taking a deep breath, Piper grounded herself before she made her way across her living room, mentally welcoming her plants to a new day before reaching the front door.

"Get your lazy backside out of bed and open up." Bryce's voice drifted through the wooden barrier.

"Keep your shirt on and tone it down." Piper opened the door and dragged Bryce inside before she woke up the entire apartment complex.

"About time, Piper Fernley." Bryce seemed totally unaware, or didn't care, that she'd become the alarm clock that Piper had refused to set last night. Their lifelong best-friends status allowed Bryce a pass, but just barely.

"I was having the best time I've had in ages with a stunning woman who was coming to the realization that I'm a sex goddess until you put me into World War III."

Bryce chuckled as she stood and checked out Piper's morning display of untamed hair and sleeping attire. "The beautiful, younger blonde who worships you for your body?"

Piper couldn't stifle a yawn. "That's her. The one and only." This was a joke they shared, the imaginary woman in her life—a life with no meaningful relationship on the horizon.

"So, where is she now, Pipes?" Bryce took an exaggerated look toward Piper's bedroom.

Bryce had called her Pipes for over twenty-five years, ever since she'd realized Piper had a big mouth and that Piper enjoyed humming and singing to plants. Piper had given Bryce the nickname Blaze because she'd always loved running and she was fast. Without her, Piper knew she probably wouldn't have taken up running.

"She's been relegated back into my vault of slumber-induced fantasies."

Piper wanted love with her lust, and that type of love eluded her. She was lonely for the piece that was still missing in her busy life. She'd had four girlfriends since coming out and some lackluster encounters in the year since Nettie had explained that polyamory was a recognized relationship practice—she'd just forgotten to inform Piper she'd changed her mind about their agreed upon monogamy. Piper had decided to focus on the things in her life she enjoyed and give dating a break for a while.

Every time she considered that maybe her expectations were too high, Piper always came back to the conclusion that she didn't want a relationship that had an expiration date stamped on the package close to the time it started, and she didn't want to just settle. Piper wanted what her boss, Cate, had found with her girlfriend, Meg. What Bryce and Hannah, her wife, had found. She'd witnessed the change in each of these women when they'd built a loving relationship with the right person, that subtle shift from engaging, active woman to one with the added aura of contentment and completion. Two people loving each other, committed to each other, and looking at growing old together.

No more wasting her time with someone who couldn't love her or who she didn't love. Experience had taught her a few things, but she wasn't going to say it in those terms to Bryce this morning.

"It's Saturday. I don't remember a plan for you to be here at my apartment waking me up at the crack of dawn."

Piper had intended to sleep in after staying up late last night writing her first blog. Her boss's girlfriend had a long-running pseudonymous personal blog with tens of thousands of followers, but new interests and responsibilities meant it was time to end that chapter. Having loved writing and kept a journal for years, Piper'd been thrilled when Meg called to ask if Piper was interested in starting a blog that she could point her numerous followers to as she wound down.

"Hey, I thought our kindergarten pinkie promise of forever friendship represented a mi casa es tu casa relationship." Bryce's smirk meant Piper wasn't going to win this discussion. "I'm here to drag you to Lake Merritt for a run this morning. Working in that San Francisco law office might pay the rent, but it's not going to keep you in shape for that woman of your dreams."

"I have to meet that woman first," Piper replied. "A run at Lake Merritt? What about coffee? And breakfast?" She and Bryce went through some variation of this routine about once a month, when they both had a Saturday morning free. She never won, having to put in the sweat before the sweets.

Bryce reached down to pet Sunny, who was back on full alert, undoubtedly anticipating the delicacies Bryce had brought him. Piper had named her cat after the sunflower partly because of his coloring, but of course because it meant loyalty, devotion, optimism, and happiness in the language of flowers. She knew it might be a bit unrealistic to expect those things from a cat, but she could hope.

Pulling a catnip-laced treat from the pocket of her shorts, Bryce dropped it down for the feline, who pounced on it.

"No wonder you have his undying love. Just reel him right in with kitty crack." Piper shook her head. "What about my starving stomach?"

"Breakfast is for your starving pet." Bryce continued to drop treats. "You don't want to eat before we put in seven miles—we can do two tours around the lake. Hydrate with water now, and let's get coffee and breakfast afterward."

"Is this payback for my doughnut derriere comment two weeks ago when we fought over the last pastry? It was just a bad cop joke, so I wouldn't have to arm wrestle you for it." Piper looked down at Sunny. "She has a lovely ass, doesn't she?" Piper asked the cat. "Just not my type, being already married to Doc McStuffins and all."

She gave Bryce a light elbow to the ribs. Doc McStuffins was a fictional character who cared for toys and stuffed animals, and it was Piper's jokey nickname for Hannah, Bryce's pediatrician wife. Piper had seen the kids' book at Wee Critter Haven when she was volunteering. Kids came in and read to the animals at the rescue. Most of the animals were good listeners.

"How is Hannah? Did she get over that cold some rug rat gave her?"

"She's completely recovered. Healthy. I checked her out last night—*thoroughly*." Bryce's gray eyes twinkled.

"Shut up." Piper fought to suppress a snicker. "I don't need to hear how healthy you two are. Let me go get dressed." Piper took off toward her bedroom.

"You need a little healthy exercise yourself, Pipes. And I don't mean running. I'll feed Sunny. Outta here in ten." Glancing at her phone for the time, Bryce headed toward the kitchen.

Piper nodded before stopping in front of the long living room table filled with greenery. Sunny never touched the plants, but she made sure she didn't have any that were toxic where he could get to them. She touched the topsoil of several pots to assess their moisture levels, satisfying herself that none of them would succumb before the evening, then headed back into her bedroom to prepare for their run instead of to continue the sweet dreams she'd been enjoying before she'd been so rudely interrupted.

She turned to look out the glass door leading to her small patio where a large planter filled with dahlias rested. In late summer, she'd cut the plants way back, collecting and storing the tubers at her mom's house in a cool dark closet before planting them outside to start their spring growth for the blooming season.

They were beautiful flowers—the visual complexity of the blooms, the way sunlight played across the intricacies of their petal formations. But it was what the flower stood for that made them her favorite flower. She loved dahlias.

Dancing in the Weeds with Pipes the unPlugged

"Writing a Life"

I need to thank Meg the unMuzzled for this opportunity to write my own blog. I almost called it Circling the Drain with Pipes the unPlugged, *rather an apt metaphor on a bad day, but I know life isn't perfect. This blog is about writing the pages of my life as I live it, and maybe offering something worthwhile as you write the pages of yours—something that brings you a stop-and-enjoy-the-blooms, stay-true-to-yourself connection.*

❖

As you write your life, you may not initially know the genre. Hopefully not horror. It might seem like a mystery, even somewhat speculative, but a lot of us are hoping for a final judgment of contemporary romance. Or at least some major component of that in our lives.

The big bold print across the title probably doesn't do your life justice. Probably not the start of the story either—once upon a time. There are undoubtedly all sorts of lines that could have worked as the beginning. It could have been a dark and stormy night. A truth universally acknowledged. The best of times, the worst of times. If it starts out by calling you Ishmael...nope. Hell nope! And while the perfect ending is happily ever after, you won't actually know that until the very last page.

There's no doubt that the body of the text is important. As some sum it up, the who, what, where of the story. And the how, when, why of the plot. The minor characters deeply enrich the telling as well, while you hold out for that other main character in your life. And you certainly shouldn't forget those scribbled notes in the margins of your life, they reveal so much. The little regrets. The antidote to heartache. A list of your longings. The doodle of temporary insanity.

But it's all just words on the page until that life-changing event. An event you might not even recognize as life-changing until you live a few more chapters. When that other main character alters the entire trajectory of your life. You'll just keep writing until you reach that chapter. The one where love finally shows up, and everything shifts from perfunctory to Pulitzer. When love knocks you flat on your ass. When you find that person who completes you. Until then, there is wishing on stars. And hope...never give up hope.

CHAPTER TWO

As Bryce drove them to Lake Merritt, Piper patted the dashboard of Bryce's Mercedes convertible. "Well, I have to admit this is a great morning for an outing in your little red chariot." Piper always enjoyed the ride but knew the vehicle was way out of her price range. "And a good morning for a run. I'm so glad I thought of it."

"Yeah. Brilliant idea on your part." Bryce side-eyed her as she navigated the road.

Piper was proud of Bryce, a police sergeant with an eye on climbing up the ranks. Bryce had met her future wife investigating a break-in at Hannah's clinic. Before Hannah had given her the Mercedes as a gift on their first anniversary, Bryce had only ever driven clunkers, well-maintained clunkers, and her last one, an older Subaru Outback, was now Piper's car.

After parking the Mercedes on a nearby street, they walked to the pathway that looped the lake, the glimmering jewel in the heart of urban Oakland. On this weekend morning, there were walkers and joggers on the pathway, and a few families already gathered on the grassy shore while morning rowers skimmed across the smooth surface.

Grabbing the back of a park bench, Piper and Bryce did a series of torso contortions and leg stretches, flexing and bending and dipping before heading onto the pathway to join the people already getting a bit of morning exercise.

"I'm starting to feel old," Bryce said. "Thirty-two and I have to get the twinges out of the cricks. I wonder what walking around the block is going to feel like at sixty."

"Quit the bitching. It's probably just a hangover from that thorough exam you gave Hannah last night. The one where you verified it wasn't a cold she'd been suffering from, but was, in reality, the hots you'd been afflicted with." Piper did a toe touch followed by a butt wiggle, just to prove her agility.

"I thought you didn't want to discuss my love life, because if you've changed your mind..." Bryce arched an eyebrow, her gray eyes laughing at Piper.

Piper stuck her fingers in her ears and took off, picking up speed. Bryce caught up and they ran in tandem. The only sounds Piper could hear were of their feet pounding the pavement and the steady intake and exhalation of fresh-air breathing. An earlier light ghosting of fog had lifted, and the sun was out, making it a perfect day for the outdoor exercise. Piper ran just to the left of Bryce, who was setting the pace. They stayed to the far right on the trail so that bicyclists and faster joggers could pass.

At almost mile two, Piper was feeling good when a woman jogging at a quick clip approached from the other direction, a tan, thirtyish-pound mixed-breed dog beside her on a leash. Piper didn't get a good look at her before a bicyclist came out of nowhere from behind Piper, sounding a loud air horn.

The terrified dog crossed the center of the pathway. The cyclist cut between Piper and Bryce, forcing Piper closer to the center too. The canine veered around Piper, taking her down with a leash-across-the-ankles trip line that left Piper no chance to maneuver. As she crashed and rolled, the woman stumbled on Piper, also falling.

"Go save the dog," Piper grunted as the frightened canine took off at full speed, leash in tow. Bryce followed in pursuit.

The bicyclist was long gone as Piper lay there, flat on her back. She was left alone to deal with the woman whose body now pinned her to the pavement, front to front, the woman's warm breath feathering Piper's ear, her jasmine-mixed scent filling Piper's nostrils. Through Piper's postaccident haze, three things registered. The pain of pavement impact on her backside, how perfectly the woman fit into the contours of her own body, and the fragrance of *Jasmine grandiflorum*: floral, fresh, sensual.

Piper ignored both her pain and cursed libido. "Are you okay?"

"Einstein...my dog." The woman's response came out as a strained groan.

"My friend Bryce went after him. She's fast. I'm pretty sure she'll get him for you." With literally no space between them, Piper couldn't see the woman. She could be twenty or she could be sixty, but whatever her age, there was a low-pitched voice beneath the pain.

The woman continued to pin Piper to the pavement, front to front. "She'd better. Einstein's a good dog."

"Einstein?" Piper wondered how he'd come by the name, then considered that she couldn't believe she was having this conversation with a strange woman stretched out on top of her.

"He's smart. Hell of a lot smarter than most people. Especially ones that can't keep to their side of the running path." The woman now had more growl than groan in her voice as she spoke directly into Piper's ear. A low appealing growl. Rich and seductive in the right circumstances. However, once Piper got past the appeal of the husky voice coming from the warm lips brushing her earlobe, the rudeness of the comment registered.

"Hey, Einstein tripped me. Not that the bicyclist didn't play a major role in it." Piper couldn't believe the woman was blaming her.

Finally, the jogger rolled to the ground beside her. Piper pushed herself up to her feet, looking down at the angry woman. Decked out in attire similar to Piper's, she wore broken-in running shoes, loose faded navy shorts, and a baggy white cotton T-shirt that offered minimal definition of the ample breasts Piper knew were present because those breasts had just pressed against her own. The woman had well-muscled legs, lean arms, light brown hair pulled back into a ponytail, and a face that was makeup-free this morning—a beautiful face, on second look. Model-worthy feminine features. Soft, clear skin. A sensuous mouth. Large, piercing bluish-gray eyes—steel blue. Not that Piper was staring at her, just a quick survey to confirm that she hadn't been badly injured.

Piper continued to assess her. Even in jogging attire, even upset, this woman had an air of refinement. She considered that the jogger was likely a decade older, not enough of a gap to be of any concern to Piper. *Younger* had been Bryce's contribution to the dream woman joke.

With her wild mop of hair and on-the-go, free-spirit personality as a child, Piper's mom had teasingly associated her with a dandelion puffball. This woman was possibly a rose, but the most significant factor—she was hostile. And she wasn't the least bit interested in Piper, if she was even interested in women. Gorgeous, but nope. No more dead-end romances. Being aloof was one thing, but Piper didn't need someone in her life with anger issues. Yup, a dandelion to the woman's rose. A rose with thorns. Sharp thorns.

Just then, Bryce reappeared with Einstein, breaking Piper out of her momentary reflections and eliciting an almost imperceptible mouth twitch from the jogger that Piper decided might be construed as affirmation that Einstein was safe. That was if the barest movement at the edges of her full moist lips could be interpreted to encompass an expression of acknowledgment, definitely not gratitude.

"He's fast, but I was faster." Bryce puffed out the words between intakes of air, handing the leash to Einstein's person. "Everyone survive?"

"I'm good." Piper dusted off her backside and winced. "Maybe a black-and-blue mark on my ass tomorrow, but nobody to notice that."

She felt her face heat with a blush as the woman almost imperceptibly elevated a perfectly sculpted eyebrow. Piper wasn't sure if the brow lift was in response to the location she'd mentioned, or the fact that she'd disclosed that there was nobody to notice the bruise.

Bryce laughed, and Piper watched the grump bite the insides of her cheeks before imparting commentary in what had calmed into smooth alto advice. "Go home and soak your"—there was an extended pause—"injuries."

Piper thought maybe the cheek-biting was to prevent a smile, but then the jogger clicked her tongue at the tan dog and headed down the trail with him, her gait a bit off. Not even a thanks to Bryce for the Einstein retrieval, much less a thanks to her for the cushioned landing she'd provided.

"Well, hell. Shall we head back to the car?" Bryce asked as the woman and dog disappeared ahead of them.

"Mm-hmm. I think a bicyclist and Einstein have me waving the white flag of surrender for today." Piper managed a smile as she touched Bryce's arm. "Nice work, Blaze. Let's go get coffee and food. Does the dog-saving cop want doughnuts or something more substantial?"

"Let's get a real breakfast. I'm famished, between last night's exercise and chasing down an ungracious woman's dog." Bryce frowned. "Sorry, Pipes. Too bad you'll have nothing to show but a black-and-blue ass for your very close encounter. Gorgeous, but so rude.

She certainly didn't see you as a sex goddess. Not the least interested in either one of us, and you're no slouch. Not interested enough to even be polite."

Bryce headed out at a slow walk along that last segment of the loop around the lake that would take them back to her car. Piper joined her, limping just a little. Dang if she wasn't going to have a big bruise by tomorrow.

❖

Piper looked around the Blissful Bean for Cate and Meg on Sunday afternoon. Meg waved and then gave Piper an inquiring look from the table where she and Cate sat as Piper limped toward them. Piper was ready for a relaxing afternoon visit with her boss and her girlfriend. Earlier, she'd been at Wee Critter Haven where she volunteered every Sunday morning. Today she'd cleaned cages and had plenty of time to think about her encounter with the woman on the jogging path the day before. The woman had been rude. *So* rude.

"Oh, honey. You're walking like you hurt yourself. What happened?" Meg asked.

Both women already had coffee in front of them. Piper slid into an empty chair next to Meg and across from Cate.

"Got tripped up by Einstein at the park at Lake Merritt yesterday morning. Long story short—horn-blaring bicyclist, panicked canine, me the stuffing between the asphalt and Einstein's owner. No harm, no foul." Then, looking at Cate, Piper added, "I guess I don't need a lawyer. The only one I could sue would be the guy on the two-wheeler with the horn, and he was in the next county before I even hit the ground." Piper paused as she retold the story, the woman's attitude still bothering her. "The dog owner seemed pretty irritable. Anger issues. But she couldn't sue me and win. I've got the bruise to prove I'm an innocent victim of the whole incident."

"Well, I'm glad it won't come to litigation then." Cate chuckled at Piper's description of yesterday's accident.

"Let me get you whatever you want." Meg stood up. "Coffee, tea, or something else? And food?"

Piper handed Meg a travel mug covered with rainbows that she'd carried in with her. "I had coffee earlier. Just some green tea would be perfect. Thanks." Piper reflected on how much she cared for the kind woman who was the best thing that had ever happened to her boss.

Cate remained at the table. Sitting with her, Piper saw a stunning woman who knew how to run a meeting and would undoubtedly run this one. Wasting no time waiting for Meg's return, Cate jumped right in. "Meg and I are getting married." There was the glow of happiness in Cate's umber eyes that hadn't been there before she started seeing Meg two years ago.

"Oh, Cate. I'm so thrilled for you two." Piper didn't try to tone down her enthusiasm as she thought again about what *she* wanted—she wanted what Cate and Meg had found together.

"I perceive you think that's good news, judging by the decibel level of your response." Piper could hear the humor in Cate's voice, even if Cate seemed to be struggling for a tone that was a bit reproving. "And now I suspect the entire coffee house has a clue."

"This couldn't happen to a more perfect couple. So, am I invited to the wedding? All of the couples counseling Pete and I offered you to get you and Meg together." Piper beamed at her boss, thinking about all that Cate and Meg had overcome as their love grew. "And I was the one who first recognized The Meg Effect. All of Meg's charm…and other winning attributes."

"I think you're Meg's biggest fan, after me." A smile played across Cate's face. "Pete sends his regards, by the way—we had lunch yesterday." Pete was now the CEO of Meg's late husband's investment company and had been Cate's best friend since college. Piper was always pleased to catch up with him when he dropped by the office.

"Thanks, tell him regards back. Ooh, here comes Meg now with my drink." As soon as Meg had set the tea in front of her, Piper jumped up and gave Meg a hug. "Cate told me. I'm so happy for both of you."

"It's going to be a small ceremony. Just people we consider to be family and best friends. Family—that's you." Meg kissed Piper on the cheek before they returned to their seats. Meg's blue eyes softened. "Not a traditional wedding party. Just those we want standing up next to us. My kids and you. Everyone else will be the audience. If you agree."

"Effing yes." Piper looked at Cate, then watched her choking down laughter without success. Piper rarely swore, unlike Cate, who sometimes punctuated a statement with a bit of color. When she'd started working for Cate, Piper had explained that she wasn't offended by Cate's occasional show of emotions, but she avoided most profanity because of a promise she'd made to her religious grandmother that she'd do her best not to be unladylike. She considered that she probably hadn't worn anything that resembled a dress since her grandmother had insisted on her baptism when she was a baby. There were a boatload of things her grandmother would probably have considered so much more unladylike that Piper had done—activities with past girlfriends would probably be at the top of the list. She might say a word like *ass* on occasion, but she avoided serious profanity, and she did her best to apologize to her deceased grandmother when she did swear.

"Effing stands for *effusive*. You know effusive. I'm giving you an unreserved, enthusiastic, uninhibited affirmative on getting hitched, on standing up front with you. I'm all in. I'm so flattered you'd ask me. Thank you." Piper was so happy for the two of them—she hoped they could hear the delight in her voice. She wiped her eyes and took a sip of her tea.

"Oh yeah. Your granny would be pleased if she was still on this planet." Cate laughed again. "Glad that's settled. With a bit of not-profanity to boot." Cate straightened and sobered. "We have more to discuss."

Piper sat up straighter too. "Is this Cate-and-Meg stuff, or boss stuff?"

"We already took care of my stuff," Meg said. "And I'm so pleased—I love the blog you posted. You're doing me such a favor. I'm eyeball deep in my art career, and I'm adding a wife." Meg winked at Cate, and Piper couldn't help but grin. "You're going to do a great job." Meg leaned over and gave Piper a squeeze.

When the hugging was done, Cate took over the conversation. "The wedding was the Cate-and-Meg stuff. Now for the boss stuff. Meg and I are going to take a real honeymoon, tour Europe for six weeks."

Piper felt her pulse accelerate, now on full alert. How would this affect her paralegal job at Cate's law practice? She picked up her tea and took several swallows as she processed what Cate had just told her.

"I've got colleagues lined up to handle any legal work that needs handling. I can even do a bit of advisement, if necessary, from Europe, but Meg will kill me if I let it interfere with our honeymoon." Cate looked over at Meg, who nodded in agreement. "What I'm thinking is that you can come into the office maybe two days a week to stay on top of things. Check the phone, and retrieve any paperwork a client might need. Business like that. And—"

Piper set down her tea and cut in. "And the other days of the week?" She tried to take control of the shock that was pounding in her chest. She knew she'd be bored to tears working only two days a week for that much time. What would she do the rest of the week?

Cate gazed across the table at her. "Don't worry—I know the thought of free time terrifies you. There's a client who needs someone with your skills for a while. Not a law office, so essentially an administrative assistant role, but you've been running my office too and you're smart, so you should do fine for six weeks. Plus, you can make some extra money and you'll add another skill set." Then she added with amusement in her tone, "Besides that couples counseling you're so good at."

Piper could only nod as she absorbed this additional information, the coming changes. A six-week honeymoon for Cate and Meg, a six-week change in her weekly work routine. At least Cate had faith in her ability to adapt. "When's the wedding?" she finally managed to ask.

"Next Saturday," Cate said.

"Of course." Piper worked to get a grip and gave Cate an exaggerated eye roll. "You're never one to waste time, Cate."

"What do you think, hon?" Meg inserted her concern, and Piper felt a bit better.

"It sounds like an opportunity. An adventure." Piper inhaled, holding her breath for a long moment as she struggled with her unease. "Who's the client I'd be working for?" She looked at Cate.

"Dal Noble. We knew each other at UC Berkeley. Most of our exchanges have been electronic or by phone and I've handled them directly. I don't think you've ever met. Dal's president of a private company and also runs a nonprofit. Relax, you can meet and get acquainted next week, before the wedding. Before Meg and I take off."

Piper finished her tea as she digested what she'd just learned. She was a bit overwhelmed but wasn't going to let the ramifications to her job get her down. She tried to focus on the wedding as they finished up. "An adventure," she repeated to herself as she left the Blissful Bean.

When she arrived home, Piper acknowledged again that she couldn't be more pleased for Cate and Meg. They'd been in love for two years, so the fact that they were making their love official and planning to grow old together was more than she could have hoped for. Especially for Cate, who had been so miserable before Meg came into her life.

As Piper sat on her couch with Sunny, thinking about Cate and Meg, she looked out the patio door at the dahlia plants, their flower representing love, devotion, dignity, and beauty. What she wanted in her life too. She wouldn't settle for less. Opening her laptop, she began to write about the language of flowers.

When she finished her second blog, Piper searched for Dal Noble on the internet. Cate hadn't given her much information, and Piper didn't find a likely match. Dal probably wasn't his legal name—but Noble certainly sounded promising. Not that Cate wasn't noble, but Piper laughed at the thought of working for someone *officially* noble. She hoped that didn't mean boring. She supposed she should talk to Cate for further clarification if she got a chance this next week.

DANCING IN THE WEEDS WITH PIPES THE UNPLUGGED

"Floriography"

Floriography—the secret language of flowers. Varied meanings have been attributed to plants for thousands of years, across many cultures. During the Victorian era, floriography was in vogue. Flowers were used to convey messages that might otherwise go unspoken. The root name, the mythology, the medicinal characteristics, the appearance—many attributes were used to assign significance to a flower. One could communicate feelings with a bloom—a petal pronouncement, a foliage forewarning, a posy applause, a budding love. Every bouquet delivery could be decoded flower by flower, each flower symbolic. Like a modern-day, emoji-laden text message.

French flower almanacs, artistic collections of illustrated blooms paired with poetry, initially added appendixes that were flower dictionaries. These addendums evolved in the 1800s into best-selling floriography reference guides, helping readers learn the symbolism assigned to each type of flower.

My favorite flower is the dahlia—a perennial, with the right care persisting year after year if its tuber heart is not frozen. The dahlia, like people, is diverse in shape, size, and color. A stunning flower, complex in form and hues, with a medley of meaning. How could this bloom junkie not connect with the dahlia and find hope in some of its symbolism? The Victorian era floriography—love, devotion, dignity, beauty. I want those things in my life.

CHAPTER THREE

A pproaching the outer door of her fourth-floor company office on
Monday morning, Dal glanced at the upper nameplate that read
Noble Animal Services and the one beneath it that read *CritterLove
Rescues* before she headed inside.

Dal hoped no one would ask about her slightly uneven gait, a
temporary souvenir from her close encounter with the rogue cyclist
and the wild-haired jogger. Having to explain falling on her face to her
clients and donors didn't fit the image she was keen for her business
to project, one of polish and professionalism. Success mattered to her.
Profits mattered. Profits meant her future would not be her past.

"Are you injured?" Dal's seventy-eight-year-old administrative
assistant asked. Viola sat at the desk in the reception area with the door
to Dal's personal office space farther behind her.

Dal considered that Viola had aged over the years into a slightly
plump, gray-haired woman who still loved life. Who still loved her. If
she'd had an unofficial foster mom, it would be Viola because *foster*
had a special meaning for Dal, a word she knew in her veterinary
profession, to nurture and care for someone or something as they grew.
Viola was now one of the few people that Dal loved and trusted. Viola
often joked that she was still overseeing Dal's growth. Dal thought
about how she'd met the woman who had become a stand-in mother
and friend over a quarter of a century ago.

Dal had left home at age fourteen but was only gone for one night.
Her father hadn't noticed, a father who had put on a charade of caring
for her just to use any attachment on her part to put her down. He'd

had run-ins with local law enforcement for his drunken behavior at local bars, but somehow, her neglect had flown under the radar. She'd decided to leave when she'd seen no reason to stay after the only saving grace in her home life had passed away, her loving dog, Sugar.

On that first night alone, Dal had thought an unlit house a few blocks away was empty and that she'd found a safe place to sleep. She'd crawled halfway through an unlocked window when a woman with a kind face and intelligent eyes had cornered her, armed with a broom.

Dal still remembered that first conversation when Viola had offered her a sandwich.

"What's the catch? Why be nice to me—especially after I broke in?" Dal hadn't trusted Viola. Not trusted anyone. "What do you want from me? I don't want you to bullshi…uh, feed me a line. I can smell baloney a mile away."

"You're right. You found me out. I laid a trap for you. Had that window installed there on the side of my house to attract some silly fool—that being you—then sat in the dark, armed with my broom. Just waiting. And along you came and fell right in." Viola had laughed. Dal had grinned too, at the obvious absurdity of Viola's declaration.

After four peanut butter and jelly sandwiches illustrating how hungry she'd been, Dal had studied Viola for a few minutes before finally deciding to share her reasons for leaving home. Even at fourteen, Dal had known that she wanted control of her life. She'd wanted to achieve independence so she didn't ever have to count on anyone again.

Now, at forty-one and looking back, Dal was amazed that she'd been willing to listen, but she had recognized that there had been nothing for Viola to gain by offering advice. Viola had convinced her that the streets were no place for a child—she'd never gain the control she craved by being homeless. After Dal had agreed to go home, Viola had told her that she could drop by for food or advice anytime she wanted. Dal had felt a connection.

Her father had died, drunk, in a one-car accident a week later, but not before he'd declared to a county child welfare service agency worker, whom the police had contacted after another drunken rampage, that he didn't want anything to do with Dal—it was a declaration that had surprised her with its impact on her guarded heart. She'd thought that he couldn't hurt her any worse than he already had, and she knew that she still carried that hurt. That it was part of what defined her.

Dal wondered who she might have been if her mother hadn't passed away when she was three. She'd had no relatives. So, starting at age fourteen, she'd experienced several short-lived foster care placements. During those years, Viola had managed to keep tabs on Dal and encourage her that those few years would pay off if she took advantage of them.

Dal knew that she owed Viola so much. When she'd aged out of the foster care system, Viola had offered her a home while she continued to pursue her education, an education that would allow her financial independence. Their bond had grown as Viola had proven herself to Dal.

In the role of administrative support, Viola had joined Dal as she moved from practicing veterinarian to president of Noble Animal Services, based in the financial district in San Francisco. It was work that Dal was devoted to, now the owner of twelve California twenty-four-hour veterinary clinics and overseeing another eight Bay Area nonprofit CritterLove Rescues animal shelters.

Viola waited patiently for Dal's answer to her inquiry.

"An accident left me a bit sore. Some harebrained jogger almost took Einstein and me out on our Saturday morning run."

"At Lake Merritt?" Viola asked.

"Yes. I should probably concede that a bicyclist was involved." Dal reluctantly remembered her initial response to the accident, a response that she knew could have been handled better. Much better.

"Bicyclist?"

"The crash wasn't entirely the woman's fault. The cyclist blared an air horn, terrorizing both Einstein and her. She went down, I went down, and the dog took off." Dal didn't feel the need to be defensive with Viola like she'd been right after the accident with the woman she'd landed on, the whole situation an out-of-control disaster.

"It looked like Einstein was doing okay when I brought Ruby home last night." Viola knew how much she loved that dog.

Dal nodded as she thought about the house where they lived in the Oakland hills, Viola in the downstairs granny unit while she and Ruby occupied the upstairs—it was the perfect solution for taking care of her five-year-old daughter. This past weekend, Ruby had gone with Viola to visit her niece and grandnieces. They hadn't had time to talk last night with Dal too busy getting Ruby to bed and Viola exhausted from her travels.

"Do you think I'd be standing here telling you this tale if my best boy wasn't safe and sound? The woman's running partner, another woman, chased him down and returned him to me while the two of us were scraping ourselves off the pavement."

Dal decided not to mention that she'd spent a bit of time pulling herself together after landing on top of the woman. Or that the woman had been fit and attractive with pale, flawless skin, expressive hazel eyes that were greenish-brown with flecks of gold, and a head of untamed red hair that surprisingly complemented her good looks. She didn't want to spark any commentary from Viola that she needed a loving woman in her life.

"That's good. How old were these women?"

"Young." Dal inwardly groaned, hoping that answer would halt the discussion.

"And how old is young in your mind these days, Dahlia Noble?"

Viola knew her too well—she could probably tell that the encounter wasn't as simple as she'd described. "Don't give me trouble just because you're retiring at the end of the week." Dal sighed. "Thirtyish," she added.

"That's not so young. Maybe compared to me, old lady that I am, but not that much younger than you. A decade or so." Viola gave Dal that look she had when she was going to launch into a lecture about Dal's life—the life Dal worked so hard to carefully manage.

"I'm still not divorced from Chantal." Dal's stomach churned in frustration and self-recrimination. "Chantal was a lesson I never want to repeat. Ruby is the only part of that debacle that wasn't a mistake."

Dal admonished herself again for lapsing from the pledge she'd made to herself decades ago, that she wouldn't ever allow herself to become dependent on another person for her livelihood, that she would maintain control of her life, and that she would protect her heart. Well, she'd blown that, at least the control piece.

It was six years ago that she'd been stupid enough to allow herself to be deluded into thinking she needed a wife to have a child, that after years of casual sex, she could have a marriage like other people had.

Build a family the way other people did. But she now realized that she hadn't needed a wife to have a child. She'd carried Ruby, and Chantal had never shown the least bit of interest in their child.

Chantal wasn't who she had pretended to be, although she'd managed a better act that first year before Ruby's birth. She'd turned out to be a complete disaster who would have wrecked almost any marriage. Dal knew now that Chantal had only seen the marriage through dollar signs. And on her part, in looking back, Dal had to admit that the marriage had been an unrealistic attempt at normalcy after a bit of initial lust. She hadn't actually risked her heart, not in a deep, lingering pain way. Maybe that was why she'd ended up with Chantal. Her heart had been safe.

Dal decided to be frank with Viola. "Even with Chantal being the death blow to the marriage—cheating, materialistic, never wanting Ruby, and walking out when Ruby was two—I suspect that with someone else the issues would arise because of my personal baggage. My fault."

"I've known and watched you for decades. You're smart. You've grown with your experiences. You have to meet a woman who you love enough and who loves you enough to make a marriage work. The right woman. Someone you trust with your heart. It's going to be a special woman." Disgust was evident in Viola's voice as she added, "Not some woman like your ex."

"Chantal put on a good show of charming and sexy when it served her, but I should have had a clue when she didn't seem to care about my emotional distance, didn't care that I didn't deeply love her. I don't even know for sure if I was just avoiding romantic love or if I'm incapable of it." Dal blew out a deep breath at the admission.

"I know you, Dahlia, and I flat out know the capacity you have to love someone, whether you recognize it or not. Probably someone as unpretentious as all those animals you love. No hidden agenda. I just hate to see you lonely."

"Well, we're getting off the issue. We were talking about my lack of a divorce." Dal redirected the conversation away from the lack of a loving woman in her life. "Chantal is fighting my full custody even though she's never once visited Ruby since she left. She's holding up the divorce, holding Ruby hostage, demanding a bigger settlement. Even her lawyer has suggested that she's delusional. She pursued me because she saw money." Dal fought to keep the anguish out of her voice.

Viola nodded as Dal vented. Dal knew that Viola understood that she was the one person Dal gave herself permission to be unguarded with.

Her marriage to Chantal was a failure in Dal's life, and she hated to fail. Dal had never risked heartbreak, and she now knew that Chantal had never wanted her love. But the woman had created chaos in her world—she'd impacted Dal's carefully orchestrated control.

"I understand. But every woman isn't Chantal. Now *there* was a fraud." Viola's disgust was evident in her tone. Dal had known that Viola had never liked the woman she'd married—she should have listened. Viola had been ready to consider her an ex when she'd walked out on Dal and Ruby. Now, another three years later, Chantal was definitely an ex in Dal's mind too.

Dal's only current dealings with Chantal were through their lawyers, working to sever that final connection with a signature on a divorce agreement. She certainly didn't consider herself married to the fortune hunter, but she needed the divorce decree to make it official. But not at Ruby's expense.

"You just need to find the right woman." Viola wasn't going to give up pushing on her to find love. "Loneliness is not a lifestyle choice."

Dal contemplated her Friday night in the bar. Of all the things that Dal would talk to Viola about, Dal never talked to her about the occasional one-night stands on nights when Viola was taking care of her daughter, although she suspected Viola had a clue. Viola knew her so well. That was why she wasn't going to mention the feelings that had led her to say no to the woman who had wanted her the other night, if only for sex. Not when she didn't understand them herself.

Dal pushed those thoughts away and gave the woman who advised her like a mother her best chastising glower. "My work is my life, besides Ruby and you and the dog. As much as I'm not married to Chantal, I don't have the paperwork to prove it yet. Never again, Viola. I don't want a wife in my future. It's for the best. I just want to be free of Chantal."

"Don't let that woman ruin your life. Figure yourself out and get on with it." Viola had never beaten around the bush with advice. It was probably why Dal loved her and why Dal was as successful as she was, both personally and professionally. And now Viola was retiring, professing that at seventy-eight, it was way past time for her to join a bridge club, learn a few line dances, and take up bungee jumping.

"You know Cate Colson." Dal changed the subject. "I talked to her after you left with Ruby late Friday afternoon. She's getting married this coming weekend. She has a paralegal who she says is outstanding. The newlyweds are going on a six-week honeymoon, and while her paralegal will hold down her office a few days a week, she's going to be floating for a bit, and she prefers to keep busy."

"So tell me the plan," Viola said.

"Cate suggested that I bring her in here as a part-time administrative assistant for those weeks while I find someone more permanent to replace you. I agreed. This takes the pressure off since I haven't found a replacement yet." Dal gave Viola a look that she hoped would tell Viola how much she'd be missed.

"I'll be impossible to replace, considering what I'm willing to put up with around here." Viola chuckled. "I think Cate's paralegal's name is Piper. I've interacted with her once or twice over the phone, years ago, when I was trying to reach Cate to sort out some legal questions regarding the nonprofit. She probably doesn't remember me, but my impression is she'll do fine as a temp."

"That's good to know. I agree—I don't think anyone can replace you." Dal turned to head into her office. She'd see Viola at home, but she knew she'd miss her here at work. "My favorite old woman," she added over her shoulder as she got down to the business of the day.

❖

Cate was busy or gone much of the week finalizing arrangements for the wedding and the honeymoon. Working mostly alone in the office, Piper had no spare time as she finalized the long list of preparations she needed to complete for Cate's absence. On Thursday afternoon, Piper finally had some free time and called to make some sort of connection to the temp job Cate had arranged for her. She closed her eyes and pushed the number she'd entered on her phone.

"Hi. This is Piper Fernley, Cate Colson's paralegal. Just calling to sort out the details for my start next week."

"Piper. So glad to hear from you. I'm Viola. You probably don't remember, but we've talked once or twice, some time ago. When I was trying to reach Cate for Dal. It's been chaotic. Tomorrow is my last day—I'm finally retiring at age seventy-eight." Viola sounded pleased that the day had finally come for her to hang up her administrative assistant's hat. "We'll be out tomorrow, as they're throwing some smaller retirement celebrations at different company locations, then a big blowout later tomorrow. I'm sure you'll have no problem filling my shoes when you show up Monday morning. Dal can help you with any questions you might have, being a hands-on sort of person. How does that sound?"

"Sounds great." Actually, it sounded kind of terrifying, but Piper swallowed her apprehension. As long as nobody expected her to walk in cold and know everything. "So, I'll be here at Cate's on Tuesdays and Thursdays. I can start there on Monday with a plan to work the three days a week that I'm not here at the law practice."

"Perfect. I'll be out bungee jumping, or whatever new retirees do, but you should be fine. Have a good weekend. And don't take any guff from Dal. Hope you've had your rabies shots." Viola laughed, but before Piper could ask what the heck that meant, or more about the company, Viola hung up.

Piper felt her life was a bit out of control, but she worked hard to appreciate that Cate had made sure she was taken care of. She didn't want Cate to worry about her while she was on her honeymoon, so she let Cate finalize her wedding plans and didn't bother her with questions. She'd focus on the fact that this would be an adventure—that you never knew what unexpected things an adventure might present.

DANCING IN THE WEEDS WITH PIPES THE UNPLUGGED

"Finding Their Way to City Hall"

There is no map to City Hall. Everyone takes a different path, but these two, they could hardly have taken more diverse routes. One stumbled around with a fractured heart, first stalling out with that poor broken organ embedded in her chest, no longer willing to beat anything but a solo cadence. Definitely not a love song. And the other, she was on a road so seemingly straight that she'd managed thirty years down that lonely lane with blinders on—until she finally pulled over for a little introspection. At last, a spot where a sharp turn allowed her to acknowledge her true self. Against all odds, they gave themselves a chance, wading through family obligations, navigating killer infidelities and religious condemnation, scaling a mountain of miscommunication—going to the only place that was right for them, to love and be loved. And two years into their shared adventure, they forged their way to City Hall, joined in holy matrimony, made the commitment to be wife and wife. It took maturity, it took humor, it took work, it took forgiveness to find that happily ever after. Two amazing women, loving each other, dancing toward stardust together. If only we all could be so blessed.

CHAPTER FOUR

The Blissful Bean was Piper's first stop on Sunday morning before she reported for her volunteer shift at Wee Critter Haven. The wedding yesterday had been perfect, and Cate and Meg should now be on a plane to Europe. Piper was going to really miss them, and she was glad she'd be busy while they were gone, even with the changes to her work. As she entered the reception area of the rescue, Piper was happy to see that Elsie was behind the front desk.

Elsie's face lit up. "One of my favorite volunteers. How are you, Piper?"

"I'm good. What do you have planned for me today?"

"I saved a special job for you. Your mission, if you choose to accept it, is to work with that shepherd mix in run number seven. But definitely not *Mission: Impossible*." Elsie offered Piper a chuckle.

Elsie had told Piper she'd grown up in the Philippines, caring for many stray animals in her neighborhood. She'd been kind and friendly when Piper had encountered her, which was on most Sunday mornings.

"I'm so glad you clarified that for me. Not impossible, huh? In that case, I'm in."

"I have faith you can get him to warm up to you." Elsie nodded. "Take a few treats and just go sit in his run. Read to him if you want. He growls a bit, but no biting. I'll have him assessed by Carrie, the animal behaviorist who works with us, but I think Fred's just so traumatized and frightened right now. He needs love and stability. Poor baby."

"I can do that." Piper selected a handful of kid books that she knew some of the local kids used when they came to read to the rescues. She made sure to grab the Doc McStuffins book because it reminded her of

Hannah. Then, retrieving some training treats, she headed back toward run number seven.

"What's his name again?" Piper called back over her shoulder.

"Fred. His owner moved away and left him in an empty house alone. He had dry food and water, but it was several days until a neighbor heard him crying. He was thin, neglected, terrified."

With that information, Piper went to find Fred. He offered her a soft, low growl that she interpreted as sadness and uncertainty. She didn't blame him.

"How are you, Fred? Will you share your space with me?" Piper spoke softly, and when he didn't object, she sat several feet from him on the concrete floor of his run. She began to quietly read to him, not pausing as he belly crawled closer, a few inches at a time. He never took his eyes off her, but she kept her focus on the book, giving him space to warm up on his own terms.

When he seemed to have relaxed some, she slowly held out a treat. "How about a snack?" Fred took it from her hand, and Piper continued to read. Eventually, he pushed himself up against her leg and settled there, offering a groan. She could feel him shaking as he leaned into her.

"It's been a long haul, hasn't it, buddy? Well, you're safe now." Piper gently stroked his head as she finished another two books. When the quivering had subsided, Piper asked, "Are you willing to come outside for some fresh air with me?" She slowly stood up, and Fred did too. She showed him the leash, and he came over to her, so she fastened it to his collar and they headed outside to the exercise area until her shift was almost up.

"You're going to make someone a fabulous friend, Fred," Piper told him when she returned him to his run. She loved animals. As she watched Fred settle down, she thought about her ambition to attain a law degree and focus her work on animal welfare and human rights, specifically LGBTQIA+ rights. Finances and time were preventing her from going back to school. But for now, she'd focus on dogs like Fred.

❖

On Monday morning, with fourteen minutes to spare, Piper approached the building where the new job was located. Her curly hair was its usual disobedient mop, but there wasn't much Piper could do about it without shaving her head. She'd taken care to apply light makeup and wear a deep green button-down shirt, a blue-and-black check-patterned vest, and her favorite pink tie. Her pants and boots were black. She didn't want to be a boring dresser, and Cate had accepted that, or at least ignored it.

Piper believed that everyone made choices as to what they liked to wear, their style. After all, everyone started out the same. Naked. If you were lucky, your clothing became self-expression. Maybe her choices were a bit flamboyant, but they made her happy, and maybe they would brighten someone else's day.

To ensure she wouldn't be late, Piper had left early from her apartment in Oakland. She'd ridden the Bay Area Rapid Transit train, BART. The trip was similar to her daily commute to her paralegal job at Cate's office, the two offices being less than half a mile apart. Sitting in a seat, cocooned in a metal box that shot through a dark tunnel under the expanse of water at the bottom of the bay, Piper always leaned back and hoped her fate wasn't a California earthquake as she spent those miles between Oakland and San Francisco in peril. At the end of each passage, it was a relief to surface in San Francisco in the same shape she'd departed Oakland.

Not knowing exactly who this Dal Noble fellow was made her nervous, but she'd been so busy that she hadn't searched beyond that initial, unproductive online effort. Besides, she knew that face-to-face impressions were so much better than what came filtered through a search engine. As she walked from the transit station, Piper told herself that she'd find out soon enough.

As she looked up at the tall building, Piper wondered about Viola's bungee jumping in retirement remark and hoped it reflected Viola's sense of humor. *Hope you've had your rabies shots*—Piper wanted Viola's comment about her boss to be a joke. Dal Noble couldn't be all bad if he liked animals and oversaw rescues. Could he?

Riding the elevator up to the fourth floor went without a hitch. Piper found the door with the plaque that read *Noble Animal Services,* and another plaque underneath that read *CritterLove Rescues*, without any problem. The morning was going well.

Entering the reception area, Piper saw the back of a white tailored shirt clad figure with light brown hair secured in a bun. A desk and chair blocked any further view from the waist down. Piper wasn't sure how many people worked here. As Piper scooted through the door, the person paused her search in a file cabinet and turned around. That was the end of Piper's morning without hitches.

Piper tried to stifle the gasp that escaped her effort at a professional initial presentation as the rude, hostile woman she'd tangled with on the run at Lake Merritt a week ago faced her. The woman's eyes widened in surprise before they narrowed. Those eyes. Steel blue. Piercing.

Piper took control of her racing heart and cleared her throat. "I'm looking for Dal Noble."

"You've found her." The woman's eyes roamed up and down Piper in deliberate scrutiny. Then she clenched her jaw before breaking her silence. "We've met. In rather an unconventional way. I'm sure you remember."

Piper closed her eyes. Dal Noble was this woman, but this was not the new boss or the welcome that Piper had envisioned. Breathing deeply through her nostrils, Piper centered herself. She could do this. She'd dealt with all sorts of people in her job, professionally. Heck, she'd dealt with Cate. Plus, she'd done the calculations. Three days a week for six weeks—she could survive eighteen days working for Dal Noble. The countdown had begun.

"Yes, we've met." Piper reassessed the accuracy of that declaration. "Or at least *run* into each other." Dal showed no indication she saw the humor in Piper's amendment. "I'm Piper Fernley, Cate's paralegal, although I've also been running the office, reception…" Piper took another deep breath. "I'm here as the temp. For Viola's job."

Dal remained silent, just looking at her. Then she spoke. "I guess *unconventional* is the word of the day. Rather unconventional attire for an office setting."

Piper knew she was unconventional in her choice of clothing, and given Cate's acceptance, she hadn't thought through what a new boss might think. Definitely not this boss. Piper was just being herself.

Looking down at her shirt, still fighting the shock of encountering Dal, Piper rambled. "Green…do you know Popeye, the cartoon spinach-eating guy, or Robin Hood?" Her mom liked Robin Hood, robbing from the rich to give to the poor. "Although I'll have to admit that it's Popeye's girlfriend, Olive Oyl, or Robin Hood's Maid Marian who are probably more my type."

Piper didn't know how to interpret the slight widening of those intense bluish-gray eyes, the subtle ghosting of revelation across Dal's face as the last comment registered. Piper hoped she didn't have anything against lesbians, or this was going to be a longer tour of duty than she was already fearing.

"Just thought I'd wear the vest to match some black-and-blue reminders of an unplanned encounter. On my..." Piper touched her backside. "The tie was bought at a garage sale to benefit an injured dog."

"Well, I guess I have to approve of the tie, then," Dal replied, continuing to study Piper. "Piper Fernley. The pathway assailant." Dal's mouth offered the tiniest hint of an upward quirk as she drew out the moniker. "I'm rarely surprised, but this caught me off guard." Then she muttered under her breath, "Ambushed." There was a hint of that park growl in her tone.

Pathway assailant? That accident hadn't been Piper's fault. The growl might be seductive, but the woman was still rude. Piper couldn't help herself, she needed to respond.

"Well then, if that's your take, I guess it's a good thing that it's your dog who's got the name Einstein." Piper gulped. She was going to get herself fired before she ever started. This woman brought out something in her. It couldn't be attraction—Dal had been so disagreeable in the park, so it didn't matter how good-looking she was or how well her contours had fit with Piper's.

As Piper started to apologize, Dal blinked and then replied, "Touché." She quietly added, "I guess you'll have to do, bushwhacker."

It was the same smooth, alto voice that Piper remembered speaking into her ear at Lake Merritt when this woman was lying on top of her on the pavement. Piper shook her head to clear it.

Dal studied her. "I'm an Olive Oyl and Maid Marian fan too."

Well, that was a relief—Piper interpreted the statement as an admission that Dal liked women. And she wasn't firing her...yet. Piper wasn't sure exactly what she'd done, but maybe she'd passed some sort of test. Then Piper noticed the nameplate on the inner office door, Dal's door. *Dahlia Noble*. Her favorite flower. Love, devotion, dignity, beauty.

"Your name is Dahlia." Piper knew her tone was incredulous. She conceded that she'd certainly have to give her new boss one out of four—Dahlia was beautiful.

"You have a problem with that? I thought you'd just clarified that my name's not Einstein." She gave Piper a pointed look. "So I guess we'd better go with the name on my office." Dal displayed the barest suggestion of a smirk. Then she added, "And my birth certificate."

Piper didn't think she sounded happy about the birth certificate. Maybe a story there? This new boss might be tougher than Cate.

"No problem." Piper managed to get the squeak out of her voice. *Dahlia.* This couldn't be a sign. The woman wasn't the younger, blond, imaginary dream woman who thought Piper was a sex goddess. Bryce had contributed the *blond* and *younger* to their shared joke, and thinking that Piper was a sex goddess—well, that might be a bit of humor on Piper's part. But she had been serious when she'd wanted the attributes to include a woman who at least liked her. That clearly didn't seem to be Dal Noble. And with that acknowledgment, the rest of what Piper truly wanted in a partner didn't matter, the love and be loved that had taken her friends to completion. No, this wasn't a sign. More like an eighteen-day test of fortitude.

"Viola is the only one who calls me Dahlia, mostly when I'm in big trouble. You can call me Dal." Piper's new boss's eyes went soft for a moment before she seemed to realize what she'd disclosed.

Interesting—*in big trouble* with her retired administrative assistant, and that was acceptable. Piper didn't know what to make of that.

"I'm sorry about what happened out there in the park at Lake Merritt, on the jogging trail." Piper didn't want to get off on the wrong foot any more than she already had, in addition to the fact she knew that her Einstein comment had been churlish. "I hope you and your dog were both okay."

Dal frowned, and then she took a breath before she spoke. "I was a bit unsettled."

"No kidding." Piper wanted to amend the *unsettled* to *a whole lot rude*, but that would undermine her effort to apologize and be the bigger person.

Dal gave her a warning look and continued, "The cyclist played a major role in the incident." She paused and furrowed her brow. "Your friend probably deserves a thanks from Einstein."

"That was Bryce. She's a police sergeant," Piper replied. Finally, the mention of a thank you that was way overdue.

"Well, now that I know your friend is the law—with the power to arrest—I guess we'd better agree that it wasn't either of our faults."

Piper thought she might have detected Dal carrying on the barest battle with a smile. Maybe the woman did possess a sense of humor that she tried to suppress. Piper had thought the same thing at Lake Merritt when Dal had made a point of advising her to soak her injuries, knowing the bruise was on her ass. But it was evident that the woman had her guard up.

Dal interrupted her thoughts. "Now, are you ready to start taking over for Viola? I have more than enough work for a full-time person, but that's not the plan. You're only here part-time, and it's temporary at that."

Piper nodded, grateful to be switching gears so she could show Dal she'd be good at her new job.

"You can use that for taking notes." Dal tilted her head toward a laptop on the desk that Piper assumed was for the administrative assistant. "SheBites!!!—one word, capital *S*, capital *B*, followed by three exclamation points—that's the password." Dal spelled out the word as she kept her face blank with no hint of amusement—well, maybe a touch in her eyes. Piper's interest was piqued. What was Viola and Dal's relationship? She wondered, was the password a serious warning? Piper was on alert. And she couldn't help herself—she liked to understand people.

Inhaling deeply as she collected the computer, Piper centered herself before following her new boss into her office. She was still having a hard time reconciling *Dahlia* with the Dal she'd encountered so far.

❖

"To bring you up to speed, as you can see, there are twelve twenty-four-hour veterinary clinics and eight rescue sites. I own the for-profits and oversee the nonprofit rescues." Dal handed Piper a printed paper listing the names and locations of each.

Dal had frequently declared that she wasn't brilliant, just focused.

She'd been focused on finding a way to guarantee that she'd never end up in such a painful situation as she'd endured in her youth. And if Dal could pay back the loving memory of Sugar while she was achieving her goal, so much the better. After passing out of high school in an alternative program at seventeen, community college, then an undergraduate degree and an MBA before a DVM at UC Davis's veterinary school, Dal had opened her first clinic. That had been the beginning of this professional life.

"So how does it all work?" Piper asked.

"I've got accountants, tax people, and Cate has advised me on legal matters, but the gist is that there are two separate aspects to what I do. Noble Animal Services includes the twelve veterinary clinics. The eight nonprofit rescue shelters are part of CritterLove Rescues. We often just shorten it to CritterLove around here. I've got a good accounting firm that manages all the monetary sorting."

"So why the rescues? I mean, I can see the clinics, moneymakers and all. Not that providing good medical care to animals isn't a wonderful thing. But the rescues?" Dal felt Piper studying her before Piper quietly added, "I volunteer at a rescue on Sundays."

Dal was surprised by the disclosure of that piece of information. There was more to the woman than she'd concluded out there on the running trail. Jogging on Saturdays. Volunteering on Sundays. She wondered if the cop she'd been with was more than her friend. Her girlfriend? Then she pushed that thought away. Why should she care? In fact, she shouldn't care—she'd made herself a promise, and it was important to keep it. A promise that worked for her when she didn't blow it.

Dal rubbed her temple as she realized she was off her game. She'd spent years working with Viola, who was the only person who knew almost everything there was to know about her. Piper wasn't Viola, and Dal needed to pull back. It was time to slow this personal chitchat down. That was the best way to maintain control. Don't let anyone get too close.

"It's actually none of your business, but I make a decent living." The need to defend her clinics and by extension her rescues overtook Dal. "I'm well equipped to take care of myself and my daughter." Dal looked over at a picture of Ruby in a frame on a table in the far corner of her office and smiled, a table with a dog bed for Einstein under it. Now why did she have to mention Ruby? That was personal.

"A daughter? How old is she?" Piper appeared surprised.

Dal decided she'd offer a minimal answer, but that was it. "Five."

Dal felt the wave of love that she always felt when she thought of her daughter. Ruby was at school, and then she'd be in the after-school care program this afternoon. She'd had Ruby with her this entire past weekend, unlike the one before when Viola had taken her to visit her niece and grandnieces, when she'd been at the bar and then out jogging with Einstein the next morning. Dal looked away from the photo and cleared her throat. Time to get away from her personal life.

"You volunteer at a rescue?"

"Yes. I just spent yesterday morning there. Wee Critter Haven in Oakland." Piper looked down at the printed list that Dal had supplied her, then looked back up, her expression transparent and pleased. "It's one of yours," she said, delight in her voice.

Oh hell, this temp wasn't what Dal had expected. Viola and Cate had indicated she was smart and competent. And she was attractive without trying, seemingly unaware of or unaffected by her features. Smooth pale skin, full lips, captivating green-brown eyes with gold flecks—not defined, but enhanced by what slight makeup she chose to wear. A look that was ultimately defined by the addition of that untamed mass of rich crimson ringlets that ignored all the rules of coiffed and cosmopolitan.

But that wasn't all to Dal's assessment—there was more to this woman sitting in front of her, not hidden layers, but the opposite. She knew that was what made her like animals more than most people— there could be any of the entire range of emotions, and they were authentic in animals. There was no hidden agenda. That's how Piper struck Dal—she was genuine. Even the damn clothing.

Dal nodded. Wee Critter Haven had been the third rescue she'd opened. Piper gave Dal a grin. Sort of a *nice job* grin, as if Dal needed her approval. She chastised herself and huffed, then considered that it was rather endearing. And sincere. Dal was drawn to Piper in a way that unsettled her.

"I worked with a dog named Fred on Sunday. Even wrote a bit about him when I got home. A shepherd mix. He was abandoned in an empty house all by himself for several days before a neighbor reported his crying." Piper seemed pleased with her memory of her morning with Fred. "Sweet boy, but he'd been through hell. He and I read books together. He agreed with me that his favorite book was Doc McStuffins."

Dal was surprised. Ruby loved Doc McStuffins. Dal would never have guessed that a single millennial like Piper would even know who the fictional character was. This young woman was an enigma. Disconcerting. Bushwhacked again.

"Bryce, my friend who chased down Einstein—"

Dal stopped her. "The cop?"

"Yep. That's her. Anyway, Bryce's wife, Hannah, is a pediatrician. I've called her Doc McStuffins since they met."

Dal didn't like the surge of pleasure she felt. Bryce wasn't Piper's girlfriend. Bryce had a wife. But that didn't matter. She didn't want to get the least bit cozy with this administrative assistant. Her work, Ruby, Viola, and her dog were her life, plus she still had to get the settlement agreement so she could officially make Chantal her ex-wife. She'd better get this conversation back to business because Piper Fernley had a propensity for invading her private life.

"The two enterprises I oversee—they're well-divided. As I mentioned, the clinics make good money. The rescues are a registered nonprofit. Smaller donations help, but the biggest fundraiser is the big annual dinner gala affair. It's the biggest factor for allowing us to keep the rescues open."

"So why the rescues?" Piper repeated the question as those hazel eyes studied Dal.

Dal knew that the *why* had to do with her past. With the pain of her childhood. With that one living creature in her childhood home that she'd trusted and loved after her mother had died, Sugar. Dogs weren't crazy drunken assholes who lured you in with lies just to rage and threaten you for no good reason except their own entertainment, as her father had done. But that was history. Now she lived in her hard-earned present, although Dal knew she wouldn't forget her past. She had a life she'd learned to protect.

"Why the rescues? I'd answer, why not?" Dal gave Piper her best flippant look. She knew it was one of her tactics to avoid a sensitive issue.

"I don't know. There are a lot of things you could do, but you chose to focus on animals. A nonprofit, rescuing them. There's a reason."

Dal studied Piper. She was rather an open book, but also so perceptive. Too perceptive.

"You even said that Einstein was smarter than most people, out there in the park. That's why he had the name," Piper said. "So, you either truly like animals or truly don't think much of most people. Or both."

Piper was obviously reading her, line by line. Dal considered that it wasn't in a devious way, but in a sensitive way, picking up on the fact that people had failed Dal. Reminding Dal of so many animals she'd worked with—attuned, straightforward, what you see is what you get—those animals hadn't let her down. They didn't play games, not even the damaged ones. Piper was unlike so many of the women Dal encountered. She was observant, with seemingly no hidden agenda. Dal found it attractive. Very attractive. Dal's life had no place for that kind of attraction.

She decided to divert the conversation. "And here you are, a paralegal and now an administrative assistant when your calling is likely along the lines of therapy or counseling."

"Funny you should say that. Cate has thoughts along the same lines. An alternative career for when she fires me." Piper's eyes lit up.

"Fires you?" Dal asked with incredulity. Cate hadn't mentioned firing her. That seemed rather alarming, but Piper was now grinning.

"She fires me a couple of times a week, but not really. She needs me. She threatened to fire me when I was advising her on Meg and suggested counseling as a new career. But she ended up with a wife. So I couldn't have been too bad." Piper laughed, a mirthful, unselfconscious laugh.

Shaking her head, Dal was unable to suppress a chuckle. She couldn't remember meeting anyone as forthcoming and unpretentious as Piper seemed to be. She'd had no previous clue that her new temp might be so open. Or so entertaining.

Dal harrumphed to change the mood. This wasn't getting work done. "So, as much fun as this little getting-to-know-each-other chat is, I need you to set up meetings with some people." Dal indicated her own computer screen. "I'm sending you the names and numbers, and my calendar. Any late morning or afternoon this week or next that

I'm not already booked. I try to keep the early mornings free in case Ruby needs…" Dal backtracked. "In case there's pending work I need to address."

"Got it." Piper gave her a knowing look.

Dal silently cursed. This woman would sneak into her private life if she wasn't careful. At least she was only here part-time for six weeks. Eighteen days total.

Monday evening, Piper left the NAS office considering that she just might survive another seventeen workdays with Dal Noble. She was getting to know Dal a little better, even if Dal didn't want to get to know her. Not that she was interested for any other reason than the woman was a puzzle. It was probably like figuring out Cate, who had been alone and unhappy. Piper remembered when Cate had been filled with self-doubt and had protected her heart by not letting anyone in who might hurt her—she'd fought a relationship with Meg until Piper and Pete had intervened. Pete had challenged Cate about her unhappiness, and she'd championed Meg to Cate, continually giving Cate relationship advice, whether she'd wanted it or not. Piper acknowledged that she was certainly better at advising other people than herself.

Wanting to check the messages and her plants, Piper swung by Cate's law office before going home. As she entered the reception area, she greeted the jungle, Cate's name for the office foliage. She apologized to her babies, letting them know that her absence was only temporary, as she hummed and checked each pot.

While Piper watered, she continued to consider her first day and her new temporary boss. She didn't know Dal's history. Piper wondered if Dal had exes in her past. If she was lonely. She cared for animals that needed rescuing, and a daughter. She preferred animals over most people—now there was a clue to the woman's makeup. Dal was private, independent, and often rude, but Piper had seen a hint of amusement in her eyes a few times today as they'd spent time together.

Piper wondered what lay under all of those hidden layers of a woman who seemed to need to shut her out. Something had put her defenses up. Maybe Piper could help Dal like she'd helped Cate. That would be a good thing, and maybe it would help her get through the remaining days of this six-week adventure.

When she checked the messages, there was an email with a photo of Meg and Cate in front of the Eiffel Tower and a message from Meg letting Piper know that the honeymoon was spectacular so far. Piper took a quick phone snapshot of the reception area and replied to Meg: *Tell Cate that I haven't burned the place down yet. I've got it under control. No worries.* She missed them both but smiled when she thought of their happiness. And for some reason, that made her think some more about Dal. And dahlias. And the things she wanted in life.

Dancing in the Weeds with Pipes the unPlugged

"Fading Those Walls"

Walls stained the color of sorrow. I think we all have them. The barricades we construct to create that closet in our hearts—perhaps the fifth chamber, a place hidden beneath the coupled cardiac atria and ventricles. Packed full of buried pain. It probably begins as just a simple framework, a corral to fence in those initial untamed tears. Before the disconsolations swell and multiply through life's events, becoming embedded behind shatterproof sheetrock. Until someone or something comes along and opens a window, offering some light that blesses those walls and helps the sorrow fade. Light the color of caring.

I spent a morning with a rescue dog named Fred. Failed by the world. Failed by his people. Miraculously not a fear biter, but owning the right to a justified deep-throated growl. Until we sat together in run number seven. Read a book. Ate some treats. Went outside and shared some sunshine. Let in a little light that faded those walls the color of sorrow, if only just a bit. And maybe someday, fully celebrated with love, Fred will become someone else's light.

CHAPTER FIVE

Piper was disappointed on Wednesday morning. She'd been hoping that Dal would appreciate her conservative light blue button-down shirt, navy vest, and no tie, but instead discovered Dal's note stating that she would be gone all day touring the Bay Area clinics with Alex, who was in charge of their oversight. Piper had seen a crack in that rude defensive shell that Dal had worn at Lake Merritt—there had been a thread of connection on Monday, even if Dal sent out silent warning signals to leave her alone.

As Piper focused on the projects Dal had left for her, Elsie, who Piper now realized managed the eight Bay Area nonprofit rescue shelters, came into the NAS and CritterLove Rescue headquarters.

"Hi, Piper. What are you doing here?" Elsie's surprise at seeing her outside of the Sunday volunteer rescue shift was evident.

Piper was thrilled to see Elsie. "My lawyer boss is off on a six-week honeymoon, and Dal is a client. Cate and Dal worked out a three-day-a-week temp job for me so I'll be busy and stay out of trouble."

"So Dal is your temporary boss?" Elsie held Piper's gaze as if she was adding this new information to an assessment of her.

"Yup. That's the state of things. Do you know Viola, who just retired?"

"Sure, I've known Viola for years. It's because of her that I landed the job overseeing the rescues. I owe Viola. I love my job."

"Can I ask you something?" Piper asked. "You don't have to answer."

"Sure. Ask away."

"The laptop that Viola left me...the password includes the words *she bites*, which is a little worrying. I'm just wondering if Viola has a sense of humor, or if I need to run for my life." Piper chuckled, but she seriously wanted Elsie's opinion.

"Don't worry. It's common knowledge around here, so I'm not giving away secrets. Viola has been like a mom to Dal, helped Dal out from the time she was a teen. Dal was in the foster care system. Viola met Dal when she was younger, then was there when Dal aged out." Elsie smiled before she continued. "She knows Dal as well as anybody does and is proud of her. Loves her. I'll let Dal tell you any more than that. But Viola would tell you not to run. I would too."

Piper digested the news. That was one piece of the puzzle. Now she wanted to find out why Dal was so wary. The clues indicated she concealed a good heart underneath all the defenses she'd put in place. From what she'd learned so far, Piper guessed that the real Dal Noble was more complex than the hostile woman she'd first encountered.

Then Elsie's eyes danced. "Let me add, Dal is a lot like Fred. She growls, but she doesn't bite."

"Good to know. How's Fred?"

"He's doing better. Getting his strength back. Improving his trust issues. You can work with him on Sunday—you did a great job with him last time. I'm just in to grab some papers. I'll see you then."

"Have a good one. See you Sunday—you and Fred." Piper couldn't suppress a grin. She always enjoyed her encounters with Elsie.

Elsie squeezed Piper's shoulder before moving on to finish her business in her office before leaving.

Piper thought some more about Dal. Something had landed her in foster care, and although she carried the scars, she had to have strength and endurance, even in the face of adversity. Look at all she'd accomplished and what she cared about—a young daughter, down-and-out animals.

❖

When Piper entered the front door of her Oakland childhood home on Wednesday evening, the delicious aroma of lasagna floated out from the kitchen, and Piper heard the voices of her mom, Bryce, and Hannah. Tux, a three-legged dog Piper helped Meg rescue off the streets of San

Francisco, came running to greet her, then followed her to the kitchen. Adopted by Piper's mom, he hadn't forgotten Piper.

"Well, Tux. Are you the lasagna chef?" Piper reached down and patted his head.

"No, just my tripod taste tester," her mom replied.

After greeting Piper, they all settled at the table to eat and chat. Bryce had been busy with work too, so Piper hadn't talked to her since she'd started at NAS.

"How's the new job?" Bryce asked.

Piper considered where to start. "Remember a dog named Einstein?" That got her mom's and Hannah's attention as well.

"The dog I chased down?" Looking between her wife and Piper's mom, Bryce said, "If this is the same Einstein, Piper and the dog owner ran into each other while running. Literally. An air horn caused the dog to trip Piper, then the woman fell on top of Piper. Nice dog, extremely rude woman."

"That's the dog. And the woman is my new boss for the next five and a half weeks."

"You've got to be kidding me." Bryce leaned back in her chair and examined Piper. "I didn't read your name in the obituaries, and I haven't arrested anyone for murder so far this week, so I guess you both survived a few days together. How'd you manage that?"

Piper knew Bryce would find this all very entertaining. "I only worked with her on Monday. She was gone today. Her name is Dahlia Noble, Dal for short, and I won't tell you that I'm willing to withhold judgment because you'd only give me a hard time."

"I would. So rude. At the top of my rude people list. Seemed to blame you, and no word of thanks to me. Ran my ass off to save her dog." Bryce shifted her gaze from Piper to her wife and Piper's mom. "She owes me a little appreciation for saving Einstein."

"She admitted that in her own way."

"Her own way?" Bryce's eyebrows rose.

"She knew she blew it." Piper sighed. Bryce had probably seen Dal at her worst, but Piper didn't want to get into a discussion of Dal's attributes. She was struggling with her own evolving assessment. "Even admitted that Einstein probably owes you a thank you."

Bryce laughed. "*Einstein* owes me? *Probably?* I guess she's still not your dream woman, huh?"

Piper could never keep anything from Bryce, so she remained silent.

"Oh my God, Pipes. You do like her."

Piper wasn't exactly sure how to define what she felt for Dal after the one full day she'd spent with her, but the more she considered the woman and what she knew about her, the more she wanted to at least make an effort to know her better. She didn't say any more—didn't tell them that Dal was very guarded, or that she wasn't sure her new boss even liked her.

"I'm so happy you came to dinner tonight." Piper's mom interrupted her contemplation about her new job. She turned toward Bryce and Hannah. "Hosting you two never gets old. After all the time Piper spent at your house when she was younger, Bryce, you're welcome here anytime."

Bryce's mom had taken her into their home when her own mom was at work, busy supporting the two of them with her two jobs. She considered how she might have turned out without the love that Bryce's family had offered her. Maybe guarded, like Dal.

Those thoughts about Bryce's family churned up buried memories of her childhood loneliness. They reminded her why she wanted a family of her own and made her consider that maybe she had more in common with Dal than she wanted to think about tonight. And she was still figuring out how she should respond to Dal's grumpiness, probably a way of keeping people at a distance. Piper didn't want it to get her down, and it might, if she let it. But if she focused on understanding Dal, maybe she could help her. She'd done that with Cate. She was good at that.

Piper was happy when her mother brought out dessert, and the rest of the evening was spent in lighter conversation and enjoying each other's company.

❖

As Piper checked on her jungle at the law office on Thursday, she paused at the cactus, the only plant Cate had shown an attachment to. Piper smiled at the names Cate had called it—*prickly plant, the barbed one, that spiky thing*. Cate had admitted she might have some affection for that plant. She'd even made a gift of one to Piper in a camouflaged thank you for Piper's support when she was dating Meg. A tiny little needle-infested twig.

Then the idea hit Piper. She would swing by the store and pick up a little greenery she could present to Dal at NAS tomorrow, just to show her there were no hard feelings after Dal had called her the pathway assailant. Something Dal Noble might appreciate.

On her way home, Piper stopped at the store and headed to the floral and plant section. This wasn't a bouquet-seeking mission. Piper loved flowers, but those were not on the shopping list tonight. She walked up and down the aisles looking at the many options, on the hunt for a specific quarry. It took some effort, not that she didn't love shopping for plants. She could probably do it all night, but she needed results because she had to be at work at NAS tomorrow morning, and she wanted to get home to spend some time with Sunny.

The victor ranked in size with that tiny needle-infested twig that Cate had given her over two years ago, smaller than she would have liked because Piper didn't know how she would manage to bring a larger cactus to the office on public transit. She could have embraced a much bigger, more travel-friendly plant, but she had wanted this type. It was perfect for the message she wanted to convey.

Dal was already in the office when Piper arrived on Friday with her hands full. Hearing a racket at the entrance to NAS, Dal came from her office to check out the commotion just in time to witness a hip-swing, door-opening motion by Piper that captured Dal's attention. Piper stopped her humming and offered Dal a grin.

"Morning, Dal."

Dal checked out Piper's outfit. She told herself it wasn't because she cared what Piper was wearing—she was just curious after Monday. She hadn't seen Piper on Wednesday and realized she was looking forward to spending time with her today. She stuffed that thought away, not wanting to deal with it.

The unconventional new temp wore a white button-down shirt and black slacks tucked into her black boots. Dal frowned as she felt a surge of disappointment. She knew Piper was attractive, no matter her outfit, but Dal realized that she had rather enjoyed the break from boring, the eccentricity of Piper's outfit on Monday.

She even conceded that the apparel likely reflected who Piper was and not what others wanted her to be. It had added a bit of color to the place. And the banter had been fun. She'd enjoyed herself. Dal couldn't remember when she'd last found anyone within decades of her own age to be both so genuine and engaging. That was appealing.

As soon as Dal had hoped that she hadn't completely offended Piper on Monday with her clothing comments, she'd chastised herself for worrying about it. For the first time in a very long time, Dal was feeling uncertainty over a woman, wanting to know her better type of confusion.

Dal pinched the bridge of her nose as a warning whispered in her head. This wasn't the time to be confused. There was no doubt that Piper wasn't Dal's usual type—she wasn't a smooth talker or someone with a carefully orchestrated and staged allure. She had an uncalculating appeal, as if her presentation simply expressed who she was.

Dal reminded herself that she had no interest in giving up any part of a life that mostly seemed to be working for her. Not for any woman. When it wasn't working, it was because she'd broken her pledge. And that brought her to her divorce. She still had to get that settlement agreement before the divorce could be finalized. Besides, Piper was an employee—there were professional boundaries Dal would not cross. But she could engage Piper in a friendly manner. Be cordial, she should be cordial.

"Good morning, Piper. No injured dogs to donate to today?" When Piper gave her a quizzical look, Dal put her hand between her clavicles. "Pink tie." She wasn't going to bring up that black-and-blue vest, a reminder of the park incident. Of Piper pointing to where her bruise was. She thought she'd done a good job of not thinking of Piper in that way. If only Piper hadn't brought up Olive Oyl and Maid Marian and declared she liked women, then she wouldn't have been on Dal's mind at all since Monday.

"Oh. The pink tie. You liked it? I thought you found it blinding, so I left it at home."

"Excruciatingly so. But I came prepared. Brought my sunglasses today." Dal decided that a little banter couldn't hurt.

"Well, I brought you something. I bought it last night for you." Piper beamed at her.

"I might still need my sunglasses for that blinding smile." Damn, the bushwhacker was growing on Dal, exuding a friendly warmth.

Piper held out a little cactus. "Just a small something to green up your day. You don't have to thank me."

Dal took the gift but didn't know what to say. An armored plant? She took control of her confusion. "So, *thank you* is the correct response, hmm? Does *speechless* work?" Dal looked down at the cactus now in her hand. Then back at Piper. "Interesting choice, thorns."

"Those aren't actually thorns—they're highly modified leaves. The cactus stands for endurance and strength. Even in the face of adversity. Also, enduring love like a mother's love. Ruby and all," Piper said. "I like plants and wanted to give you one. This one spoke to me as the right plant for you. Floriography, the language of flowers." Then she added, "You're welcome."

Dal knew that she needed to keep this on a professional level. Piper was skilled at moving a conversation into the realm of chitchat. And she was finding that chitchat addictive. But chitchat was how she'd divulged to Piper the fact that she had a daughter named Ruby who was five years old. And revealed some insight regarding her affinity for animals versus most people. Dal needed to get the morning back on course. After she set the little cactus on the filing cabinet to give herself some space from the thoughtful gift, Einstein wandered out from Dal's office, tail wagging.

"Well, aren't you a good dog?" Piper kneeled and gave him a hug. His tail beat harder, whacking the side of the receptionist's desk.

"He's only here today because nobody's home with him. When you two are finished with the lovefest, I surprisingly have some work-related things to discuss."

Piper laughed. "I don't think I've left Cate's legal practice after all. You sound just like her. Always keeping me on track. Just focus me, and I'll get the job done."

Dal thought that was exactly what was needed. Not that Piper wasn't accomplishing the work she'd been hired to do—she was excellent at it. Cate was lucky to have her. But Dal needed to keep Piper out of her private life. Out of her head. Out of her heart. She'd walked away from no-strings-attached sex in that bar almost two weeks ago because she was starting to feel that she needed something different in her life, although she didn't need something that was a threat to maintaining a life that worked. One that had worked until the Chantal disaster, which just proved what happened when she lapsed from the promises she'd made herself. This wasn't about Piper. This was about Dal. With that, Dal gave Piper several more assignments to complete. Assignments that should keep Piper busy for at least another week or more.

❖

When she arrived on Monday, Piper noticed that the little cactus was no longer on the filing cabinet but had been moved to a bookcase in Dal's office where Dal could see it while she worked. Dal seemed to be avoiding directly engaging with Piper, although on her more than usual number of trips up and down the hallway passing Piper's office door, she would slow down and spend longer than necessary glancing in at her. Either Dal was constantly checking up to be sure she was on task with the work Dal had given her, or she had an interest in Piper. Dal finally came into her office just before she left for the day.

"Hi, Dal. Busy day?" Piper looked up from her computer as Dal entered.

"I've been very busy all day." Dal cleared her throat. "I'm predicting a busy week. Probably no time to chitchat." Dal paused as if she was at a loss for words.

"Got it. No chitchat." Piper waited patiently. "Can I help you with something?" Piper waited some more, struggling with her intuition that Dal was making this all up and losing that fight. "Maybe a little personal talk?" Piper grinned, and Dal's lips pursed before a hint of a smile graced her lovely mouth.

"As I just made perfectly clear, I don't have time for chitchat. However, if there are any work-related issues that you'd like to have a serious discussion about, maybe I can manage that."

Piper put her hand on her chin and furrowed her brow, pretending she was thinking. She had to stay within the bounds of their professional roles, and she didn't want to shut Dal down with a question that would trigger her protective reflex. Then she snapped her fingers. During her volunteer time at the rescue yesterday, she had learned more about Fred.

"Burning question about adoption fees," Piper said. "Nonprofit related. Fred, the dog in run number seven at Wee Critter Haven, has a family who loves him, and Elsie says they're perfect for an adoption, but the dad lost his job and the fee is worrying them. The kids in the family are two boys, twelve and fourteen. Losing Fred will break their hearts."

"Ambushing me again." Dal's accusation carried no bite in her tone. She put her hand on her chest. "A blow to the heart—if I had one." She paused for a moment, then said, "There might be a Fred Fund if you give me a day to check it out."

Piper felt a ripple of delight. "A Fred Fund, huh? I'll bet you know right where you can get your hands on it. Can I make an additional suggestion?"

"As long as it's not chitchat." Dal couldn't mask the twinkle in her eyes, even if she had schooled her expression to neutral.

Piper had appreciated Dal's bluish-gray eyes, but when they twinkled, they were dazzling. The blues came out. The sky. The ocean. The delphinium or larkspur bloom—grace, dignity, and protection from the dangers in life so nothing stood in the way of success. Piper suspected that was fitting.

"Maybe it would be good for those two kids to come and volunteer at the shelter as well as offering a little Fred Fund support. It would help the shelter and probably make the entire family feel good about helping cover Fred's fee in donated time. Make it seem less like charity." Piper shrugged as she waited for Dal's response.

"As if the Fred Fund is charity. It's in the best interest of the rescue, prevents overcrowding by keeping animals moving to new homes." Dal's reply came out as a defensive grumble, but Piper knew there was no designated Fred Fund except the one Dal was about to create. "I have it on good authority, though, that you're experienced in counseling and therapy, so making people feel good is probably right up your alley."

Piper nodded as she fought to suppress her pleasure that Dal was willing to have this conversation with her. "I'll accept the counseling assertion, as long as you don't fire me. Now I'd better finish up my day job here before the chitchat gets me terminated."

Dal cleared her throat but didn't manage to suppress the amusement Piper could hear in her voice. "Good night, Piper. Go home, and I'll see you on Wednesday." And with that, she turned and left.

❖

As she was heading down the NAS hallway to her own rescue management office on Wednesday morning, Elsie stopped at Piper's office to let her know that money had turned up as an anonymous targeted donation that would ensure that Fred would end up in the home with the family who loved him. Piper kept her mouth shut, but Dal was certainly growing on her—touching her heart in a way she couldn't deny.

And this wasn't just about her heart. Dal had met her definition of physically stunning from that first encounter out there on the running trail—her own body's reaction had told her so—even when Dal's rudeness had derailed Piper's thoughts of that physical attraction. If it was just about arousal, touching Dal's body in places that would make her plead for more…well, Piper's dreams were filled with those images as she spent time with Dal.

But Piper wanted more than sex. She wanted a chance at love when she decided to become involved with a woman again. And although Dal's guard was still up, Piper was catching glimpses of what was underneath—someone who might be worth trying to know better. Piper decided that she'd attempt to put her feelings into a blog tonight.

It was close to noon when Piper heard the main office door open and went out to the reception area to see who had entered. The visitor acted like she knew the place, and she did. The older woman cheerily introduced herself as Viola and told Piper she was there to collect Dal for lunch. Piper let her know that Dal was on the phone. Viola walked to Dal's door and waved, then returned to talk to Piper while she waited.

"Just so you know, she growls, but she doesn't bite." Viola chuckled as she tilted her head toward Dal's door.

That was exactly what Elsie had told Piper about Dal. "And the laptop password? Just your sense of humor?"

"Just me giving Dal a bad time. As her stand-in mom and her friend." Viola seemed to want to offer Piper information about Dal, but Piper wasn't sure why.

Piper waited to see what else Viola might disclose about Dal.

Probably inappropriate at a boss-employee level, but she couldn't help it if Viola wanted to talk. And Piper wanted to listen.

"I've loved her since I met her when she was fourteen, a mix of hurt, determination, and independence. Hurt by her childhood with a terrible father, determined to be a success and never be dependent on anybody or hurt again." Viola studied Piper, and then her dark eyes warmed as if she'd decided that Piper measured up to some secret standard. "Dahlia can be a pain sometimes, but I suspect you can hold your own."

Dahlia. Dal had said on that first day that only Viola called her that, usually when she was in trouble. Piper guessed that being a pain qualified as trouble. Now Viola had filled in a few blanks.

As Piper was absorbing all of this information, Viola continued, "Take good care of her, Piper." Then Viola winked.

Piper wasn't sure what to think, but she knew she wanted to know Dal better personally. She was beginning to suspect Viola wanted that for her too—she wasn't usually too far off in reading people, but she didn't want to be presumptuous. She didn't want to be pressured either.

Dal was complex, and Piper didn't want to get hurt. She didn't want to fall for someone who couldn't love her, but how would she know without taking some risk? She was contemplating her growing feelings for her new boss when Dal emerged from her office, shepherding Viola out the door. Viola had a big mouth, or Dal's best interest at heart. Piper couldn't miss Viola's love for Dal. Yes, there was so much more to the woman than Dal wanted to present to others.

DANCING IN THE WEEDS WITH PIPES THE UNPLUGGED

"The Leap"

Have you ever stood on the edge of your future? Of course, every individual moment of your life you've got your past at your back and your future right there in front of you. But today, yours is offering a flashing-lights, danger-sign detour from that route you had planned. A chance to put yourself on a possible red-eye special and fly straight over a cliff in the dark. A detour that offers no clue how the landing will go. Not even a clue if it's really a detour or actually the only way home.

Your ass warns you. Don't be a dumbass. Don't get kicked in the ass. Don't let your ass end up in a sling. But that other passenger accompanying you, the one called your heart—it's whispering a dare. Challenging you to jump, because you aren't finding true love on the route you've been taking. It tells you that it's time to risk the splat of another bad landing.

Your dream woman is only a mirage, existing as an imaginary destination, an excuse after you've been to that place where you tried to play the game of love and lost. Where you stayed too long, even after you knew it was time to move on.

And now, there's someone who is not a mirage. She's real. And sometimes rude, difficult, and layered in state-of-the-art protective gear. There's a gauntlet of other reasons this isn't a good idea. But she's already carrying on a conversation with your heart. That damn heart, telling you that she knows how to love—animals, a child, a stand-in mom. So, you kiss your ass good-bye and agree with your heart. It's time to take the leap, wherever it lands you.

CHAPTER SIX

D al sat in her office on Thursday and contemplated the previous day. Over lunch, Viola had grilled her about how Piper was working out, about her love life—subtly linking the two as if Viola could read her emotions. Well, she probably could. That was a red flag for Dal. She knew she needed to stay away from Piper, even if she was a bit weak.

Piper was connecting with her, working her way past Dal's carefully constructed walls. Dal wanted it to be just a silly little plant, but no woman had ever given her a gift like that small cactus, simple and handpicked and heartfelt. And it irritated her that the memory of her body pressed to Piper's out there on the pavement kept coming to mind when Piper looked at her with those enthralling, laughing eyes as Dal tried to avoid chitchat because they had important work to do... and because chitchat could only lead to trouble. There was no place for Piper in her life. Hell, she needed to remember that she was still dealing with her last relationship mistake.

Dal mentally replayed the conversation that she'd just had on a phone call from her attorney, Nora Lowry.

Lowry had said that Chantal's lawyer had indicated Chantal was now talking one million instead of two million for a signature on the divorce settlement, on top of the alimony Dal had agreed to.

Dal knew what a million bucks would do for the rescues, but she couldn't hurt Ruby to save that million dollars either. She could get the money from some of her investment funds, but she still hated the thought of handing it to Chantal.

She'd told Lowry that she believed Chantal was fishing and beginning to realize how out of line her demands were. Dal didn't want a court battle, but she told her lawyer that she wanted to wait and see whether Chantal would sign for less.

And now, Chantal was only one of the current issues in her life because Dal also needed to figure out what to do with Piper when the load of work she'd assigned her was finished. How would she keep Piper at a distance with the thirteen workdays to go? Dal had counted them. She figured Piper would probably be done by tomorrow with the tasks she'd been given.

Dal was correct. On Friday morning, Piper leaned in and knocked, then waited in the doorway with a stack of papers in her hand.

"I've got the report finished for you, collating the information from all of the computer records you gave me," Piper said. "I'll email everything to you, but I printed out some of the clinic data summaries you were interested in seeing right away, going back five years. In case you have any questions."

Piper wore a lilac button-down shirt with brown slacks and boots. Her untamed hair framed her intriguing face. Dal couldn't help herself—she focused on Piper's full sensuous mouth as she continued speaking about data summaries.

Dal nodded, the words barely registering as they escaped that mouth. Dal refocused. Her accounting firm tracked most of her bottom-line money flow—gross and net revenues, expenditures, taxes—but she'd had Piper collate additional useful information when she'd realized she wanted to keep Piper busy in that back office. The fact that Piper was capable of doing the work was very helpful for NAS, but Dal didn't want to admire how capable she was. She didn't want to admire her mouth either.

"Come in and let's see." Dal beckoned Piper in and motioned for her to sit in a chair across from her at her desk. A full desk between them—two hundred pounds of solid oak. That should work. And she'd put a halt to any talk that would reveal personal information about herself. She'd been doing a fairly good job of avoiding that type of interaction. Except for Monday.

Okay, she'd concede that she'd wanted to pull Piper in close, weave her fingers through that head of gorgeous red hair in a moment of weakness. Stroke it back, exposing that spot just below Piper's ear…that very kissable spot. She might have been upset out there on the jogging trail, but she hadn't forgotten the feel of her lips brushing against that smooth soft skin.

It had to be her hormones because Dal had done everything right on Monday. That had been her, the boss, asking an employee if there were any issues that needed serious discussion. Then they'd discussed the Fred Fund. So, no, that wasn't chitchat. Just in case Piper assumed a softer side to her, she'd needed to make her point. The fund was not charity. Charity offered too much personal insight. Plus, having the two boys volunteer to help at the rescue clarified it wasn't charity, only a bit of earned assistance. Even if that hadn't been her own brilliant idea. But the bottom line was that there was no place in her professional life or personal life for thoughts of something more with Piper. She wouldn't let her mind go there. She'd focus on the fact that the woman was an employee. End of discussion. Dal took a deep breath. That little cactus on her bookshelf wasn't some sentimental gift. Hadn't Piper declared that it represented strength? And endurance? She had this under control.

That was before Piper accidentally touched Dal while exchanging paperwork, and Dal's body told her it was no ordinary touch—even though it was. It was nothing more than Piper's knuckles sweeping along the length of Dal's arm and across the back of her hand as they both reached across the desk at the same time for the paper transfer. The friction of skin to skin, a caress that spread from her limb to her fluttering heart, then a rush of arousal that traveled downward and settled between her legs. Desire that stopped her breathing for a moment.

As she looked into Piper's hazel eyes, she saw that it hadn't been done on purpose. Piper was too transparent. While Piper's face initially displayed surprise, her eyes darkened and mirrored the same yearning she knew her own were conveying. It was mutual, at least the desire. And Dal suspected the emotional draw too.

Dal had promised herself she wasn't going to make any decision about what to do with Piper until Monday, and she wasn't going to let her friggin' libido control that decision. Or her heart. She gritted her teeth and worked through the information with Piper, hardly absorbing a thing. She'd have to study it later. She'd take it home and look it over this weekend when Piper wasn't sitting directly across from her. So much for a two-hundred-pound desk. *Fuck.*

❖

Dal left after lunch to meet with Elsie. She had to admit that if she was going to keep feelings she didn't understand and couldn't control in check, it was rather fortuitous that she'd had this meeting scheduled. She'd toured some of the nearby twenty-four-hour for-profit clinics with Alex over a week ago, and this afternoon she was focusing on the nonprofit rescues. She didn't have time for more than a tour of the San Francisco rescue with Elsie, and after that tour, Dal asked her if any of the other animal rescue centers were having any issues.

"The Oakland rescue shelter, Wee Critter Haven, has experienced an increase in the intake of animals that is stretching the capacity. We're already fostering out all the animals we're able to find foster placements for and offering as much pet support as we can to keep animals with their families. The Oakland shelter's already handling more animals than we'd like, and there's no space at the other shelters for significant transfer," Elsie told her.

As a veterinarian, Dal knew that adequate space with an appropriate configuration was important in limiting the spread of disease through a shelter. Dal had set up protocols to maximize the health of the animals—quarantine areas, intake vaccinations, testing, sanitation, stress reduction, foster care when possible. Dal didn't want overcrowding to cause problems for her rescues.

"Knowing you, Elsie, I suspect you might have some ideas for solving the issue." Dal had worked with Elsie for several years and found her to be competent and caring.

"The property next door would make a perfect expansion area. It shares a wall with our rescue shelter that could easily be opened up. With some modifications, I think it could be what we need, and it happens to have just gone up for sale," Elsie replied. "I think it will sell fast, so if you think the nonprofit might be interested, you should probably contact your real estate agent and see it asap."

The real estate agent had said that the seller's agent was only taking offers through Sunday at four o'clock, planning to accept one on Sunday evening. Ruby had a morning family fun run at her school and an afternoon ballet class recital on Saturday, with a follow-up pizza party. Dal refused to miss that time with her daughter, so Saturday wasn't an option. She needed to see the space Sunday morning so she'd have time to consider and detail an offer with the agent if she wanted it.

Even if it meant running into Piper, she had to do what was in the best interest of the animals.

Not that her heart and her libido didn't want to encounter Piper, but her head knew it would only make keeping her at arm's length harder if they spent any personal time in each other's company. Dal frowned in frustration. It seemed that circumstances were conspiring against her.

❖

"Get your shoes on, Ruby, and we'll go see the dogs and cats." It was Sunday morning and Dal had realized that she needed to bring Ruby along to Wee Critter Haven because Viola was gone today visiting a cousin and couldn't watch her.

"Can we bring home a cat, Mom? Or maybe a rabbit and a duck." Ruby looked at Dal with that calculating sideways glance that came with her teasing grin. "Wait. I don't want those. I think we should get an elephant." Ruby squealed with laughter.

"An elephant? Only if you promise to keep it in your bedroom." Dal teased her back as she leaned down and handed Ruby her other shoe before looking at her watch. "Let's go, Ruby-Doo. Those dogs and cats are waiting for you."

After calling Einstein back inside before locking up, they walked out to Dal's hybrid Lexus. She was aware that there were many people who were surprised when she didn't drive up in some sexy luxury sports car, but they didn't really know her. She'd said good-bye to that sports car with no regrets when Ruby was born.

After checking to make sure that Ruby's car seat harness was secured, Dal moved to the driver's door, hopped in behind the steering wheel, and drove to the rescue. When they arrived, she helped Ruby out of the car and they walked into the reception area of Wee Critter Haven. A few people were being helped, and the sound of robust barking to the accompaniment of more muffled meows drifted up to the front from the back. Dal looked around and didn't see the real estate agent there yet.

As she was waiting, Elsie and Piper came through the door from the back area where the cages and runs were located. Piper's entire face lit up, as if seeing Dal had just made her day. Lit up in a way that Dal hadn't experienced from another woman in…maybe ever. Shit. It made her chest constrict as she felt the effect right to her core.

Piper was wearing tight black jeans and an orange T-shirt that didn't hide her shape, and pink Converse that clashed with her already clashing shirt and red hair. Dal could find no rational explanation for why she found that so alluring, except that Piper was an attractive woman who didn't work at it, who was that way without effort, that way because she didn't worry about what others thought. She was just being herself. Dal looked away because she knew she was staring.

Elsie came straight over to Dal, Piper right behind her. "The real estate agent isn't here yet," Elsie said before turning to Piper. "Dal's here to check out the place next door that's for sale, as an area for expansion of this place." Elsie's gaze moved down to Ruby. "I haven't seen you in ages. Your mom keeps you tucked away. You've grown." Then she looked back at Piper. "This is Ruby, Dal's daughter."

"Hi, I'm Piper. I've seen your photo in your mom's office." Piper gave Ruby a wave.

"I'm Ruby," Ruby repeated. "Do you know my mom?"

"I do," Piper replied, turning toward Dal and offering her a smile just as Barbara, the real estate agent, walked in.

Barbara already knew Elsie, and after shaking Piper's hand, they prepared to head next door to view the property for sale.

"I can keep Ruby here with me if that's okay," Piper said. "She might enjoy seeing the dogs and cats more than where you're headed. I won't let her get hurt. I know the perfect old cat we can visit."

Dal fought to block the surge of emotion that flooded her at the realization that Piper was a kid person. Of course she was—she liked kids, liked Ruby. Then Dal considered that she'd never dated a kid person, not that the women she'd dated were more than short-term or one-night stands, except for Chantal, who was in no way a kid person either. Dal mentally slapped herself back into reality—she wasn't dating Piper, wasn't going to date Piper.

"Can I, Mom? Can I go with Piper?" Ruby tugged on Dal's shirt.

Dal knew it was the better option for Ruby. Her daughter would have a better time, and she trusted Piper to take care of her.

"*Pleeeeze.*"

Dal looked down at Ruby. "Yes. I'll come find you in the back when I'm done."

Ruby let out a whoop, then grabbed Piper's hand as she pulled her toward the door to the animal area. Dal heard Ruby ask if they had any horses and Piper telling her that this rescue wasn't big enough to make a horse happy, but they had an old resident cat named Boris who needed to be petted and would love a reading of the Doc McStuffins book. Dal shook her head, and Ruby never looked back.

❖

After Dal toured the property and discussed what a reasonable offer would be with Barbara, the agent left to draw up the paperwork for Dal to electronically sign in a few hours. Dal headed to the back to collect Ruby so she could take her to get some lunch. She knew Ruby would love that.

Damn if Dal's heart hadn't already done enough cheerleading related to Piper for one day. She'd spent part of the real estate tour reminding herself that Piper was the office temp—that was it. That was all she could let her be. But her heart went into overdrive when Dal rounded a corner in the shelter and found Piper and Ruby in one of the animal visitation rooms. Ruby sat on Piper's lap as Piper read a book to both her daughter and the cat. Not that the cat was paying much attention, but Ruby was.

"Mom, we're reading this book to Boris. Piper and me. Can we finish, then get some lunch?"

Dal nodded and watched the scene in front of her. When they finished the story, Piper returned Boris to his bed for a nap, and they headed up toward the reception area. Stopping in front of a run, Piper stuck her hand in to scratch a mature dog who came right up to the wire door. The tan and black shepherd mix arched his neck up so Piper's fingers could stroke under his chin.

"Fred?" Dal asked after looking at the run number. It was run number seven.

"The one and only. Beneficiary of the *not-charity* Fred Fund." Piper's eyes danced. "Elsie said that he'll probably be ready to go home with his family late this next week. The boys were in today, and Fred loves them. After he's home with them, they're going to put in some extra time helping around here."

"Hello, Fred. Nice to meet you." Dal put the back of her hand where the dog could smell it on his terms. He looked up at Dal with his dark soulful eyes. She reached between the wires and offered him a chin scratch too.

"Can we take him home, Mom?"

"There are already two boys who are going to give him a good home. Besides, you've got Einstein."

"Okay," Ruby said. "Then let's go to lunch with Piper. I'm hungry, and Piper is my friend. I like her. A lot."

Dal knew lunch with Piper wasn't a good idea, not for keeping her emotions in check. She noted that Piper was polite enough to let Dal decide without commenting. There was no good excuse not to invite her along—only good reasons not to. Dal felt the mounting anxiety associated with getting to know Piper even better. But she could find no honest explanation she wanted to offer Ruby.

"You've probably got other plans," Dal said. When Piper remained silent, Dal admonished herself for getting into this position before finally asking, "Would you like to join us?"

"I would if it's not intruding on your day with Ruby." Piper looked at Dal.

"Piper! Piper!" Ruby clapped her hands and cheered.

Dal felt nothing but conflict. This was getting complicated. She didn't want Ruby getting attached to someone Dal couldn't include in their lives without making compromises that would only create issues she didn't want. And there were already issues she had no control over. If she just wanted to be Piper's friend, that wouldn't be a problem, but simple friendship wasn't her reaction to Piper.

"Bye, Fred," Ruby called over her shoulder, running toward the exit sign above the backroom door. Dal wanted an exit sign too. But she was feeling the echo of Ruby's cheer. *Piper! Piper!*

The three of them loaded into the car, Piper in the front seat next to Dal, and Ruby in her child seat in the back. Dal hated how normal it felt, Piper talking and laughing with Ruby while she drove and listened. Like Piper was a piece of their lives that Dal hadn't known was missing—not missing until she came along and filled an empty place that Dal didn't want to admit was there. Dal decided that she'd make it through today and then figure it out tomorrow. In the meantime, she'd just enjoy lunch.

After stopping at a deli and picking up some avocado and cheese sandwiches with drinks to share, they found a park.

Ruby took her sandwich apart and traded her avocado for Piper's cheese. Dal watched the negotiation and trade, feeling torn at how easily Piper interacted with Ruby and alarmed at how easily Ruby might become attached to her. Not that the prospect of her own attachment crossed her mind for more than an absurd second.

"She's cool, Mom."

No, Dal thought. *She's hot.* But that thought was totally inappropriate. Piper had no place in her plans for her life. "Yes, Piper's cool."

"Hey, I'm sitting right here." Piper grinned, that joyful, sexy grin that connected with Dal's heart.

❖

Piper was sitting on a small rock wall next to Dal, her now cheeseless sandwich laid out on its open paper wrapper on Piper's other side. The park was small, without tables, but it was a beautiful little green space and had a swing set for Ruby to use.

Piper was having a wonderful time. She was pleased that Dal had been willing to let her watch Ruby at the rescue and that she'd been included in their lunch plans. That Dal had been willing to offer Piper this glimpse into her private life.

She could tell that Dal had been experiencing some reservations about bringing her along for sandwiches. Dal was good at keeping her emotions hidden, so much better than she was, but Piper had spent two weeks working for Dal now. She had noticed that pronounced swallow, the color shift in those steel-blue eyes as a storm front gathered strength when Dal wasn't happy. Piper had seen the heat of attraction in those eyes too. Piper was having trouble reading Dal. Or maybe she was reading her accurately, and the mixed messages were Dal's conflict, conflict reflected in her warm and cool interactions.

"I'm sorry if I'm intruding on your day." Piper shifted and looked at Dal, sitting next to her on the wall.

"Don't be ridiculous. I'm just surprised you'd want to waste your day with us. You must have better things to do."

"Nothing better than this," Piper said as Dal turned and studied her.

Just then, Ruby came running toward the short rock wall that Piper and Dal shared, sitting about a foot apart. Dal's daughter climbed up on the end where Dal sat, forcing Dal to move toward the center to make room for her daughter, pushing Dal against Piper.

Piper had been feeling an increasing draw toward Dal over these two weeks she'd been working for her. They'd been dancing around their chemistry for several days now—at least Piper thought that's what they were doing. She was pretty sure Dal felt it too.

But sitting here pushed up against Dal's side in an unplanned closeness, she wanted to suspend the tap dancing around each other, at least for a few minutes on a Sunday afternoon. Yeah, she would love to plant that impossible kiss on Dal's mouth, but Dal wasn't ready for it—if she ever would be. Plus, Dal was her boss and Ruby was here chaperoning. All of those things were saving Piper from that impulsive act that she had no business considering. An act that would get her fired. For real.

But there was still the possibility of getting to know Dal better. The real Dal. Piper's private life was wide open. Dal's was closed off, hammered shut as tight as Dal could manage. She was guarding a daughter, a past, a heart—Piper did not know the extent of the list or where to start, so she decided to go with the moment when Ruby headed back over to the swings.

"Ruby's a great kid." Piper broke the silence.

"Are you surprised by that?"

"Yes and no." Piper didn't want to offend Dal or cross any lines.

"That answer covers a lot of territory," Dal dryly noted, her right foot drifting against Piper's left as she remained close to Piper after she'd moved over for Ruby.

Piper wasn't sure if Dal had noticed the contact or not. They were sitting thigh to thigh, hip to hip, shoulder to shoulder, and now foot to foot. Piper stared down at her own pink sneakers next to Dal's expensive black flats. She thought about how different they were. Their shoes might be a metaphor for the two of them. Holy heck, that would make quite a pair of shoes. Probably not Dal's style, but Piper acknowledged that the image appealed to her. The dandelion and the dahlia.

"Surprised? No, because I have a clue how much love has gone into your daughter's life," Piper replied. "And the yes probably isn't a yes to my statement. I'm not surprised she's a great kid. I'm just a bit surprised that the public image you seem to want to project isn't one of a loving mother. I think you're a great mother, but I also think you work to keep it all compartmentalized."

Dal didn't answer for at least half a minute. Strange, it didn't even feel like an uncomfortable silence to Piper. Just a natural pause while Dal was gathering her thoughts, while their bodies still touched almost the full length of one side, and that felt natural too. Not that it didn't bring back thoughts of their physical encounter in a different outdoor setting, one that happened when Dal wasn't a woman she worked for with hidden depths, but a total stranger. A rude, beautiful, total stranger.

Then Dal spoke. "I'm not ashamed of being a good mother to Ruby. Case in point, I brought her with me today."

"I didn't say you were ashamed. I don't think you are, at all. But did you have a choice of whether to bring her today?"

Dal stiffened, and Piper had her answer.

"The best way to keep control of my life is to keep my private life private. You don't know all that I've had to deal with. That I am dealing with."

Piper had already surmised it, but Dal had just clarified that keeping control of her life was a top priority for her. "Fair enough. But I'd get lonely keeping everyone out." Piper lifted her head and turned to face Dal. They were less than a foot apart.

"I can live with lonely," Dal told Piper, but her eyes, the color of deep desire, suggested otherwise.

Piper didn't just read it as the deep desire of lust—there was more to the expression on Dal's face, a tenderness mixed with the yearning. Then Dal leaned closer to Piper, close enough for the jasmine-mixed scent that Piper had noted at Lake Merritt to flood her nostrils. So close their lips were centimeters apart. Dal lowered her lids and pressed her lips firmly together for several seconds, then took a deep breath and pulled back. Piper knew that Dal had wanted to kiss her. She wanted to kiss Dal too. But there was so much in the way.

DANCING IN THE WEEDS WITH PIPES THE UNPLUGGED

"The Park"

I can't tell you exactly how and when it happened, but I can tell you that in the park where a warm breeze blew, where flowers bloomed on a sunny day, where I sat on a wall next to a beautiful woman, I knew that something was growing.

I might say that before we came to the park that day, what was between us was the hidden tissue before the bud, meristem tissue, present with potential. Or maybe when we first sat, the bud was already a small protuberance, but only teasingly present.

Then I felt it, as we shared sandwiches side by side on the wall, a child happily swinging several feet away. What was between us could not be denied. The promise of a budding bloom, one that might become a beautiful flower—it whispered in that breeze between us. Almost, almost a kiss.

CHAPTER SEVEN

Before trying to go to sleep last night, Dal had paused to think about her urge to kiss Piper, how close she'd come before she'd stopped herself from making that terrible mistake. Bushwhacked by an unpretentious, kid-friendly, animal-loving, fashion-afflicted, smart, sensitive, engaging woman. If she hadn't let herself spend time so close to Piper, her resolve to simply view Piper as an employee wouldn't have been tested. She wouldn't have wanted to explore and taste that mesmerizing mouth. Luckily, Ruby had been there. Dal had concluded that the best way to stop this unwelcome growing chemistry between them was to limit her interactions with Piper—she needed a plan. She'd spent a restless night trying to figure one out, and this morning she was ready.

When Piper arrived, Dal was waiting for her.

"Please come on into my office, Piper. I have something I want to talk to you about."

"Let me dump my stuff in my office and I'll be right there."

Dal had Einstein with her at the office but warned him to stay in his bed as Piper came in on this Monday morning. She didn't stop for pleasantries once Piper sat on the other side of her desk. She needed to set this plan in motion. She'd felt that pressure all night long. Now looking directly into Piper's appealing hazel eyes, that alert but guileless face, Dal felt the urgency even more.

"The big fundraiser is going to be here before we know it. I'm starting to think that I may need to hire someone for mornings to cover the day-to-day stuff, someone I can expand into a full-time position later. With your time constraints at three days a week, it might be best that planning and organizing the fundraiser event should be your major focus. You can lock yourself in your office, away from the rest of us, and get the job done. It's critical to financing the rescues."

Dal mentally patted herself on the back. That was a great pitch to sell the job to Piper without upsetting her by indicating it was a way to give Dal some much-needed space from this threatening temptation that was Piper Fernley. Dal had discovered that she'd wanted to be careful not to hurt Piper's feelings, which only served to emphasize that her personal appeal was a problem. Hell, this was only the beginning of Piper's third week here at NAS.

Dal knew her concern wasn't simply about not hurting someone unnecessarily, which she did try to avoid because that never went well and there was no point in alienating people. No, this concern was about something far more unsettling, her growing feelings for Piper.

Dal struggled to ignore the provocative woman waiting patiently across from her. Provocative because Piper didn't seem to know how appealing she was. Dal fortified herself with the imperative of putting this plan in place and continued with her presentation.

"Viola started the planning and made several contacts for the fundraiser before she left, but there's still a lot to be done. She left extensive notes on the budget, the venue, the caterers, corporate sponsors…it's a long list." Dal kept her eyes on her notes as she plowed ahead. "And if you need advice, Viola's reachable by phone."

Daring to look up at Piper's attentive face, Dal kicked herself as her heart pounded faster and then that pulsating dropped lower. She told herself it wasn't about needing *this* woman—it was about needing any woman because it had been too long. There were plenty of women with smooth pale skin, a tantalizing shape, inviting lips. Now, if she could only forget that those engaging features were only part of a unique package that also included genuine, amusing, intelligent, ebullient, kind…And she definitely wasn't going to think about those audacious, untamed curls that suggested Piper just might possess an uninhibited wild streak that carried over into the bedroom. Nope, Dal wasn't going there.

She cleared her throat and fought to focus. She knew just how perceptive Piper was, and Dal didn't want her believing that she was the least bit interested because she wasn't. She couldn't let herself be. Instead, she struggled to keep her attention on the fact that Piper was efficient and smart, and with Viola's notes, the fundraiser ought to pull together just fine. This project would consume Piper's time for the next four weeks while she was here, and that was Dal's intent.

Dal continued to lay out the details for Piper. The gala event was six weeks away from the upcoming Saturday, so Piper would need to finalize everything she could, and then her replacement could complete the job in the three weeks after she was gone. The one important missing piece was the entertainment. Viola had left ideas for that too.

"You'll need to find a keynote speaker, or whatever recognizable personality you can manage. In the past, Viola found some local politician or civic-minded citizen to give a speech, a mouthpiece that probably bored the crowd a bit but fleshed out the event program. I know you can do a great job." Dal had covered her presentation, and she held her breath as she waited for Piper's response, not that it should matter what she thought. But damn, it did.

"If this is what you want me to do, and if I can talk to Viola with any questions, I should be able to get it under control in the time I have left with you, and I'll leave all of my information for the person who follows behind me. Plus, they can call me. I know that the fundraiser is critical to the rescues, and I'll do my best for them." Piper appeared a bit overwhelmed but remained professional.

Dal breathed a sigh of relief at Piper's response. She knew the fundraiser was in good hands and that Piper would be kept very busy with all that needed to be done. Mission accomplished. This was the right course of action for both of them. Even if Dal's divorce had been finalized, Dal was not romantic-love material. Piper would only end up hurt if Dal pursued her. Piper needed so much more than Dal's baggage. Cutting this off before it could develop would save them both a whole lot of grief.

Taking the notebook that Dal had given her, Piper told Dal she was heading down to her office to study it, and that she wanted to set up a spreadsheet to track each component—to help her, and hopefully, her successor. Piper left her office door open, and even though Dal could hear Piper working, she managed to avoid Piper most of the rest of the day. She chastised herself for not feeling more elated.

❖

As she was finally preparing to leave on Monday evening, Dal congratulated herself. She had everything under control. She'd had a meeting with her financial advisor after lunch, and when she'd returned, she could hear Piper down the hallway on the phone or occasionally making a sound as she worked on her computer. Not that she'd been paying attention.

Finishing up the work she was doing, Dal texted Viola, who had collected Ruby from after-school care. She wanted to touch base with her regarding dinner. She could still hear Piper and decided that before she went home to Ruby and Viola, she ought to at least check in with her. That was part of her role as the boss. It was after five o'clock, and she didn't want to be accused of overworking her temp. Or to be more honest with herself, Piper deserved to have a personal life, and Dal knew she couldn't be part of that. Plus, if she knew that Piper had a girlfriend, maybe she wouldn't be dealing with these feelings, or maybe she'd be jealous as hell. She'd never actually experienced strong jealousy, but she'd deal with that in a rational manner—yes, she'd see a girlfriend for Piper as the gift it was.

Dal paused outside Piper's doorway, in the hallway, out of sight. Piper was talking on the phone. She'd let her finish the call.

"Hi, this is Piper Fernley with CritterLove Rescues. I'm glad I finally reached you. I'm following up on the nonprofit's annual gala fundraiser event, six weeks from this upcoming Saturday. Just confirming we're still set for your catered steak or lobster dinner menu, with a vegetarian option."

Dal was pleased with how organized Piper was. She congratulated herself on her decision to hand the fundraiser off to Piper—two birds with one stone and all that.

There was silence for a moment, Piper listening to the other person on the call before she continued, "Yes, that venue's been confirmed." After another pause, Piper responded, "That's perfect. We'll keep in touch, then." Piper was silent for another moment, then, "Great. You've got my number. Thanks."

As Piper ended the call, Dal stepped forward and leaned on the doorframe until Piper looked up.

"You ready to give up for the day?" Dal noted that Piper's hair was mussed in every direction and she looked tired, but she had a smile for Dal that caused a momentary pause in Dal's respiration.

"I guess I am." Piper leaned back in her chair and steepled her hands. "I think I'm figuring most of this out. It just seems like there must be ways to maximize the profits from the fundraiser. You did pretty well last year for the rescues, compared to the net profits from the event over the past several years." Piper pointed at her computer screen. "I'd just like to know that I'm doing the best that I can for the shelters. It's important for me to line up a big entertainment draw, rather than the mayor or some suit, but no luck so far."

"It sounds like you're doing a good job. Since you're busy with this, I called an agency this afternoon and arranged to have someone here to handle the office stuff, mornings. To see how they work out as a possible person to replace Viola. They start next week."

"That sounds good," Piper replied, "since you've got me busy with this. I think we were doing okay with me covering for Viola three days a week before, but now I'm here in this office all day and have little time for out front."

"Exactly, and I do need to look ahead at filling the position permanently. You're going back to Cate in less than four weeks, and I need to get things settled. Have you heard from Cate?" Cate seemed like a safe topic.

Piper appeared pleased at the mention of Cate's name. "I've been getting emails from both her and Meg. From the photos, it looks like they're having a great time. They've finished touring France and should be in Italy today."

Dal paused, then decided it wouldn't hurt to visit with Piper a bit more. Just to be polite. "Have you been to Europe?"

"No. But I'd like to, someday."

"I've always been too busy too. Maybe someday." Dal doubted she'd ever make it to Europe. She was too busy, and she wouldn't want to go alone. "What else do you want to do in life?" As soon as that question was out of her mouth, Dal chastised herself—where the heck had that come from? She was supposed to be keeping her distance. But at least it was a pretty general question. And she wouldn't have to reveal any private information about herself.

"I'd like to get my law degree." Piper flashed Dal a hint of a frown.

Dal was surprised. She knew Piper was smart and very good at her job. And now she knew that Piper had ambition too. "Why don't you? And what would you do with it?"

"I'd like to focus on animal welfare and human rights, LBGTQIA+. But I'm supporting myself and had been assisting my mom a bit—she had minor surgery and needed a medical leave while she recovered."

Dal could see Piper advocating for animals, and people too. Especially the down and out. And helping her mom—that was totally in line with who she'd observed Piper to be. Damn, it just made her like the woman even more.

"My mom worked so hard to keep the two of us afloat all those years when I was a kid. Even now that my mom has recovered, I'm just not sure I could manage law school with full-time work, needing to do well and pass the bar and all. And the cost is out of reach for me without going into a lot of debt. I'm trying to figure it out."

As her admiration for Piper grew, Dal decided she'd better head home and stop the chitchat with her because that was definitely off the agenda. She didn't want the feelings that were stirring. Every time she engaged in personal exchanges with Piper, she seemed to learn something or share something that only made her want more from Piper than just these six weeks. But she didn't trust that it wouldn't have the inevitable ending that only concluded in rejection and pain. She'd had enough of that in her past. Now was the time to avoid making even a bigger mess of her life. There were plenty of willing women who would be happy to satisfy her basic needs and not make her heart vulnerable. She could live with that. She needed to accept living with that.

"Well, I guess I'll see you on Wednesday. Go home and have a nice evening." Dal made sure that her tone was simply collegial. Boss appropriate.

"You too. Please say hi to Ruby for me," Piper replied. "And give Einstein a pat."

Dal returned to her office, shut off her computer, grabbed her purse, and turned out the lights before closing her office door. As she headed into the reception area to leave, her cell phone dinged with a text. Looking down and seeing it was a return message from Viola, she was reading as she headed to the door, not paying attention. Viola was letting Dal know that the chicken she'd cooked would be ready in about forty-five minutes. She ate most meals with Dal and Ruby, and now that she was retired, she'd taken over frequently cooking nice dinners for the three of them.

Dal was still focused on the text when she bumped into Piper and stumbled before she ended up pressed front to front against Piper, who was pushed back against the door. Dal inhaled a deep involuntary intake of air and then fought to suppress a gasp as she reacted to Piper's closeness. Her heart stampeded in her chest. She knew this position, this body—she'd lain against it on the pathway at Lake Merritt. It was familiar and fit the contours of her own body just as well now as it had that Saturday morning. Before she'd known Piper.

"*Fuck.*" Dal tilted her head back a fraction. She silently cursed some more as she looked at Piper's lush, full lips, fighting not to touch hers against them. Dragging Piper across the receptionist's desk and taking her right there flashed across Dal's mind. She blinked to clear that thought, then looked into Piper's dark hazel eyes, now green and sienna with their unmistakable reflection of Piper's yearning. A deep and intense ache throbbed low in Dal's pelvic region, but she recognized a strong emotional desire as well, to know Piper better.

Suddenly, Dal had the answer to the question: What did she want? She'd contemplated that question when she'd walked out on the woman at the bar a few weeks ago and hadn't been back. Dal wanted more.

She could tell by the look in Piper's eyes and the rate of her respiration that this accidental encounter had affected Piper in much the same way it had just affected her. But what pissed Dal off the most, besides the fact that office sex was not going to happen between her and an employee, was that her wanting more seemed to be focused solely on Piper.

Dal didn't want to do this with anyone else. She wanted to kiss Piper. Gently hold her. Just spend time with her, exchanging banter, watching her with Ruby and Einstein. Goddammit, this wasn't just about sex. Dal was dealing with that lonely piece of her life, that empty spot in her heart that she had tried to silence. That place that Piper was speaking to. And that was why she needed to stay away from her. Shut this down. Piper could break her heart. Take the control she had over her life. What was the point of her past if she hadn't learned its lessons?

❖

Cate's office was very quiet on Tuesday. Sitting here alone all day, just the music and the plants for company, Piper tried to shove last evening's door incident with Dal out of her mind because she'd already analyzed it to death. It had been a repeat of the Lake Merritt scene, Dal up against her body, sparking everything to life. She'd felt the fullness of Dal's breasts, the press of Dal's hips and firm, muscled thighs, and her own nipples hardening, with her core clenching and wanting more.

Piper had thought she'd been lucky watching that rude woman walk away after the park encounter, but Dal was so much more. She was multilayered, contradictory in her fluctuations between no chitchat, teasing, and revealing pieces of herself.

There was a growing physical chemistry between them, and Piper felt an emotional connection as well. Last night, Piper had experienced the heat of a scorching flame that ignited between them when Dal's eyes had met her own, and the stirring emotional sentiment that nested in her chest and also wanted a chance at more. As much as Dal fought it, she knew Dal wasn't immune. Dal's one-word profane pronouncement last evening had sounded like a call to everything from fury to need.

Piper had caught the moment when Dal had looked over at the desk as they were pressed against each other—she'd noticed the hunger in Dal's eyes and surmised what Dal was thinking because she'd had the same thought. And the halt to banter and assigning Piper to focus on the fundraiser served as roadblocks to personal time together.

Piper knew she'd never had much trouble reading most people, and Dal certainly wasn't a closed book, hard as she seemed to be trying. Piper had sensed the war going on in Dal, the confusion that had been so clear on her face. She'd wanted Piper, then couldn't get away fast enough after their accidental encounter last night. Dal had yanked her out into the hallway, slammed the office door shut, and headed for the elevator, leaving Piper watching her hip-swaying jog in a tight skirt instead of those faded running shorts.

Dal was like Fred and Cate, assessing the risk of being hurt, but with seemingly formalized ground rules that wouldn't give that risk a chance. Piper understood, although her closet of emotional crap wasn't nearly as full as Cate's or Fred's or Dal's was. Besides, there could be nothing between them as long as she was employed by Dal. They both recognized that.

It was two o'clock in the law office when emails came in from both Meg and Cate, and Piper was grateful for the distraction. Cate was checking on the law practice, and Meg was sending photos of their day in Rome. With Italy nine hours ahead, Piper could picture them at eleven o'clock at night, probably sitting side by side in bed, shoulder to shoulder, keeping in touch with their normal lives—Cate communicating with her dad and Meg with her kids. Piper wasn't going to think about what they'd been doing or were about to do at this time of night. They were in love. Thinking of them only reinforced what Piper wanted, that same kind of love in her life.

Piper replied to Cate: *All's well, nothing to report here. Focus on Meg—and Italy if you have time.* She sent a photo of the prickly plant in the corner of the reception area to both of them, with an added note that she missed them. She did. They were family.

Piper knew that she and Cate were a good team as lawyer and paralegal. And Cate had taken an interest in her life, cared about her. Cate had told Piper that she'd think about Piper's goal to attain a law degree, how she might be able to help her. Then she'd grumbled about not wanting to lose a good paralegal. But Cate's eyes had projected warmth and caring as she'd said that.

As Meg had become the perfect fit for Cate's personal life, she'd also become another amazing mother figure in Piper's life. Meg had taken the time to invite her over for watercolor sessions, and she took time to listen to Piper, to support her. If things went anywhere with Dal, Piper could see asking for Meg's advice.

Piper was just finishing up for the day when she had a text from Bryce.

Bryce: *You up for a run tonight?*

Piper: *If I won't end up on the pavement under my boss.*

Bryce: *No guarantees. How are you and the new boss lady doing?*

Piper: *Meet me at 6—my place. We can talk on the run.*

Bryce: *K*

❖

"Will you forgive me if I go out for a run with Bryce, little lion? I'll make it worth your while with some tuna on top of your dinner. I'll be back before you know it. And Bryce will probably have catnip-laced kitty crack when she gets here." Sunny agreed, leading Piper to the kitchen to make good on her fish promise. He wolfed down the food.

Forty-five minutes later, after fighting rush hour traffic and no chance to talk without distracting Bryce, they stretched at their normal bench, then took off at a jog. When they'd reached the spot where the accident had occurred, at almost mile two of the loop around the lake, Bryce slowed to a walk.

"Okay, I want to hear about Dal Noble," Bryce said. "Is she treating you right? When we had dinner at your mom's, she was growing on you."

Piper considered what she wanted to disclose to her best friend. Not that there was any kiss-and-tell action. Even if there had been, she wasn't the kiss-and-tell type, at least not in any detail. Piper was always honest with Bryce. But being honest didn't mean she couldn't censor what she disclosed.

"What can I say? We have a professional relationship. Dal's the boss. I'm the employee."

Bryce didn't say anything, just raised an eyebrow.

"Dal respects the line." Piper reiterated her comment for Bryce's benefit because she knew Bryce. That line was good protection from Bryce's push to get her laid, at least by Dal when Dal was off-limits. Bryce might think a quick trip into bed was what Piper needed, and Bryce might push for it to be with almost anyone. Piper was tired of the singles bar and nightclub scene, and she'd never fallen into bed with just anyone. She just wasn't the person to navigate those places. Not anymore, and probably not before—Piper knew she didn't do it well. She wasn't enamored with online dating either, so she'd taken a break while she'd been considering her options. Then Dal had come along and started growing on her. Dal with all her armor. And now, here she was acknowledging the most obvious roadblock to Bryce, the work constraints.

"And you? How are you feeling about respecting that boss line?" Bryce shoulder-bumped Piper, looking at her with a sideways glance as they walked.

"I like her. A lot. But I wouldn't want to put her in a position that would compromise her integrity." Piper knew that was the truth. Not that she wouldn't want to end up in a compromising position someday when lines and rules and integrity weren't an issue. But not if there was no chance for love. She wanted love in her life. But she was getting way ahead of things.

Then Piper decided to share a bit more. Maybe Bryce would have some insight. After all, she'd met Dal at her rudest. "Besides, she works so hard to be a closed book. To maintain control of herself and her life. I don't know that I'll ever break through that completely." Piper tried to explain her understanding of Dal to Bryce. "Or if she even likes me that way. I don't know that she's willing to allow a place in her life for anyone else. Or in her heart."

"I checked around, and she's hard to figure out. I heard that she had a wife for a few years. And has a kid." Bryce locked her gaze on Piper.

"I know about Ruby. Met her at the rescue on Sunday. Great kid. I didn't know about the ex-wife, but I'm not surprised, with Ruby and all—not that she couldn't have decided to have a child alone."

Bryce raised her eyebrows. "What else do you know?"

"Nope. You're the gumshoe doing the investigating."

"I'm just trying to help you, Pipes. I've heard she can be a player, but then I've heard that she's a great mother. That she'd spent time in foster care as a kid. That she's made a success of her life. That she's guarded and can sometimes come across as impolite. *Rude.*" Bryce stopped and nodded as she emphasized *rude.* Piper had to concede that was how they'd initially labeled the woman in the park before she'd actually begun to know Dal better. Bryce wasn't done. "That her nonprofit is based on her fervent feelings for animals. That keeping control of her life is paramount. A mixed-up mess of information." Bryce shrugged as she finished. "All those things don't usually go hand in hand."

Piper listened to Bryce but didn't respond. She didn't like hearing Dal was a player—she knew there was so much more to Dal. But Dal certainly didn't have a loving partner that would prevent it.

"Hey, let's go get a quick bite to eat and a beer before I drop you off. There's a new place that serves food and drinks." Bryce changed the subject.

They finished their run and headed over to the bar and grill Bryce had in mind. It was a bit crowded, but they found an open table and settled in. They ordered the veggie burgers and craft beers that their waiter suggested. They were sipping their drinks and waiting for the food when a woman suddenly appeared and addressed Piper, who hadn't been paying attention.

"If it isn't Piper Fernley. I thought that was you."

Piper looked up to see Tanya Janzen. She'd known Tanya in

college, even dated her for most of their final year. Tanya had been girlfriend number two. It had been several years since Piper had heard from her.

"I'm in town on a consulting job this week. Also visiting my folks," Tanya said.

"Tanya. I haven't seen you in ages. How are you?" Piper remembered that Tanya had never met Bryce because Bryce had been abroad the year that she'd dated Tanya. She introduced them. "This is my friend Bryce. We were just out running at Lake Merritt, so the attire."

"Bryce, huh? So nice to meet you." Tanya slowly looked Bryce up and down.

Piper recollected that she and Tanya had made better friends than girlfriends. She'd had fun with the woman but never loved her, and Tanya hadn't been ready to settle down. Tanya had been an unapologetic flirt. It had worked for the college year because, at that point in her life, Piper hadn't been ready for a life partner either. She hadn't even known what a life partner looked like, the deep love she'd seen complete her friends.

"Bryce is my best friend from childhood. Married to Hannah, a local pediatrician." Piper remembered the direct approach was best with Tanya, so she made sure to clarify her friend's status.

"Excuse my manners." Tanya laughed as she continued to look at Bryce. "I've been on my own too long, getting older and older, and all the good ones are taken—except for Piper, and she wouldn't have me, except as a friend. Smart woman. It's nice to meet you, Bryce." Then Tanya shifted her attention to Piper. "What are you up to these days? I know you're a paralegal. Last I'd heard, you were working for a lawyer in San Francisco."

"Cate Colson. But she's on a long honeymoon, so I'm also doing some temp work helping out a client," Piper replied. "It's helping me out too."

"That sounds busy. What's the temp job about? Anything interesting?" Tanya asked.

Piper looked at Bryce, who communicated consent with a subtle nod, so Piper pointed at the empty chair next to herself. "Join us?"

"Sure." Tanya sat down and waved the waiter over for a daiquiri order.

"I'm working at Noble Animal Services, on a project for the associated nonprofit, CritterLove Rescues. I'm trying to organize their annual gala fundraiser, learning all I can to make it a success."

"You know I went into event planning, right?" Tanya asked.

"I remember." That's why Piper had invited Tanya to crash her time with Bryce.

"Fundraisers are my specialty. Next week up in Sacramento, I'm part of a day-and-a-half conference on maximizing fundraising. The focus is on nonprofits. It might be worth your time."

"I'm not sure what my new boss will say, but can you send me the information and let me know if there's still room?" Piper hoped Dal would at least consider letting her attend. She was confident it would help her improve the fundraiser for the rescues.

Tanya agreed before they settled in, enjoying their food, drinks, and additional conversation. Piper didn't get home until almost ten o'clock. She spent some time with Sunny on the couch and did a little writing, read through the information that Tanya had sent her, and then turned in for the night.

Dancing in the Weeds with Pipes the unPlugged

"Some Things I've Learned About Running"

1. Hit the ground running *might leave you black-and-blue.*
2. *Don't discount an air horn, a jogging trail, and a dog as a way to meet someone.*
3. *Include a little walking and talking with the running—good for the soul.*
4. *Running off at the mouth might be my sport.*
5. *Run with a friend—they can help you hobble home.*
6. *When they said running was good for the heart, I was thinking cardiac and not cupid.*
7. *Running—a form of terrestrial locomotion. Except when referring to risk aversion.*
8. *It doesn't have to be a marathon.*
9. *Every lap around the lake should be rewarded with a beer.*
10. *Broken-in running shoes, faded shorts, a baggy T-shirt—she was beautiful.*

CHAPTER EIGHT

A few minutes after she'd settled into her office on Wednesday morning, Piper heard Dal come into work and head directly to her own office. Piper wanted to discuss the conference information that Tanya had sent to her last night. She headed down the hallway and knocked on Dal's door.

"Come in." Dal didn't look up from the papers she was studying.

Piper stood and waited patiently, not sure of the reason for Dal's delay. Finally, she asked, "Can I talk to you for a second, Dal?"

Dal was so good at hiding her feelings, but when she looked up, her eyes gave her away. Those bluish-gray portals to Dal's emotions were open, revealing what lay beneath her impassive exterior. More of a dark stormy-gray hue than blue, they betrayed her stress.

"Is this about what happened on Monday evening?" Dal crossed her arms over her chest.

Piper was confused. Then Dal's comment refocused her. The door collision. She appreciated that Dal was so straightforward and willing to address what she thought was an issue, probably a professional issue.

Piper had been so caught up in presenting the news of a conference that might help them learn how to sponsor a more successful fundraiser that could impact the rescues for years to come that she'd completely pushed their very close encounter aside for the moment. Not that she'd forgotten it. Not that she hadn't thought about it all day yesterday. Or hadn't dreamed about it the last two nights.

After realizing what Dal was referring to, Piper replied, "No, Dal. It's about something else. That was an accident." It was the truth, and

Piper hoped that was what Dal wanted to hear, but Dal only eyed her and rubbed the back of her neck.

"Yes. An accident." Dal echoed Piper, then opened and closed her mouth without speaking before finally launching into an unnecessary explanation. "One of those things when two people try to go through a door at the same time. Laws of physics. Matter occupying the same space at the same time—or not."

"Hey, I'm not complaining."

"I should hope not. It wasn't on purpose." Dal had a definite defensive edge to her tone.

Piper decided to see if a bit of levity would work. "What if I meant that I'm not complaining about your technique? Smooth moves. Getting to know you better. I'll have to remember the push the girl against the door and fall into her technique. It's hot."

Dal's eyes widened.

"Gotcha." Piper grinned. "I know what you meant. I'm not complaining about the incident. As I said, I know it was completely an accident."

Dal relaxed, and Piper watched her struggle to prevent a smile. "So, what can I do for you, Piper? I thought I'd given you a big enough project that you'd be too busy for chitchat for weeks."

"And I thought the new fundraiser assignment was about fundraising and not just the obstruction of chitchat between us." Piper was hoping this line of conversation would lead Dal right down the path to a conversation about the conference. She'd just laid the groundwork.

"The assignment I gave you is all about fundraising and the biggest event of the year for CritterLove. As you know, it's critical for the rescues." Dal gave her an annoyed look.

It was all Piper could do to suppress a little victory jig. "That's exactly why I'm here. To talk about an opportunity to make the fundraiser better than ever."

"Suckered me right into that, didn't you? Bushwhacked again." Dal shook her head before she leaned back. "Go on."

"I went jogging with my friend Bryce last evening. Afterward—"

Dal cut in. "The Bryce who's the cop and married? The one who caught Einstein for me?" Dal paused, maintaining a passive expression, but her eyes were dancing. "You know—after the dog leash trip wire in the park technique?"

Piper couldn't hide her amusement, but Dal was so good at keeping a straight face. Only her eyes gave her away. This was the kind of chitchat that Piper loved having with her.

"Yes. That's Bryce," Piper said after she quit laughing. She looked at Dal to make sure Dal was ready for her to go on.

Dal nodded, so Piper continued, "Afterward, we went to this new bar and grill, and we ran into a woman I used to know in college. Tanya."

"Tanya?"

"A former girlfriend." Piper kicked herself for oversharing as Dal displayed a hint of a frown. Piper sighed. She wasn't one to keep secrets, and now there was no reason not to put Tanya into context for Dal. "She's a former girlfriend. Emphasis on *former*—we did much better as friends. But I hadn't seen her in years. She recognized me and came over to the table where Bryce and I were sitting."

"And I need to know about this *former* girlfriend who did better in the role of a friend because…" Dal watched Piper, visibly waiting for her answer. She'd picked up her gold pen and was tapping it.

"Because she's an event planner. She told me about a conference next week in Sacramento on the topic of maximizing fundraising. All day Thursday and Friday morning. She's involved with the conference. She said there will be single presenters, larger panels, and breakout sessions for discussion with a focus on nonprofit fundraising."

"You think it will be worth the expense?" Dal bit her lower lip.

Piper hadn't thought the money would be a big issue, so she was wondering what Dal was fretting over.

"The registration fees aren't that bad for one person. I can get up very early and drive to Sacramento the first day, stay in a cheap hotel for one night, and then drive home the second day. I'm sure I can skip a day at the law firm or rearrange my schedule. I'm completely new at planning a fundraiser, but I think the information would benefit CritterLove, although I can't make any guarantees and have no idea how much net gain there might be over last year."

Dal studied her desktop as she contemplated the information. Finally, she looked up at Piper. "Is your former girlfriend going to be there?"

"Don't tell me you're jealous." Piper rolled her eyes. "Yes, she'll be there. I think she's either a presenter or on a discussion panel. If

I follow her suggestion and go, she'll know I'm serious, and I can probably call her if I need additional advice."

Piper was feeling a bit pleased that Dal might be jealous. That meant she cared. Piper waited for her to respond as Dal continued to tap away on her desk, thinking—the gold pen held between a delicate forefinger and thumb ticked away the moments while the movement of her slender wrist drove the action. Then she gave the pen a final decisive tap and set it down.

"I'm going too, as long as Viola can watch Ruby and Einstein."

Piper hadn't expected that. This whole conference idea was taking on a life of its own. She and Dal going together. What happened to the space she knew Dal had been trying to maintain between them? The no chitchat rule?

"*Okaaaay*," was all Piper could get out. She couldn't have asked for a better outcome.

"We can drive up the night before, stay in the conference hotel for the two nights, and drive back the afternoon the conference is over." Dal looked at Piper and raised her eyebrows in question at Piper's surprised expression. "Well?"

"I do see the advantage of you going too—you'll gain the information for future years when someone else besides me is organizing the fundraiser. You can provide year-to-year continuity." Piper was trying to rein in her enthusiasm. No point in driving Dal's guard up.

"Year-to-year continuity." Dal drew out the words like maybe they hadn't been foremost on her mind, but she was owning them now. "Exactly." Then she cleared her throat. "Two rooms at the hotel."

"Of course." The thought of sharing a single room with Dal flashed through Piper's head. She tried to contain her thoughts to just images of spending time talking, teasing, and laughing because she wanted those things with Dal, but her traitorous brain had her imagining more. She couldn't suppress images of clothes dropped on the floor where they'd been discarded while she and Dal took full advantage of that lack of attire, Dal's flawless skin pressed against her own as they kissed and stroked and moaned their way through a conference that was going on in some other part of the hotel. If it had been one room, even with two beds, they might not ever leave it if her body had any say. Then Piper scolded herself. She had to stop thinking those thoughts, or she wouldn't be taking full advantage of the information the conference could offer CritterLove and the animals it served.

"Clean up your thoughts," Dal said, and Piper watched her fight the upward turn of her lips. "You're an open book. This is a professional trip. But I do expect you to spend evenings with me"—Dal cleared her throat again—"so that we can compare notes." Dal paused, and before Piper could say anything else, she asked, "Is that all?"

"That's it." Piper stood and started backing out of the room before Dal could change her mind about the conference. "I'll go back to my office and get the information you'll need—the dates next week, the exact location, the costs, the agenda with a listing of the panels and sessions we might want to attend."

Dal nodded, then focused back down on the paperwork she'd been studying before Piper came into her office.

Piper turned and started to leave. She looked over her shoulder. "Thanks, Dal."

"Enough chitchat," Dal grumbled, Piper feeling Dal's eyes on her until she was completely out of the office.

❖

Dal arrived home Wednesday evening in a conflicted mood that she was having a hard time explaining, even to herself. So when Viola seemed to want to discuss her state of mind at the dinner table, Dal didn't want to address the topic of her churning emotions. After all, such a discussion was best avoided in front of Ruby. Dal put Viola off, shifting her eyes to her daughter, so Viola would get the message not to go there.

"How was your day, Ruby? Did you get your turn to share?" Dal asked.

"I did, Mom. I told them about how you save animals. About the weekend. How Piper and I read to Boris the cat. How Fred liked Piper. And how nice Piper is."

The feelings that Piper's name evoked translated as pressure across her chest, thrill and threat playing an internal tug-of-war. She gulped, and Viola studied her. Once Dal regained control of herself because that was paramount, she told Ruby it was bedtime and accompanied her to the bathroom where Ruby had a quick bath.

After tucking her in, Dal kissed Ruby on the forehead and headed for the light switch.

"Can we go to the zoo this weekend, Mom?" Ruby offered Dal her most engaging, exaggerated eyelid flutter, the one Dal couldn't turn down. "I want to visit an elephant since I can't have one."

Dal lectured herself about being played by a five-year-old. Her daughter knew she was a sucker for that eyelid flutter. "Yeah, I think we can probably work that in. I have to see when a contractor can meet with me at the rescue property I just bought, to make more space for dogs and cats. So we'll have to work around that."

"Promise?" Ruby asked.

"Yeah, I promise. Unless there's a ginormous monster emergency, we'll go see the elephant, Ruby-Doo."

Ruby clapped her approval. "Can you come over here so I can give you a kiss?"

"Sure. I never turn down a kiss." Well, that wasn't exactly true—Dal remembered how close she'd come to kissing Piper at the park. Okay, so she had turned down that kiss. But she hadn't wanted to. Dal went back to her daughter and bent over her in bed.

Ruby pulled her close and kissed her on the mouth. A sweet kid kiss. "I love you, Mom. And can we take Piper?"

Dal choked, then coughed. "You're a bushwhacker too. Like someone else I know."

"I don't whack bushes," Ruby proclaimed indignantly.

Once she had the cough under control, Dal laughed at her daughter's indignation. "Good night, Ruby."

"Piper?" Ruby didn't give up.

"Elephant," Dal told her. "That's all I've promised. Are we clear?"

"Yeah." Ruby stuck out her lower lip.

Dal turned out the light and headed back out to the kitchen where Viola was waiting for Dal. First manipulated by her daughter, now subjected to an inquisition by the woman that she considered a mother. No wonder she was fighting for control of her life.

"Okay, Dal. I can tell something's going on. Out with it." Viola was standing by the sink, a damp dish towel over her shoulder. "I'm not leaving until I know what it is. Is everything at the office okay?"

Dal cursed the close bond she had with Viola. The decades of love between them. The fact that Viola was the one person who knew her, could read her like a book. Well maybe not—Piper could read her pretty well too. Oh crap.

Dal directed her attention to Einstein before she quickly glanced across at Viola. Her unofficial mom. Her friend. "I'm just wondering if you can watch Ruby and Einstein next week from Wednesday evening until Friday evening. Friday's a release day, so no school, but she can go to the childcare program. There's a conference."

"Dahlia. You're sugarcoating something. I'll be happy to watch them. But what's the conference about? And I mean the details."

Viola would get the details out of her, one way or another, so she dived in. "It's a conference on maximizing fundraising with a nonprofit focus."

"I thought that you'd handed that off to Piper. Not that you said it in so many words, but you were trying to give Piper a wide berth, to maintain space between the two of you." Viola studied her. "You're attracted to her." There was no doubt in Viola's tone.

Dal knew she was attracted to Piper. That was the whole reason for putting space between the two of them. And Dal could agree that the reasons Piper gave for attending the conference had been legitimate. Rational.

But what had been irrational had been the green deluge of jealousy that had overcome her when she'd heard that the former girlfriend was going to be there. All of Dal's resolve had dissolved in a flood of possessive emotion. She'd never felt that before, and now she had to deal with the consequence. A consequence that would be so much easier if she could just relegate it to one of life's mistakes, but her heart was doing the same little victory jig that Dal had seen in Piper's eyes when she'd led Dal by the nose right into that discussion about the conference improving the fundraiser.

Dal was in turmoil, but she wasn't ready to admit that to Viola. And she couldn't blame Viola for this newest mess she'd gotten herself into. She'd do her best to maintain her distance from Piper in the meantime and just keep everything under control at this conference.

"Someone has to organize the gala"—Dal couldn't help but give Viola a pained look as she tried to filter what she was willing to tell her. Then she reminded herself again that this wasn't Viola's fault—"with you retiring at the ripe young age of seventy-eight." Dal paused and took a deep breath, then smiled kindly at her. "Not that I'm begrudging you your retirement. But Piper came to me today with this request to attend, and it made sense, a way to learn about how to raise as much money as possible for the CritterLove shelters."

"And you just happened to decide that going with her was also in the best interest of the rescues—the reason you need me to watch Ruby and the dog." Viola tilted her head at Einstein.

"Piper will be gone in another three and a half weeks. Not that she won't do an amazing job of trying to organize the event," Dal said. "She's already started. But she wants more guidance. Up-to-date guidance. I thought it would be good for me to have that too, for future reference, so the fundraiser continues to bring in the money that the rescues need." Now that she'd explained it to Viola, Dal decided her own attendance sounded perfectly reasonable, even advisable.

"Where is this conference?"

"It's in Sacramento."

"How did Piper hear about it?" Viola asked.

"She ran into a friend of hers who is an event planner last evening, in a new bar and grill downtown." Dal warned herself not to mention that surge of jealousy that had led to her decision to attend too. "I hear the food is good. We should go and try it sometime."

Viola grinned. "Nice try. I'm not that easily distracted. This friend of hers, was she more than a friend?"

"How would I know?"

"Because I can tell that you do, Dahlia Noble." Viola gave her a stern look, the only person in the world who could do that and likely get the response she wanted.

Dal sighed. "She happened to have been a former girlfriend of Piper's. Years ago."

"Mm-hmm." Viola nodded. "And is this former girlfriend going to be at the conference?"

"Maybe—as a presenter or panelist. I think this stuff is her area of expertise." She couldn't lie to Viola, but for crying out loud, this woman who knew her so well was going to read more into her responses than what she wanted to reveal.

Viola's eyes softened. "Dal, there's nothing wrong with being a bit jealous. With liking Piper. I'm not telling you to marry her." Then she chuckled. "And I'm not telling you not to marry her, but first you need that blasted signature on the divorce settlement from your ex."

"I wasn't planning on marrying her and becoming a bigamist. And one marriage was enough. Taught me my lesson." She wasn't telling Viola, but she clearly hadn't learned her lesson well enough because that lesson had taught her that when she lapsed from parts of her personal pledge—like maintaining control of her life—disaster followed. And that was exactly what had happened with the absurd momentary bout of jealousy that now had her attending this conference with Piper. She'd let herself lose control, and that was the dangerous part. And worse than losing control, it was lapsing from the part of the pledge that safeguarded her heart that really scared her.

"I can't tell you what to do, although I try. I just don't want you ever using me as an excuse not to move on. Not Ruby, either. There's no doubt in my mind that Piper's passed the Ruby test. Ruby has told me all about her. How did that happen?"

Dal purposely rolled her eyes at Viola's persistence. There was no escaping the entire Sunday story. Well, maybe she'd skip the lunch at the park. Absolutely skip the almost-kiss. Damn, if that almost-kiss didn't keep surfacing.

"Piper volunteers here in town on Sundays, at Wee Critter Haven. I took Ruby with me on Sunday morning to look at the expansion property for the rescue that Elsie wanted me to see. Piper watched Ruby while I went next door with Elsie and the real estate agent."

"Okay," Viola replied, hanging up the dish towel. "Enough for tonight. I'm glad you're going to the conference. It'll be good for you, for several reasons." She started to head to her apartment. "Give the woman a chance, Dahlia. She's not like a lot of other women. Nothing like that ex—Piper's just the opposite."

That's what's scaring me, Dal thought.

❖

Wednesday evening, Piper had gone home in a good mood. She couldn't believe that Dal had volunteered to go to the conference with her, especially after Monday's move to assign her to the fundraiser and essentially tuck her away in her office. Maybe being in charge of the fundraiser wasn't going to isolate her as much as she'd expected. Not such a bad thing after all. It came with a conference. A conference with Dal.

After watching TV for a while with Sunny and doing some blog writing, Piper decided to stretch out on her bed and read for an hour before getting ready to turn in for the night. Sunny had joined her, and at first she presumed what she was hearing was coming from the cat. Then she heard a distinct human voice. After a moment of fumbling, she located her cell phone in the side pocket of her sweatpants.

"Hello? This is Piper," she said into the phone.

She heard chuckling. "Piper Fernley, butt-dialer." Pete's voice was on the other end of the line.

"Gosh. I'm so sorry, Pete. I had your number up on my phone this afternoon to call and ask if I could add you to my emergency contacts. With Cate and Meg gone, my mom with travel plans, and Bryce and Hannah sometimes unreachable, I got to thinking I should do an update. I got busy and didn't get a chance to call you. I hope I didn't wake you up." She looked over at the clock. It was only a few minutes after nine. Thank goodness. "I was just here on top of my bed reading. With Sunny."

"Sunny, huh?"

"My cat, unfortunately...Not that it's unfortunate that he's my cat. He's a good cat. An exceptionally good cat."

"I get it, Piper." She could hear Pete chuckling some more. "Unfortunate that it's just you and Sunny. Your cat."

"Exactly. Again, I'm so sorry for butt-dialing you." Piper felt her face flush.

"It's only a little after nine o'clock. No problem. Most fun I've had all evening. Matt's off at a meeting tonight. Besides, I was planning to call you anyway. Can we get together?"

"Sure. If you have time for me."

"Are you kidding? You have to bring me up to speed on Cate and Meg's honeymoon travels. I'm sure you've heard from Cate. No way she'd just walk away from her law office," Pete said. "Besides, you and me, we're a team, getting Cate and Meg together. We're the Pete and Piper Matchmaking Service. And I want to hear about your life. Besides Sunny. The cat."

"Yeah. I've heard from Cate. And Meg. They're in Italy right now. After France. I can show you the photos. When do you want to get together?" Piper asked.

"It might be more relaxed to do coffee on a weekend rather than trying to squeeze in a lunch on a workday. I'm over in Oakland on Saturday to pick up a chair we ordered. Do you want to meet for coffee then?"

"Sure. Is the Blissful Bean good?"

"At ten o'clock?"

"That's perfect," Piper replied. "Again, sorry for the butt-dial. Except I'm not...because coffee plans."

"Looking forward to it."

"And, Pete, I still think the Piper and Pete Matchmaking Service has a certain ring to it."

Pete laughed. "You might be right, kid. See you then."

DANCING IN THE WEEDS WITH PIPES THE UNPLUGGED

"It's Not Rocket Science"

I have a confession to make. I thought I was terrible at physics. I would have said that I'm terrible at chemistry too, but that seems to be improving a bit. Not H_2O or CO_2 chemistry, but We2 chemistry. The kind of chemistry between two people.

I probably would also have said that I wasn't a biology person either, but I'm leaning into cardiology, matters-of-the-heart biology. Tugging at my heartstrings, heart's desire, stolen heart, heart on fire, broken heart...

But it's the recent physics lessons that make me think I'm not so bad at that subject either. It started with a beautiful woman and a dog named Einstein. The dog's name was probably the first clue. Then a chain reaction—or in this case, not a chain, but a leash. Plus, there are the properties of matter, when two objects can't occupy the same space at the same time. Not quantum stuff, but real objects of matter, like humans. She and I have accidentally, momentarily, serendipitously tried to occupy the same space at the same time on a few occasions now. The space between us reduced to no distance at all—touching.

And now, I want more in my life. I want to get to know her, spend time with her, discover who she really is. I want the We2, tugging at my heartstrings, touching. I want a shot at over-the-moon, out-of-this-world, to-the-stars-and-beyond love with her. It's not rocket science.

CHAPTER NINE

Dal spent most of Thursday thinking about Piper. What she meant for Dal's heart. Dal worried that her heart might just let Piper right into her life, and she needed to let her mind rule. She hadn't felt like this about any woman before. Chantal had been more of a calculated decision, albeit a bad one when she'd overrated her need for a wife. She knew she'd initially been drawn to Chantal's sexy and charming exterior, and been deceived by a gold digger. Piper wasn't a decision—she was an unfamiliar, irrational, growing emotional need. Dal had the feeling that letting Piper into her life could leave her heart shredded and bleeding. And that was unacceptable. Her childhood had left its scars and taught its lessons.

Dal decided she could make it through the conference next week—that was in the best interest of the rescues. There were three weeks to go after this week, and then after the conference, only two additional weeks with Piper, her temp. Because that's what Piper was, *temporary.* Dal could walk away after that. In the meantime, she needed to get on with the expansion plans for the Oakland rescue. Dal picked up the phone and called her contractor late Thursday afternoon.

"Hey, Joanne. Dal Noble here. I've just purchased an expansion property adjacent to the Wee Critter Haven in Oakland, and I'd like to have you take a look at it with me."

"Good to hear from you, Dal. Sure, no problem. When did you have in mind?"

"I was hoping we could meet there on Saturday," Dal said.

Elsie had indicated that they'd be turning away needy animals soon to prevent overcrowding. While Dal wanted to take action to avoid turning away rescues, she also hoped to avoid meeting the contractor on Sunday when Piper would be there. There was no point in inviting temptation.

"Jeez, I'm so sorry, Dal. I've got a wedding to go to on Saturday, and I'm booked up tomorrow. I'm heading up to Humboldt for a week and a half on Sunday, midafternoon. I could meet you on Sunday morning. That way I could start laying out ideas while I'm up north."

Dal silently cursed. She knew she'd have Ruby on Sunday because Viola already had plans that day, and the elephant visit was scheduled for Sunday too.

Dal took a breath. She could do this. "Sure. What time on Sunday morning?"

They settled on ten thirty. Dal hung up, hoping she'd get lucky— maybe Piper had other things to do on Sunday. But Dal realized that wasn't what her traitorous heart wanted.

❖

Piper walked into the Blissful Bean on Saturday morning at ten o'clock thinking about the fact that Dal had mostly been out of the office yesterday. During the little time that she was there, Dal had avoided her, only telling Piper to finalize plans for the conference, before leaving Piper alone for the rest of the day and leaving early.

Pete waved Piper over to his table. He had his coffee and a croissant, and she told him she'd be right back with the same.

"So, how's my butt-dialing partner in matchmaking crime?" Pete asked as Piper sat down with her thermos and food.

"I'm good. Do you want to see the photos from the honeymooners?"

"Only the PG ones." Pete grinned.

"Nothing X-rated on my phone. Meg wouldn't allow that. Neither would Cate. Although I don't doubt that they're having a memorable honeymoon."

They looked at the photos and noted how happy their friends appeared, then congratulated themselves on a matchmaking job well done.

After they finished, Pete studied Piper. "So, what about you? We need to get you settled down. I think you want that. Any prospects?"

Piper knew that Pete could be discreet—maybe not with Cate and Meg unless she asked him to keep it to himself, but beyond that he wouldn't talk. He could offer advice, and she needed advice, or at least an ear.

She told Pete a bit about Dal. No specifics about her history, but that she was beginning to like her new temp boss. About the businesswoman Dal Noble was, as well as the nonprofit that she'd founded. Her admiration for Dal came through, but Piper figured that was okay. Dal was someone who should be admired.

"Likes women? Single?" Pete was a CEO, and he knew how to get right to the heart of a matter. Her heart. Plus, Piper knew that she wasn't exactly good at hiding her feelings.

"Yes," Piper replied.

"I can tell you like her. So, you work for her for three more weeks. Boss-employee constraints. But after that?"

"I don't think she wants the kind of relationship that I want. I want to settle down, but not settle, if you know what I mean." Piper knew that Pete had offered Cate such good advice concerning Meg. "I don't want to get hurt in a one-sided relationship."

"You want what Matt and I have, what Cate and Meg have. I get that."

"I can usually figure out most people, but I'm having trouble with her. We'll seem to be getting along, and then she'll close me out. She works really hard to shut me out."

"Hot and cold, huh?" Pete drank some coffee. "The positive spin could be that it's encouraging—sounds like it's not all cold. Maybe hang on to the hot and see what happens." He waggled his eyebrows when he said *hot* and gave her a smile. "Remember Cate with Meg? My take would be that she could have history that's driving her actions. That she's conflicted."

Piper shrugged, not sure what to add. She agreed that Dal seemed conflicted and had a hint of that kind of difficult history. But Piper wasn't ready to divulge that to Pete, and she was feeling conflicted too. She'd convinced herself no more dead ends. The problem was, she just didn't know if Dal was a dead end or not. Piper didn't want to get her hopes up only to find out she'd been wasting her time, but she could live with that. It was the potential for substantial pain that worried her. She suspected if given time, Dal could hurt her.

Pete took another sip of his coffee and looked over the top of his cup at her. "My advice—give it time, kid."

Well, darn. Pete was telling her to do the very thing that she sensed had the possibility for real consequences. Negative ones. But that was what her heart was telling her to do too. She wouldn't find what she wanted if she didn't listen to her heart and risk something. Piper concluded that she'd have to accept that.

"And if there's anything I can do to help, just ask."

"Thanks, Pete. Just having coffee with you is nice. We'll see if Dal and I go anywhere once my temp job is up. It'll be what it'll be. I know a relationship can't be forced."

They chatted some more, finished their coffee, and promised to do it again.

❖

Viola had taken Ruby to her grandniece's birthday party yesterday and kept her for a sleepover, so Dal was drinking coffee on Sunday morning alone. She thought about yesterday when she'd been free all afternoon and night. After running errands in the afternoon, she'd seriously entertained heading out to a bar. God, she'd needed some physical release. But she just wasn't interested in sex with some random woman anymore. Not with the few women who had left her their phone numbers after a night together either. That upset her. She didn't want to need emotions involved in order to share a little physical enjoyment with another woman.

And Dal knew it was because she wanted Piper. She couldn't get her out of her head, and not just the blast of heat between her thighs when the thought of desktop sex had crossed her mind after she'd accidentally pinned Piper against the door last week. Oh, she wanted that Piper, the Piper who had known exactly what Dal had been thinking and wanted it too. But she also wanted the one who took her teasing, her moods, and gave it right back to her. The one who rarely played games like so many other women. Who was unpretentious, but not naive. And who liked animals and kids. Dal groaned, disgusted with herself. And now she'd undoubtedly see her at the rescue when she met up with the contractor.

Dal had finally finished her coffee and was scrolling through emails and the news when Ruby and Viola came upstairs. After saying good morning, Viola left to join her cousin for the day and Dal helped Ruby pour some cereal, then get ready to leave. They drove to the rescue, where the contractor was waiting. Elsie was there too and held up a finger for Dal to give her a moment while she finished with a visitor.

When Elsie was done, she joined them. "Piper's here, and she said she'd watch Ruby when Joanne explained that she was meeting you to discuss construction plans for the expansion."

Dal heard the panicked voice in her head that wanted her to simply declare *hell no* and avoid personal time with Piper as Ruby jumped up and down, chanting Piper's name. "Okay, I guess that will be easier."

The words came out of Dal's mouth as the call from her heart drowned out the voice in her head. When had her heart ever carried on this loudly before? Where was cardiac laryngitis when she needed it? Dal resolved that she'd enjoy the rest of the day and then shut down this growing vulnerability.

Elsie went and found Piper, who came out front and smiled at Dal before taking Ruby's hand. Dal tried not to let that smile affect her. She thanked Piper, took the lead, and led Joanne away to the new property.

When they returned, Elsie led them back to one of the visitation rooms where Piper and Ruby were again reading to the old cat, Boris.

As they all left the area, Piper told Dal that Fred had finally gone home to his family. Piper hip-bumped Dal in celebration. Dal wanted to grab her and hold her close for more than a hip bump, but that wasn't smart. Or appropriate.

"The Fred Fund clearly didn't hurt in getting him home. Wherever that money came from." Piper winked at Dal, a friendly, knowing wink that increased the pounding in Dal's chest. Then Piper grabbed her hand along with Ruby's and led them both down to where two boys were cleaning out an empty run. It was all Dal could do not to continue to hold Piper's hand when they reached their destination. Damn, it all felt so natural. Like family. A complete family.

Piper introduced her to the boys. "Dal, I'd like you to meet Nick and Jeremy. They're Fred's new family. Fred's home with the boys' parents, but they're here helping out today. Aren't you, guys?"

Then Piper told the boys that Dal ran the rescue and that Fred had been one of her special projects. Dal felt herself blush as the younger boy, Jeremy, ran over and hugged her around the waist before telling Ruby that she had one of the world's best moms.

Dal thanked the boys for giving Fred a loving home, and just as Dal thought that she and Ruby would manage their escape, Ruby became adamant that Piper should come to the zoo with them. Again, Piper didn't put Dal on the spot but answered honestly that she had no other plans when Dal tried to give Piper an out.

It wouldn't help Dal keep her distance if she spent several more hours today in the company of this woman that she didn't want to find so appealing. But Ruby didn't let up, and Dal had no excuse to prevent it. Well, she'd already told herself that she'd enjoy the day, so it was finally decided that Piper would join them. Dal's head was still in turmoil, but her heart and Ruby were ecstatic. It was just an afternoon, she reminded herself.

❖

The San Francisco Zoo no longer had elephants because they didn't have adequate habitat, so the Oakland Zoo was their destination. The zoo currently had one elephant, a male, in a six-and-a-half-acre enclosure. As a veterinarian and animal lover, Dal worried about the fate of elephants in the world. She knew ivory poaching and habitat loss threatened those in the wild, and those in captivity needed proactive programs to make their lives humane and minimize exploitation. She was satisfied that the Oakland Zoo was proactive in its programs. Thinking about the elephants brought Dal's thoughts to Piper, seeing her becoming involved in legal advocacy if she became an animal welfare attorney.

After parking Dal's car and walking to the entrance, Ruby held Piper's hand as they moved into the zoo. As they strolled the grounds along with all the other guests, Dal enjoyed the fresh air and the view of Piper's swaying hips as she and Ruby walked ahead. The squeal of Ruby's glee always made Dal happy, and the accompaniment of Piper's melodious laughter only added to the experience.

They wandered the pathway to the children's zoo where there was a reptile house and an area where sheep and goats could be petted.

The river otters kept them entertained for quite a while. Dal couldn't imagine doing this with Chantal or any of the other women she'd spent a Friday or Saturday night with.

They finally reached the elephant enclosure at the back of the zoo's African Savanna area. Looking beyond the fence, they could see the male elephant, Osh, near the pond. Ruby was thrilled. The zoo once had a pair of female elephants, but after one passed away, the surviving female had been driven to an elephant sanctuary in Tennessee. Dal reflected on the fact that female elephants were deeply social and created lifelong bonds of friendship—they needed those relationships. Dal closed her eyes for a long moment. So many other species were so much better than she was at bonding and relationships.

As they continued to watch the massive beast, Dal and Piper stood a few feet apart, and Dal felt every inch of the distance. It was good that they had Ruby as a chaperone because she imagined coming up behind Piper, putting her arms around Piper's waist, pressing against her, and nuzzling her smooth alabaster neck just below that mass of red curls as they watched the pachyderms through the fence. Going home and making love…Dal shook herself out of her thoughts. Thoughts she couldn't pursue. Putting aside their workplace relationship and Dal's marital limbo, there was all the rest that Piper would want that came with too high a price. The laughter and talking and heartstrings. Dal slowed her breathing and cleared her throat. She didn't do romantic heartstrings.

"Think one of those would fit in your bedroom, Ruby-Doo?" Dal asked, pointing at Osh.

"We could take out my bed," Ruby said hopefully.

Piper gave her a poke. "Then where would you sleep?"

"With Mom," Ruby said.

Piper locked eyes with Dal, and Dal surmised that they were both thinking of a different partner for Dal. Then they looked away from each other.

"I don't think so." Dal couldn't suppress the husk in her voice. Piper laughed as Dal growled, "Are you having fun, Piper?"

Piper grinned. "*Almost* the best time I could imagine."

❖

They rode the gondolas over to the Landing Café where they settled in for a late lunch, then off to the California Trail with bald eagles, bears, and bison, followed by a final ride on the train because none of them was ready to leave, a train ride where Ruby sat on Dal's lap, Dal sat pushed up next to Piper, and nobody complained, at least about sitting so close to each other. Dal wanted to complain when the ride was over and Piper's warmth was no longer there—not just the physical heat, but the warmth that was Piper's humor and geniality and kindness and all of those things that had made it a day to remember.

When it was finally time, they left the zoo, and Dal drove them back to the Wee Critter Haven where Piper had left her car. Ruby had fallen asleep in her car seat in the back of Dal's Lexus.

Dal pulled up next to Piper's old Subaru and turned off the ignition. With Piper in the front passenger seat next to Dal, they sat in silence for a bit. It wasn't dark, but the glow of the day was starting to fade and the interior of the car felt like a safe capsule removed from their day-to-day lives and the rest of the world, insulated from all the pressures, past and present, that pushed on Dal's feelings.

She wanted to enjoy Piper's company in silence, not wanting the day to end, and not wanting to think about all the reasons she shouldn't be enjoying this situation. Piper just fit, made them a trio without any effort. It wasn't just watching the way Piper connected with Ruby, her daughter chattering and laughing as they moved through the zoo, refusing to let go of Piper's hand. No, Piper had engaged with Dal in chatter and laughter too, and Dal had wanted to hold her hand—more than her hand because her body seemed fixated on this woman being the only one she wanted in her bed. But in addition to those things, Dal's heart was telling her to savor her time with Piper. This had been the very best day she'd had in a very long time. She didn't want anything to spoil the day, but that didn't mean it could last. There was so much that could go wrong, with herself at the center of it.

Dal turned and looked across the center console at Piper as she prepared to leave. "I guess I'll see you tomorrow. Although I'm going to be out of the office much of the day because the end of the week is a bust for work, with the conference. I have things I need to do with Alex for the clinics."

"Thanks. For taking a chance on me today. I know you didn't want to."

"Ruby can be pretty persuasive." Dal chuckled.

"I know that you know how lucky you are…to have her in your life."

"Yes, I do."

"Are we going back to no chitchat tomorrow?" Piper asked. "Just so I know the rules. I'm not very good without the rule book."

"I'm still your boss. So that's the first rule—appropriate professional relationship. Then there are all the other things going on in my life. And I need my life a certain way to make it work." Dal let out a breath. But it was a relief to have just said it to Piper—she needed her life a certain way to make it work. And that couldn't include Piper, so Dal wasn't going to initiate a discussion about her issues with her divorce because she and Piper had no future together.

"So do I get a free pass for a few more minutes while we sit here?" Piper leaned back in her seat and waited for Dal's response.

"That depends on what a free pass entails." Dal wondered what she was getting herself into. Not that she'd have to do something she didn't want to do, but that she'd have to stop something she didn't want to stop. Hell, with Ruby in the back seat, this was under control. She could handle this.

"Okay. I'm not going to kiss you. Even though I desperately want to." Piper looked at her with those gorgeous dark hazel eyes. Green and sienna this evening. "No kissing. You're my boss."

"No kissing," Dal echoed. Even she could hear the lack of conviction in her delivery. She wanted to lean over and kiss Piper so badly. A perfect conclusion to a perfect day, short of taking Piper home. The thoughts that she'd had earlier at the elephant enclosure resurfaced. Undressing Piper. Planting kisses all over her naked body…Dal cleared those thoughts again. Piper was looking for something more. Something more that would only complicate Dal's life. Something Dal couldn't give her.

"No kissing," she repeated.

"Can I ask you about Ruby?" Piper changed the subject.

Dal nodded. That seemed safe enough.

"Were you the one pregnant with Ruby? Did you carry her?"

Dal didn't answer for an extended moment. She didn't want to get into all the issues in her life that the question represented. "All I'm going to say is that I did."

Piper nodded. "So, are we back to no chitchat tomorrow?" She asked the question again.

Dal looked at Piper. Right at this moment, she didn't know what she wanted. Shit. She'd known what she wanted her entire adult life. She'd set the ground rules, charted her life out, and followed through. That was what had worked as long as she'd stuck to it. She'd protected her heart, ever since her father, including during her marriage, but if Dal let her, this woman could break it.

"I think that would be for the best," Dal told her.

Piper looked sad. Dal took a risk and quietly asked her, "What are you thinking?"

"I was just thinking of Fred. I know he's happy that he's been able to move on, to fetch his forever. Thanks to you, Dal. That's the beauty of being a dog. Naive? No, I think it's wisdom." Piper talked as she took ahold of the car door handle. "It was a wonderful day. I just wish it could last. That you could give us a chance when I'm done being your temp."

"That I wasn't so screwed up," Dal dryly clarified.

"Everyone is screwed up in some way. We all have our baggage, but some handle it differently than others." Piper remained in her seat.

Dal fought a smile. "Fred, huh? It's just too bad I'm not a dog."

"I'm kind of glad that you're not." Piper waggled her eyebrows at Dal. Then she climbed out of Dal's car. "Say good night to Ruby for me when she wakes up."

"I will, Piper."

DANCING IN THE WEEDS WITH PIPES THE UNPLUGGED

"If Only Given a Chance"

As I looked at my pink canvas sneakers next to her expensive black leather flats while we sat on a wall in the park, we seemed so unlikely. So inconceivable. So unfeasible, the two of us.

She wears a thick protective skin stretched over the scars she holds inside. Her heart and mind at war. I want to know her heart, if only there weren't so many elephants in the room: the past, the present—parading through a far-fetched, improbable, preposterous future.

Then I stood there next to her, looking at a real elephant today. The elephant—an enormous beast that presents like God's implausible experiment. Or a mouse blueprint followed by a batshit-crazy, magic-mushroom-smoking jokester who read the instructions upside down and backward, or maybe not at all. An oversized boulder placed on pillar stumps wrapped in a dense dermis more wrinkled than last week's dirty laundry. A skinny string tail behind and a tree trunk leading the way. Ears like misplaced wings protruding from the head. A smart, sensitive creature that thrives when the rest of the world doesn't get in the way. When only given a chance.

I knew while standing there looking at that elephant, implausible doesn't matter. I need to hang on to hope—under all of that thick defensive dermis that she wears is a woman who just might last forever. I know she felt it too. The two of us. If only given a chance.

CHAPTER TEN

When Piper arrived at NAS on Monday morning, she was shocked to find her ex-girlfriend Nettie standing outside the door in the corridor, looking exceedingly bored. The nonmonogamous, forgot to tell you Nettie. Piper had no problem if polyamory had everyone's understanding and consent—it just wasn't what she wanted.

Piper couldn't believe this was happening, and her ex looked just as surprised as she felt. First Tanya at the bar and grill, and now Nettie today. That was two of her four exes in a week. Without saying a word, Piper used the key that Dal had given her and unlocked the door before pushing it open, allowing Nettie to precede her. Once they were inside, Piper waited for her to turn around and face her.

"What are you doing here?" Nettie's delivery projected a tone between accusatory and incredulous.

"I work here. While Cate is away on a honeymoon, I've been filling in here part-time as a temp. I'm working on the annual fundraising project, and I would guess that you're here as the morning person for reception and admin coverage." Piper was piqued at the undercurrent of Nettie's animosity. What the heck? Nettie was history and Piper could make this work. She knew how to interact on a professional level. She was proving that with Dal...at least if you didn't know what she was thinking.

As she considered it, Piper wasn't surprised that Nettie was here for the morning job that Dal had mentioned. Dal had indicated she'd contacted an employment agency, and this was the type of work that Nettie did.

Nettie's mouth compressed in contemplation as she processed the information, and then she shrugged, an indication that working here near Piper didn't matter. Piper was over her too—she'd never loved Nettie. Not even close. Nettie had pursued her two years after Piper had broken up with girlfriend number three. Dee had been a few years of on-and-off togetherness. Piper had liked Dee and found herself stalled in that relationship, waiting for a love that never bloomed. She'd kept hoping. Dee had ended things, finally announcing that she'd taken a job in England. They'd both known the relationship had more than run its course, and Piper had been disappointed but not devastated. She now understood that Dee wasn't who she was looking for, would never have completed her, and she would never have completed Dee.

With Nettie, Piper had suffered for about three minutes, and the turmoil hadn't been about her feelings for Nettie so much as disgust with herself. Piper had known the relationship wasn't what she wanted, but she'd been complacent because she'd had no desire to head back into the singles scene again. It was Nettie who had clarified for Piper that she was done wasting her time on relationships that offered no real prospect for a future. She now knew herself well enough to be able to recognize in a reasonable amount of time the seed of an emotion that might bloom into love.

Tanya, Dee, and Nettie had each helped Piper realize what she didn't want to settle for. She'd rather be alone than settle for a relationship that didn't hold her heart. She wanted to love and be loved. The kind of love that you knew was exactly what was missing in your life once you found it. Meg and Cate, Bryce and Hannah, Pete and Matt had shown her what she did want, and she'd been waiting to find it. Now Dal was talking to her heart.

Standing there next to her former girlfriend, Piper almost laughed out loud, thinking that she probably owed Nettie a big thanks for cheating on her.

Nettie interrupted Piper's thoughts, rapping the receptionist's desk with her knuckles in an impatient manner. "Okay. So, I'm here until noon. You going to show me what to do?"

Dal wasn't in yet, which didn't surprise Piper because Dal had said she'd be spending most of the day meeting with Alex.

"Hang on a minute and let me check to see if Dal left me any instructions regarding you." Piper turned to head to her office, then she turned back to Nettie. "You okay with this? We parted on okay terms, so I can handle it." Piper thought she should at least ask, although Nettie was the one to cheat and cause the final breakup.

Nettie rolled her eyes. "No problem." Nettie plopped herself down in the receptionist's chair as Piper retreated to her office.

There was a message from Dal on Piper's office phone asking her to orient the new temp to the receptionist and administrative assistant duties that needed attention and reminding her that the temp would be there until noon each day. Dal had listed some projects, and Piper had no problem getting Nettie started.

Piper had most aspects of the fundraiser under control, including sending out requests for silent auction donations, but she was still struggling with the big draw, a celebrity that would attract the attention of possible attendees and bring in the big donors who probably had several worthy nonprofit functions they could attend. She'd left a message and number with several prospects last week, and most hadn't returned her call or had left a message expressing their regrets. The few she'd reached had also turned her down. So, Piper continued her pursuit of an entertainment celebrity name into the afternoon. She looked at Viola's notes again and reconfirmed that she didn't want to settle for the usual politician or other second-rate speaker who was usually invited to fill out the program. She wanted a big-name draw, someone who would engage the donors.

Just as Piper was ready to depart for the day, Dal finally came into NAS. She whooshed past Piper in the reception area and entered her office.

"How was the new hire?" she called to Piper.

"Fine." Piper worked hard to sound completely natural. She was feeling despondent. She knew she had no business wishing Dal would make time for her. Personal time. Dal had been pretty clear about where she stood. And now there would be Nettie at the receptionist's desk every morning—she'd thought she'd never need to put up with Nettie again.

"But?" Dal appeared in her office doorway with one eyebrow cocked. Piper knew she wasn't good at hiding things, but how could Dal tell in one word that something was going on?

Piper sighed. "She's a former girlfriend."

Dal raised the other eyebrow as she leaned against the doorframe.

Her steel-blue eyes locked on Piper. "How the hell many former girlfriends do you have?"

Piper thought she heard that tinge of jealousy in Dal's tone, and she couldn't help the shot of pleasure she felt in her chest that maybe Dal cared, the same feeling she'd had when Dal seemed to be jealous of Tanya. You didn't feel jealousy unless there was some emotion there, right?

"I could ask you the same, although I guess your answer might depend on how you define *girlfriend*." Piper had the feeling Dal's definition might vary from her own. "I've had four girlfriends. The first in high school, and three since. With dating between." Piper shrugged—it was all history. "So those last three have been over the span of a lot of years." Then Piper looked at her boss. "Your turn, Dal."

"Nope. That qualifies as chitchat." Dal glowered, obviously trying to maintain control of the conversation. Piper noted that Dal had repeatedly insinuated she wanted to avoid personal interaction that could bring them closer, but she showed signs of jealousy. Piper decided that Dal was conflicted. Piper couldn't ignore the challenge, the draw of Dal.

"But you asked first." Piper offered a smile at Dal's avoidance. "That many, huh? Well, never mind then."

Dal looked away from her before responding in a hushed tone, "I don't do girlfriends, Piper. Not like you define the term."

Piper nodded but decided to ask anyway. Bryce had told her that Dal had been married. "How about an ex? Someone who helped you figure out what you want in life."

Dal stood a moment, like she was going to say something but decided not to. Instead, she muttered, "Or what I don't want." Then she turned around and headed back into her office as she spoke back over her shoulder at Piper. "Would you come into my office, please?"

Piper walked into Dal's office and took the seat across the desk from her, waiting.

Dal studied her. "Are you going to be okay with your former girlfriend working here in the mornings?"

That wasn't what Piper had expected from Dal, and she didn't hesitate in addressing the question. "I'm way over Nettie if I was ever into her. She just reminds me of mistakes I've made, lessons I've learned. The only girl I ever thought I might love was my first girlfriend in high school, and we both moved on because neither of us was very mature. I'd define it as puppy love. I know some people find true love in high school, but that wasn't us." Piper drew a deep breath, then released it. "I'm still waiting for true love." She didn't break eye contact with Dal. "The kind that starts slow, that you build together and it blooms, that will last forever."

Dal didn't break eye contact either. Her gaze was a mix of desire and debate before she took control of her emotions and Piper couldn't read her.

Piper swallowed and continued. "The kind that works its way through all the crap in life. That works in spite of all the crap in life."

Dal nodded. "An optimist, huh," she dryly suggested, a touch of humor in her tone.

"That's me. Pink sneakers and all."

Looking down at her desk, Dal broke their visual connection. "You know I like the pink sneakers, don't you? They're so you. And the pink tie. Even the black-and-blue vest." Then she shut up as if she'd decided that she'd said too much.

Piper offered her a big grin. "I'd almost think that you like me."

A ghost of sadness, or maybe regret, traversed Dal's face, landing in her eyes before she straightened her posture. "Enough fashion talk, bushwhacker. I brought you in here to make sure we're set for the conference. You're gone tomorrow and Wednesday to Cate's office because of the conference. So I'm thinking I'll collect you on Wednesday after work and drive both of us to Sacramento. Unless you plan to hitchhike."

"My thumb's aimed at your car."

"Well, now that's settled, head on out and I'll plan to see you Wednesday. Say about five thirty. You can text me your apartment address."

"Got it." Piper stood up to head to the door. She needed to get home and do her laundry before the trip.

"Have a good night, Piper," Dal said softly.

"Through the crap and all, Dal."

Dal shook her head as an upward turn tugged at the corners of her mouth. "Pack your pink sneakers, hitchhiker."

❖

Piper headed to her mom's house after work on Tuesday to have dinner. She hadn't seen her mother in a few weeks—not since she, Bryce, and Hannah had been there. Piper had known the rest of this week wouldn't work for getting together, so they'd made a plan for tonight.

She swung into a floral shop on the way to pick up a bouquet. Piper had thought about a cactus, representing a mother's enduring love along with other things, like she'd given Dal, but then she'd decided that her mom might appreciate some blooms more. The cactus seemed a better fit for Cate and Dal—both a bit prickly. Piper considered pink carnations. They represented gratitude as well as love. She was grateful for all her mother had sacrificed for her, even if that had meant long hours apart when Piper was a child.

Piper knew the Renaissance oil painting by Leonardo da Vinci called *Madonna of the Carnation*. The art piece depicted Mary with the baby Jesus on her lap, holding a red carnation out to the baby. Piper wanted to bring her mother a bouquet that expressed their bond, so she bought a mix of red and pink carnations combined with baby's breath.

On the sidewalk outside her childhood home, Piper paused. She'd spent a lot of years in that little box with the dark blue shutters. Her mom had worked so hard to buy the place so they'd have a permanent home. There was no way she could have worked enough hours in today's market to purchase the house. As lonely as things had been sometimes, this house had always been filled with love—no matter the ups and downs in her life, Piper had always known she was loved. Piper moved up the slate walkway and admired the flower boxes on the porch. Then she opened the door and walked inside. Her mom left it unlocked when she knew Piper was coming.

"Hey, Mom. I'm here. I brought you some flowers." Piper headed into the kitchen to grab a vase. "Whatever you're cooking, it smells delicious. Tux thinks so too."

Piper looked at her mom, a khaki-colored apron covering her shirt and jeans as she stood in front of the oven checking the casserole she was baking. Piper knew that she resembled her. There was no question where Piper had gotten her red hair, except her mom's had become a slightly softer tint with age. Piper only hoped that she'd be as attractive when she hit forty-nine.

Piper's mother looked up from the oven, closing the door on the browning dish. "Oh, Piper. Such beautiful flowers. Thank you, sweetheart. Let's have a glass of wine and relax until the food's done."

"You have any juice? I'm worn out, and I'm afraid a glass of wine will knock me out." Piper rarely drank, except for the occasional beers with Bryce, and she still had to make it home and pack for the trip.

"Sure thing." Piper's mom poured a glass of red wine and a glass of cranberry juice. They headed into the living room, the three-legged Tux escorting them and then plopping on the floor at Piper's feet. Reaching down, she scratched his head.

"As you know, I'm flying out Wednesday night next week to visit Aunt Kay. With you gone later this week and me gone the middle of next week through the weekend, maybe we can do dinner again after I return." Her mom picked up her drink and took a sip. "I'll email you my flight information. You know my friend Mildred—lives at the end of the block. She's taking Tux to her house."

"That sounds fine. Like I told you, my plan is to leave tomorrow night for Sacramento." Piper sat up from petting the dog.

"So, you didn't tell me exactly what you'll be doing there. What's up?"

"I'm organizing the annual gala fundraiser at Noble Animal Services for the associated animal rescue nonprofit, and I'm going to a conference to learn how to maximize the fundraising for the event." Piper focused on the business aspects of her trip. Nothing about Dal. She needed to keep her focus on the fact this trip was about her job.

"That sounds interesting. Are you going alone?"

Piper hesitated a moment too long. "I'm going with Dal Noble. My boss."

"Is this the woman you mentioned last time? The one with the dog named Einstein?" Her mom held her gaze.

"Good memory." Of course her mother would remember their dinner with Bryce and Hannah and the discussion of the pathway encounter. Unfortunately, that discussion had included Bryce's description of Dal as an extremely rude woman.

"Who could forget a dog named Einstein?" Her mother laughed.

"Yup, she's the one with the dog." Short answers were best if Piper didn't want her mother reading too much into it.

"The rude woman that you sort of liked?" Well heck, her mom remembered that rude label too, and her expression said that she wasn't ready to let it go.

"That's her. But she's not so rude. Just a lot of history that's impacted her."

"You *do* like her. You know what I mean by *like* her." Her mother smiled. She'd followed Meg's blog, so Piper wouldn't be surprised if she was now following *Dancing in the Weeds*. And her mom was no dummy. But she pretty much stayed out of Piper's love life except for offering occasional advice that Piper knew was grounded in love. Piper didn't want to discuss her blog—she wanted to at least pretend she had the freedom of anonymity in her writing, except for Meg and Cate knowing.

Piper decided to keep her response to the facts. "Yeah, I like her. But Dal's my boss for another three weeks. She has a five-year-old daughter—she's a great mom. And she has vet clinics and animal rescue shelters and had a difficult childhood. Like I said, a lot of history."

The facts profiled Dal, but Piper knew they didn't capture so much of what was attracting her: her secret generosity, her sense of humor, her intelligence, her projected self-assuredness overlaying her vulnerability, her devotion to those she loved.

"We all have a history."

"I know. It's not my issue. It's hers." Piper shrugged as she acknowledged what she had no control over. "I'm not even sure how she feels about me. It's hard to tell." Piper finished her juice. "Mixed signals."

"Okay. I take it you've met her daughter. You always were good with kids. I'll butt out but know I'm here if you need me. I love you." Piper's mother emptied the last of her drink and stood up.

"You too, Mom. Now, is that casserole ready? I'm starving." They headed to the kitchen, empty glasses in hand, Tux on their heels.

As she helped her mother set the table, Piper thought about the different kinds of relationships between mothers and daughters. Piper knew very little about her father, who wasn't even on her birth certificate. He'd been young and disappeared when her mom became pregnant at seventeen, and with that decision, he'd been out of their lives. Piper understood that the pregnancy had been a youthful mistake, and she had no interest in him. Her mom was enough, and she just might need more of her mom's advice regarding Dal in the future. And she knew she could count on Meg's and Cate's advice. Piper was grateful for the women in her life.

❖

On Tuesday night, Piper debated what to pack. She wanted to look good, telling herself it was about the conference and not Dal. She selected a few white shirts for the daytime and a pale green boatneck sweater for Thursday evening. She decided to bring her black blazer, sticking to a less flamboyant look. For the trip tomorrow evening, she'd wear her skinny black jeans with a plain blue button-down shirt, and boots. And because Dal had mentioned them specifically, Piper threw in her pink sneakers, just in case there was an appropriate time to wear them.

She called Bryce to confirm pet sitting. "Just checking in with you, Blaze. Making sure you and Hannah are still on for watching Sunny while I'm in Sacramento."

"In Sacramento with your hot boss. Anything for your love life, Pipes."

Piper rolled her eyes. "*Boss* is the keyword. You're the law—you should know there are rules about boss-employee relations, at least very strong advice defining the lines, and Dal isn't crossing any of them. I'm not either."

"I can hear it in your voice. You want to cross those lines." Bryce's tone indicated how much she was enjoying the conversation.

"I don't know what will happen when I'm back at Cate's full-time. I don't think Dal is willing to consider having a girlfriend, and I don't want to just fill time."

"There's nothing wrong with filling your bed, Pipes."

"Says my former *I'm playing the field forever* friend who is now ecstatically married. Stop trying to get me laid. I want more." Piper had never been drawn to Bryce's wild single lifestyle. And now look at Bryce, settled and happy.

"I get it. I want more for you too. I just don't want you to get hurt. There's no way you could mistake Dal for that imaginary dream woman."

"That's okay," Piper said. "That was just a way to give me an excuse for the state of my dating life. A joke. Dal is real. Complex, but with things I like. Hidden layers."

"Yeah. And it can't hurt to like someone who is probably rich." Bryce chuckled.

"I bet you didn't marry Hannah for her money."

Bryce sighed. "You're right. I'd have married Hannah if she was up to her eyeballs in debt. So broke she was marrying me for *my* money. So poor she couldn't afford a stitch of clothes. Even a naked Hannah would have worked for me." Bryce laughed. "You just can't fight love."

Piper snorted. "A naked Hannah. Such sacrifices you'd have been willing to make." Then she sobered. "I won't call it love yet, but I'd like to see if it goes there. I don't care about her money. I like her as a mother, as someone who runs rescues and looks out for her unofficial foster mom. She's smart, funny, honest—when she lets down her guard."

"You've got it bad. If there's anything I can do to help, ask," Bryce offered. "Plus, you forgot to mention beautiful. I noticed that at Lake Merritt—the most beautiful, totally rude woman I've met."

"This boils down to her and me. I'm probably off the mark with hoping she likes me the way I like her. And even if she does, I know there are no guarantees. I just want a chance." Piper decided that they'd discussed Dal enough, so she switched topics. "Speaking of chances that are now in the trash can of history, guess who's the new hire running the front office at NAS in the mornings."

"No idea. Who?"

"Nettie." Piper waited for Bryce's reaction—she knew the saga of Piper's former girlfriend.

"Your last ex? Neglected-to-inform-you Nettie?"

"That's the one."

"I don't know how you do it. You, ex number four, and dream woman Dal in the same office. Then there's you, ex number two, and dream woman Dal at the conference. You live an interesting life."

"I'm way past Nettie and Tanya. I learned things about myself from both relationships. There's a silver lining to those relationships that didn't work out, even the total mistakes, like Nettie."

"I know," Bryce said. "Speaking of way past, it's way past my bedtime. Hannah's waiting for me."

"Well, don't let me keep you from any healthy exercise." Piper ribbed her friend, so glad that Bryce had found Hannah. "And thanks for taking care of Sunny while I'm gone."

"Hannah will stop in and feed him both mornings on her way to work, and we have plans to watch TV at your place with some takeout both tomorrow night and Thursday, so don't worry about the little lion."

"I'll set his food out for you guys right now." Piper headed toward the kitchen with her phone.

"Have fun with the hot boss lady. Even if you don't do what I'd do."

"Good night, Blaze. Thanks. You're the best."

DANCING IN THE WEEDS WITH PIPES THE UNPLUGGED

"Mothers"

I am only writing about mothers because I have been lucky in my life, and I know other women who have been the same—I want to acknowledge the role an older, caring woman can play in the lives of many of us, even when we're adults. So much has been said about motherhood, most of it better than anything I can say, some of it worse. I know that some mothers are far from perfect, maybe even the lesson in what we don't want to become. But for every older woman who has shared nurturing and good advice, whether she carried us under her heart or in it, there is a younger woman who would not be who she is without that love.

I have a couple of mothers because picking up chosen mothers has only been to my benefit as I've tried to find my way—I need all the help I can get. And I know a woman who has a chosen mother who saved her in her teens, who learned how to be a fabulous mother herself through example—a generational gift. So, set all of the societal definitions, expectations, and bull aside about the role—simply go with your heart and your head. You can't have too many smart and loving mothers.

CHAPTER ELEVEN

Dal was preparing to leave work on Wednesday afternoon a little early, so she could head home and collect her luggage and touch base with Viola and Ruby before she departed to pick up Piper. She shoved her nervous thoughts about spending so much time in close proximity to Piper down deep, where she planned to ignore them. This was a business trip to benefit the nonprofit, and that was all it was.

Nettie had left at noon and Piper had been at Cate's all day since she'd be missing her usual Thursday there, so Dal was there alone as she shut down her computer. When her phone rang, she didn't recognize the number and decided to pick up. It might be something important, and she was going to be gone for a few days.

"Dal Noble. How can I help you?"

"Hi, Dal. It's Chantal."

Dal was shocked when she realized who was on the other end of the line. She should never have answered. She remained silent, waiting for Chantel to proceed.

"How are you doing?" Chantal's voice was low and seductive, her signature purr. The one that did nothing for Dal because she now knew this woman. Chantal had left her to deal with so much turmoil.

"Why are you calling? This is inappropriate. Our lawyers are dealing with the divorce." Dal kept her tone neutral, not wanting to give Chantal the benefit of seeing how exasperated she was with the divorce negotiations.

"Now, that's no way to greet me." Chantal offered her a teasing laugh. Dal knew she wanted something. "I'm still your wife, Dal, until we reach an agreement. That's why I'm calling. We can work this out between us."

"Chantal." Dal paused, wanting to make sure that she had her attention. "I'm not giving you a million dollars on top of the generous alimony. We can go to court first." Not that she wanted to go to court, but Dal would bet Chantal didn't either.

Chantel remained silent a moment, clearly calculating her approach to the topic. "We've got so much history—that has to count for something."

"And it's best relegated to the past." Dal didn't want Chantal to know how all of this was affecting her, currently causing her chest to constrict and her stomach to churn. "Please just say what you need to say. I need to be somewhere."

"How about five hundred thousand?" There was a note of desperation in Chantal's voice.

Dal closed her eyes. She wasn't giving Chantal half a million dollars plus alimony if she could help it. "We need to let our attorneys handle this."

"One hundred thousand, then?" Chantal fell into what she probably thought was a sexy drawl. Dal acknowledged it as a drawl, but no longer sexy. In hindsight, she was convinced that her money had been important to Chantal and that her belief that she could have a normal life and leave her past behind was ill-conceived. The marriage hadn't been what it should have been on either of their parts, ultimately a failure. Chantal certainly hadn't chosen her or Ruby in the end, but it could be so much worse. While she was dealing with a loss of control, Dal reminded herself that her life had shown her multiple times why there were important reasons for not allowing her heart to be vulnerable. The devastation of a shattered heart would be so much worse.

This call made it clear that Chantal was intent on resolving the divorce as quickly as possible. But why? Dal took a wild stab. "You've got someone else in your sights."

The prolonged silence and then the sound of Chantal clearing her throat gave her away. She'd learned to read the woman in the years they'd spent together. Dal had hit the mark—Chantal had her crosshairs on someone else.

"Chantal. We'll talk through our lawyers," Dal repeated. "That's what we pay them for. Have a good evening." She ended the call, grabbed her purse, and flipped off the lights before heading to the door.

When Dal finally reached her car, she sat for a full five minutes, her eyes closed as she fought to retake control of her emotions. Chantal hadn't asked about Ruby in the three years she'd been gone—that fact left Dal torn between anger and relief. She was still $100,000 away from retaking control of that piece of her life, but she had a glimmer of hope.

❖

Dal knocked on Piper's apartment door, and a moment later, it swung open.

"Hi, Dal. Come on in and meet Sunny. Let me pack up my laptop and grab my suitcase in the bedroom."

Piper waved Dal inside. Piper's grin was radiant. She wouldn't be able to sell indifference if her life depended on it. Dal felt her tension start to dissipate, enjoying the fact that Piper was excited at her arrival. It was a simple thing—a person happy to see you. But it was a bright spot following the call from Chantal at the office. Dal thought she could get lost in Piper's glow, then chastised herself for even letting it cross her mind.

Dal looked around and focused on two small, beautiful watercolors hanging on the living room wall.

"Cate's wife, Meg, painted those for me," Piper said. "A painting of Lake Merritt because I love to run there, and the potted plant is a maidenhair fern."

Dal took note of the large array of greenery in the living room. "Got enough plants?" She didn't try to hide her interest, touching one.

"I love plants." Piper chuckled. "As if you couldn't tell. That one you're touching, a maidenhair fern like the watercolor Meg gave me, signifies the secret bond of love. My last name, Fernley, is derived from *f-e-a-r-n*, which is old English for ferns, and the rest is *l-e-a-h*, a clearing in the forest." Piper gushed on. Gush, that was the appropriate word, Dal thought. "In Victorian England, in the 1800s, young women had ferneries, and the fern craze was called pteridomania."

Dal looked at Piper and shook her head at the enthusiasm, and the fact that Piper never ceased to amaze her.

As Piper slipped back into her bedroom to grab her suitcase and laptop, an orange tabby sauntered out of the kitchen, plopped down, and began licking his paw as he used it to clean his face. Botanicals, a pet cat, a cheerful multicolored area rug, an overstuffed moss-hued couch with an array of floral pillows, watercolor art—all *so* Piper. And charming. Again, Dal chastised herself. Charming wasn't in her playbook. Charming was for puppies and kittens and things she wanted to take home to Ruby—she sure as hell wasn't taking Piper home to Ruby. Dal realized the unexpected confrontation with Chantal had affected her more than she wanted to admit. It wasn't charming she needed. It was stability, with no surprises. Piper was just a momentary antidote to Chantal's conniving games.

Piper had stepped back and Dal caught her surveying glance, Piper's hazel eyes shifting from a light sage and honey saturation to that darker green and sienna. Dal knew how she looked. She'd studied herself in the mirror after a quick shower when she'd changed from work clothes before she'd left home. She wanted to look adequately put together for their conference arrival. That's what she'd told herself.

She'd applied fresh makeup, and her hair was pulled back into a relaxed bun at the nape of her neck in an effort to contain it. She was aware there were a few renegade tendrils battling for independence, always a sprinkling that refused to be controlled unless she wore a tighter bun, and that wasn't her mood—Dal wanted to relax. She'd put on a pale mauve cashmere sweater that she knew didn't hide the fact that she was decently endowed, and she liked these tight black jeans that clung to her hips. She'd worn her expensive black flats to complete what she'd assessed as a casual but elegant look.

"Sunny, I presume." Dal tilted her head down toward the cat.

"That's my boy, the one and only. He's my little lion. Just finished dinner."

"Who's watching him while you're away?" Dal shouldn't be interested, but she wanted to know more about Piper's life. Four exes for sure. Maybe someone was on the horizon, volunteering cat care. Dal cursed her curiosity.

"Bryce and Hannah are going to spend both evenings with Sunny.

Hannah will feed him breakfast on her way to her clinic. He'll be fine."
Piper stopped and studied Dal. "Hard day?"

Dal told herself that her divorce was none of her temp's concern.
She needed to keep Piper in the temp category. Even if she did look
rather enticing in that blue button-down shirt with those skinny black
jeans and boots. Even if she'd freshened the minimal makeup that
accented her engaging eyes and full, moist lips. Even if they'd shared a
terrific time at the zoo together last weekend—not a date, just checking
out the elephant and the other animals with Ruby. After all, animals
were Dal's profession.

"Nothing I can't handle." The words came out harsher than Dal
intended.

"I know there's not much you can't handle, Dal. I'm sorry if I
upset you."

Dal felt bad. "You didn't upset me. You don't upset me." Then
Dal muttered, "At least not in the way you think." She grabbed the
handle of Piper's suitcase and headed toward the door. "Let's go," she
commanded as Piper grabbed her blazer and laptop, then kissed her
feline good-bye.

❖

"Have you eaten?" Dal asked, navigating the freeway heading
northeast toward Sacramento in the evening traffic.

"I haven't. I didn't have time." Piper turned and smiled at Dal,
sitting there next to her so close Piper could touch her. Piper wished
she could. "Have you?"

"No, I didn't either." Dal signaled and moved around a slow truck.
"Viola was getting Ruby some dinner as I left, but I didn't have time to
join them." Dal flexed her fingers on the steering wheel, then added, "I
got caught up at the office just as I was getting ready to leave."

Piper was curious because she could hear a touch of strain in Dal's
tone, the something that was likely the *nothing I can't handle* that she'd
revealed before they'd left the apartment. Piper didn't know what had
happened, and Dal didn't want to discuss it. Piper decided she'd just
try to keep things light as they shared the evening, so she took out her
phone and studied it for a dinner destination.

"There's a Little Larry's Diner on the way. They've got burgers, quesadillas, that sort of thing. It would probably be fairly fast if you don't want to spend too much time on the road getting to Sacramento."

"Okay, then. You and me and Little Larry." Dal glanced over at Piper.

"You and me. Little Larry isn't my type." Piper offered Dal a side-eye look as she smiled and let amusement infiltrate her tone.

The corner of Dal's lip twitched. "Not my type either, but I'm happy to have the chaperone." Then a grimace played across Dal's face, and she fell silent.

Dal was probably thinking she said too much. "I know the rules, Dal. I want to have a good time on this trip with you, share a little chitchat. But we both need to get the most out of the conference for the fundraiser."

"That's my girl," Dal replied before her coloring flushed. "My *temp*," she corrected. "*The* temp," she amended again as her cheeks turned a deeper red.

Piper laughed. "If you say so, *boss.*"

"Oh, shut up." Dal laughed too.

They drove along in comfortable silence before following the GPS directions to the restaurant. Once inside Little Larry's Diner, they each ordered a vegetarian quesadilla and dived in when the server brought their food. They talked about the conference and the fact that there was so much to learn regarding modern nonprofit fundraising: current fundraising trends, best practices, donor preferences, how to present your organization's story, networking, maximizing the use of technology...The list was extensive.

Because the CritterLove shelters were fairly well-known and had raised decent amounts of money at their past fundraisers, and the upcoming one was fast approaching, Piper agreed with Dal that she should continue with the organization of the fundraiser this year, but they discussed the idea that Dal might want to hire a professional event planner next year.

"I hope I'm a success at this. I know how important it is to you and the animals. My biggest concern right now is landing that big name." Piper tried to swallow down her anxiety about finding a worthy guest speaker, one that would attract big donors.

"Just do your best. I have faith you'll do what you can."

"I will. I promise." Piper was pleased that Dal believed she'd do a good job. She knew how important the fundraiser was to the nonprofit and to Dal. She'd give her very best effort for both.

"Okay. Let's hit the road, so we're in bed before it gets too late."

Piper pressed her mouth closed, so she didn't say anything that might embarrass herself. *So we're in bed*—her image of that phrase definitely wasn't inside the box defining their working relationship. Trailing touches…fingers, tongues. Caressed and craving contours… hers, Dal's. There was no way that setting sensitive skin on fire was in her job description, and she wanted more than just sex, although Dal and sex had certainly been crossing her mind. Besides, she'd promised herself that she'd be on her best behavior—she didn't want Dal to be sorry she'd come. "I'm glad you came with me."

Dal gazed at her for a long moment, finally responding, "I'm glad too." Then she cleared her throat. "I needed a break from the office… and other issues."

"Happy to help. Anytime." Piper closed her eyes and swallowed hard. Darn if she wasn't going to have a wonderful, miserable two days in Dal's company.

❖

The skyscape heading into Sacramento was gorgeous, the last remnants of the evening's glow bathing the tall buildings that made up the downtown. She and Dal found the conference hotel and arrived at the check-in area without issue. Dal handed Piper the key card to her room on the seventh floor, which was next door to Dal's. They rode the elevator up, Dal punching the number to their floor, seemingly preoccupied. She'd done fine during dinner, but Piper knew something was bothering her.

Piper decided she needed to let it go unless Dal wanted to bring it up. Pushing her to reveal things, especially if Dal considered them part of her private life, only closed Dal down. Piper was just thrilled that she'd been willing to share some time that included Ruby and seemed to be willing to carry on some casual conversation. Piper was hoping this conference would give her an opportunity to continue to get to know Dal better.

Several other hotel guests entered and exited the elevator as it moved from floor to floor until they reached the seventh floor and exited with another couple who headed off to the left as she and Dal went to the right. They found their respective room numbers and stood outside their doors looking at each other. Piper didn't want the evening to end, and apparently Dal wasn't ready to wish her a good night yet either.

Dal finally broke the silence. "Would you like to go down to the bar and get a drink once we get settled?"

"I'm not much of a drinker, but I'd like to join you. If it's permitted—drinking with the boss." Piper couldn't help but push on Dal a bit about the constraints that were defining how they interacted.

Dal nodded, looking at Piper for a prolonged moment. "I think sharing a drink in a public bar is safe enough."

"I'd hate to break any rules. Cross any lines. I'd never be able to forgive myself." Piper fought to keep a straight face as she teased Dal.

"Sure you wouldn't." Dal softly grumbled her response under her breath. "I'll knock on your door when I'm ready. I need to make some calls, so maybe between thirty and forty-five minutes. Okay?"

Piper nodded and headed into her room. The space had a king-sized bed, as well as a table and a TV in a cabinet. She retrieved the luggage stand from the closet and lifted her suitcase onto it. After debating whether to change her top, Piper decided to save her sweater until tomorrow night. Then she settled in and did a little blog writing before brushing her teeth and combing her hair. There was a knock on the door—Dal was right on time. Piper pulled it open.

"Oh, good. I've got the right room." Tanya stood there and took her time looking Piper up and down. "You look good," Tanya said when she'd finished her inspection.

"Thanks. I thought you were my boss. I was just getting ready to go downstairs to the bar with her." Piper wondered how her former girlfriend already knew her room number.

As if reading her mind, Tanya said, "I managed a glance at the computer screen at the front desk." She smirked, not revealing how she'd accomplished that. "And I'm just checking to make sure you didn't have any issues so far with the conference setup. It looks like you arrived without a hitch. I was going to see if you wanted to get a drink, but it looks like you've already got that covered." Tanya propped herself against the open doorframe, obviously in no hurry to leave, wearing a very short dress that rose even higher on one side as she leaned, exposing more than half of her thigh.

Piper heard Dal's door open and close, and a moment later there was her boss standing behind Tanya, a scowl on her face. Tanya glanced over her shoulder to see who was behind her and, seeing Dal, she shot a quick glance at Piper with a raised brow and then turned to offer Dal her hand in greeting.

"You must be Piper's boss." She paused to study Dal before shooting Piper an approving look. "I'm Tanya. Piper's—"

"*Ex*-girlfriend," Dal said. There was an undertone of pique in her voice that most likely only Piper could discern.

Piper's first thought was that she didn't want this to escalate into something negative, but her second thought was that Dal had no right to be jealous, or need to be either—not that she minded a little jealousy. Piper knew Tanya was in her past. Plus, Dal had made it fairly clear she didn't want a future with Piper, so Piper was still unclear as to just what Dal did want. Then she considered that Dal didn't know either. That wasn't all bad. It allowed hope.

"I told Tanya we were just heading out," Piper told Dal.

Tanya jumped in. "I hear you're going to the bar. I was just coming to see if Piper wanted to go there." Tanya waited expectantly while silence filled the hotel hallway.

As the seconds ticked by in the uncomfortable pause of conversation, Piper looked at Dal for help, but there was no relief offered.

"Would you like to join us?" Piper finally asked Tanya.

"I'd love to." Tanya smiled as Dal's scowl intensified and Dal looked away for a moment.

Piper stood and observed as her boss turned back, letting out a long, controlled exhalation of air. Dal shifted what had momentarily appeared to be anger into her expressionless mask as she apparently decided that she was revealing too much, and then she marched down the hallway toward the elevator. Grabbing her purse, Piper shut the door to her room and joined them at the elevator door.

❖

Piper watched Dal and Tanya as she waited for her drink. She rarely drank anything besides beer, but she'd decided that the situation called for something that would relax her, so she'd ordered a strawberry margarita. Dal had ordered a glass of white wine and taken the seat next to Piper, while Tanya was across from them with a daiquiri in front of her. Dal had shifted into her professional mode, engaged in a discussion with Tanya on the topic of nonprofits, talking about the rescue shelters with her. Piper's margarita was delivered in an oversized, bowl-shaped cocktail goblet. Piper took several gulps, and with its generous amount of alcohol, she began to relax and finished it while the other two women talked. She listened but didn't enter the discussion. When the server came over and took her empty glass, he asked if she wanted another, and she decided she would enjoy a second.

Dal cocked an eyebrow and offered a subtle shake of her head. Her knee drifted against Piper's under the table, and the soft pressure only made Piper wish it wasn't an accident as the alcohol washed through her. Dal's chair was very close to hers, but Dal must not have noticed their proximity because she didn't shift away from Piper. That only made Piper consider what she wanted from Dal—a chance at something more than accidental knee bumping under a table. She sat there imaging heading upstairs, not to their two rooms, but to that single room she'd envisioned Dal sharing with her. Then Dal was gently guiding her to the bed. No, Dal was pushing her back onto the bed, then falling on top of her. Reaching down between them…

"So, what do you think, Piper?" Tanya asked as she finished the last of her daiquiri.

Piper pulled herself back from her thoughts, feeling heat flush her face. From hip to foot, her entire leg was pressed tightly against Dal's limb. A smile ghosted Dal's mouth, the first real hint she was enjoying the evening since Dal had encountered Tanya upstairs.

With the alcohol buzzing through her body, Piper tried to bring herself back to the moment from the bedroom-scene haze where she'd allowed her mind to wander. No wonder she didn't drink. There was no way she could stay inside the clean, clear lines of that boss-employee box with two margaritas pushing her out, creating a soft cushion of insulation all around her, but clarifying a tunnel right through the middle of that haze. A tunnel that led straight to Dal.

"I think those are the best two margaritas I've ever had," Piper declared.

Tanya and Dal both laughed. "I think it's time we said good night to Tanya and headed back to our rooms so we're ready for the conference tomorrow." Dal stood up.

Standing up too, Tanya told Dal how nice it was to meet her. She left money on the table for her drink and took off. Dal had given the server her room number when they'd entered the bar, so the bill would go on her room tab.

Collecting their purses, Dal took Piper's hand and led her toward the elevator. Piper felt the connection as a maelstrom of sensations hit her—cardiac arrhythmia, pulmonary paralysis, and a wave of need that flooded well below her chest. She was positive it wasn't just the alcohol as she looked at their intertwined fingers.

"I don't think two margaritas were about seeing your ex again since you'd seen her at the bar and grill a week ago," Dal said. "If anyone was going to have an excuse to be drinking too much, it should have been me."

Piper blinked and focused her attention on Dal. "It wasn't about Tanya. You can have Tanya. Well, not you, but someone who needs her." Piper paused, still hanging on to Dal's hand as they rode the elevator upstairs. "So, tell me why you need to be drinking."

Dal glanced at their joined hands, not letting go of Piper's. "Good question." Shaking her head, she muttered, "My normal bar drink, vodka and tonic, just wasn't feeling right tonight." After a prolonged silence, Dal finally settled on another response. "Because I like wine."

"I think I like margaritas too." Piper hiccupped.

Dal's tone shifted to one of amusement. "A little too much. But your fondness may not be the same in the morning. Now let's get you to your room."

"I also like you, Dal." Piper looked into Dal's gorgeous eyes, transformed to an intense darkened shade more deeply blue than gray at the moment. "A little too much." The elevator chimed that they'd reached the seventh floor, still holding hands. "Saved by the bell," Piper chirped.

They stood in the elevator for a moment and looked at each other. "You need some water and Advil." Dal released her connection to Piper and searched around in her purse, then pulled out a small packet with two Advil in it. "If I get you to your door, can you get yourself ready for bed?"

"I'd like to say I can't." The appealing image of Dal helping her flashed through Piper's mind.

"But you're no liar. One of the things I like about you." Dal looked at Piper, then out the open elevator door into the hallway, then back at Piper before giving her a nod, indicating the way to their rooms.

"You like me too?" Piper couldn't prevent herself from slurring her words a bit.

Dal chuckled. "Let's get out of this box and get you to your door."

"Yeah, out of this box. This friggin' box," Piper lamented. "Friggin'," she repeated, then added, "Sorry, Granny."

Dal's mouth fell open. "Granny?"

Piper laughed. "Nothing to do with you, Dal. I'd *never* confuse you with my granny, never. Just an apology to my deceased grandmother for swearing. She always abhorred such unladylike behavior." Piper looked at Dal. "She never knew how unladylike I can be." Piper wanted to be unladylike with Dal, but she wasn't so inebriated that she'd say it out loud.

Dal took Piper's hand again and led her to her door before letting go and extending her open palm for Piper's hotel key card. Piper slid it from her back jeans pocket and held it out. For a moment, a long moment, she did not relinquish it as she held one end and Dal held the other end of the plastic rectangle. Their eyes locked, a potential night of passion connecting them. Piper could read the storm behind Dal's eyes and relinquished her end. She was full of alcohol and Dal was in turmoil, not the circumstances she wanted for a first night together. Dal opened the door and handed the card back, along with Piper's purse and the Advil. After allowing her gaze to linger on Piper and frowning, Dal gently pushed Piper inside before pulling the door closed between the two of them.

DANCING IN THE WEEDS WITH PIPES THE UNPLUGGED

"Lines and Boxes"

We all know lines. There's the straight line we learned in school—that shortest distance between two points, the dot that took a stroll. And the metaphorical line we learned by living—the one you don't cross, the blurred one, the one you put your life on, the one you stand in, the ones you read between. There are creative ones that can define an image without perspective or shading, or run renegade in wild dancing doodles, or become the ones spoken to tell a story. And then there are the character ones you earn with concern and even laughter as you age.

Love has lines, often bent. The upward arc of a smile that makes your day, the body-scape contours of two individuals melding into one, the cardiac curves shaping a heart longing for more.

And then there are the multiple lines that outline a box. Those box lines are written in rules defining the dynamic at hand, sometimes so no one takes advantage. A box that holds a heart confined, waiting, waiting, waiting for the time when there is no box. To see if that box made all the difference. To see if the future has been waiting outside that box.

CHAPTER TWELVE

Piper woke up from a sound sleep to three sharp raps on her door. It took a moment for her to realize she was in the hotel and not in her own bed at home. After she'd come in the night before and followed Dal's advice regarding hangover prevention, she'd crawled under the covers and never even rolled over, as best she could remember. Piper had to admit that setting her alarm had escaped her attention in the fog she'd found herself in last night, and she had no clue what time it was now.

Hoping she hadn't overslept and missed the start of the conference, she climbed out of bed and pulled on the almost knee-length hotel robe she'd dumped at the foot of the bed the night before. She ran her hand through her hair in an effort to tame it a bit as she walked to the door—a hopeless gesture. Then she pulled the door open to find Dal standing there, fully dressed in a white silk blouse and light gray pantsuit, a paper cup of coffee in her hand. Piper couldn't have asked for a more welcome sight.

"Good morning. You appear to be in better shape than I would have predicted." Dal scanned Piper's robe-clad body before stopping at her eyes. "Anybody need a chaser for last night's margaritas?"

"I like the way you say good morning. I just might love you." Piper reached for the paper cup. She wasn't sure that it was just about the coffee, but she'd stick to that excuse. Dal was too many layers to figure out this morning. Piper recalled the key card exchange last night. The turmoil she'd perceived.

Standing in the open doorway, Dal handed the cup to Piper. "Aren't you easy," she drawled. "All it takes is a cup of coffee, huh?"

Piper laughed, suddenly feeling better than she had any right to feel this morning—minimal hangover and Dal hadn't completely shut her out. "Oh no. I'm not that easy. Now if you had a little cream and sugar…" Piper let her tone drift to a hint of suggestive.

"Well, hot damn. It is love." Dal's eyes twinkled as she reached into her blazer pocket and pulled out two packets of sugar and three single-serving containers of cream. Then her eyes widened and she swallowed, obviously reconsidering the mention of love, even though Piper's intent had been to inject some jocularity into her cream and sugar request. Dal straightened her posture before putting on her no chitchat face, reining in the teasing mood.

Piper accepted the coffee enhancers. "Thanks for your help last night, boss." Piper wanted Dal to know she still recognized there were boundaries defining their interactions, even if she remembered Dal holding her hand to guide her to her room, the connection between them. Maybe she was misinterpreting that gesture, their exchanged look—Dal had done nothing to indicate she wasn't simply helping her arrive back at her room safely. She was enjoying Dal's company so much and didn't want to push Dal away.

"Do you want to come in?" Piper asked, looking back into the room with its unmade bed and yesterday's clothing still sloppily slung over a chair where she'd dumped it last night.

"No, I just thought I'd make sure you're awake and feeling okay. I need to go back downstairs and get a cup of coffee too." Dal remained in the doorway watching Piper.

"I'm fine, thanks to two glasses of water and your Advil. I'm sorry I don't hold my margaritas better—I'm just not much of a drinker. Let me get a shower and have this coffee, and then I'll meet you down there." Piper looked over at the clock on the night table. "The welcome speech is in half an hour, so can I meet you if you'll save me a seat?"

Dal nodded in agreement. "Get your shower. I'll see you downstairs soon." Dal turned to leave, her expression blank and unreadable, her tone even and controlled. Then she added more softly, "I'm glad you're feeling okay."

Once Dal was out the door, Piper gathered her clothes and headed to take a shower. As she stood under the warm flow of water, she thought about Dal. Their drive and dinner talk had been great because any time with Dal left her happy, although it was their interactions after their arrival that she wanted to consider now. Not just about how Dal had made sure she'd reached her room last night, or even the hangover therapy. A boss might do that. But the more she thought about Dal's leg pressed against her own under the table in the bar when there'd been plenty of space, how could that have been just an accident?

And Piper had been sure, even in her inebriated state, that she'd read deep desire in Dal's eyes outside her hotel door. There'd been more turmoil than she would have attributed to plain old lust, so that meant feelings. Piper chalked *feelings* versus *just lust* as a positive, even warring ones because that meant one side of whatever was going on inside Dal was on Piper's side.

Then Piper added in the fact that Dal hadn't given her a wake-up call this morning like a boss might do. Dal had gone downstairs and collected coffee, and also cream and sugar like Piper drank it. But even better, Dal had stood there and flirted with her, even said the love word in her joking about coffee condiments before she stepped back into her no chitchat mode.

Piper decided that a hangover was a small price to pay for these interactions with Dal. Maybe she'd see more of that unguarded version as they spent additional time together at this conference. God, she hoped so. Piper couldn't suppress a fist pump and grin before she turned off the shower.

❖

The morning went well with good presentations and interesting panel discussions. Piper knew that she was here for the rescues, so she focused on the information being offered. At lunchtime, Dal accepted a lunch invitation from some Bay Area acquaintances.

"It helps to have connections. Even if you prefer animals to people, you need to network." Dal gave Piper a side glance that revealed she was enjoying referencing the statement she'd made to Piper on that first Lake Merritt encounter.

One afternoon presentation in particular caught Piper's interest, a panel discussion focused on how to tell an appealing story about your nonprofit that would connect with donors. Piper took notes and decided she'd give the idea more thought because she was sure she could incorporate it into CritterLove's fundraising event.

For the last agenda item of the day, Piper found herself at a round table exchange, seated next to Dal, all the participants talking about their own large fundraising efforts and sharing advice. Piper walked away realizing that she was competing with so many other organizations to secure a celebrity personality, and celebrities already had other commitments. She felt discouraged after all the unsuccessful effort she'd already expended to line up someone special, but the message at the table was clear—a big attractive name got the attention of donors. Piper promised herself that she wouldn't give up on the idea because CritterLove's animals deserved her best effort.

Dinner that evening was affiliated with the conference, set up in the hotel's banquet hall. It was a large area on the ground floor, an expansive high-ceilinged room filled with burgundy-tableclothed seating and a small podium. As Piper and Dal entered, Tanya waved and walked over as if she'd been waiting in the wings for them to appear. Piper noted the exaggerated sashay of Tanya's hips as she shifted her focus solely on Dal.

"So, how's it going? Are you learning anything?" Tanya offered Piper a cursory glance before looking back at Dal.

They both assured her that they were benefiting from the conference.

"Is it okay if I join you for dinner?" With Tanya's gaze not deviating from Dal, Piper deferred to her boss.

Because she knew Tanya's moves and had witnessed them in the past, Piper wasn't surprised. However, she would be very surprised if Dal succumbed. Dal was so much more sophisticated than Tanya. Dal was probably way out of her league too. Suddenly Piper felt tired, but she maintained a pleasant demeanor. She was at this conference for a reason, and it wasn't Dal—even if she wished that there was more time for just the two of them to simply relax and talk. She'd thought they'd at least find time to share notes on the conference. Maybe when they were back in the office next week.

Dal looked a bit wistful as she turned and glanced at Piper before nodding her agreement, so they found three adjacent places at a table toward the exit side of the room and watched the other seats fill up.

"I'd like to hear more about how you're going to improve your fundraiser based on what you've learned here." Tanya again directed the comment to Dal. It was so obvious to Piper that Tanya was enamored with Dal, but then who wouldn't be? Dal was polished, professional, and beautiful, and that didn't touch on the things that drew Piper to Dal—the things that Dal cared about in her life.

When Dal didn't answer right away, Tanya went on to rave about what a wonderful nonprofit CritterLove Rescues was, how generous Dal was with her time and energy in overseeing the nonprofit, how Tanya was sure Dal had saved so many animals' lives...

Piper remembered that in the past, Tanya hadn't cared for animals at all. Tanya had complained about the neighborhood cats nonstop when they were together. The upside, Piper reminded herself, was that the girlfriends of her past had helped her grow. Yup, while her friends had shown her what she was looking for, Tanya was someone who had helped make her aware that she didn't want to try to sustain a relationship that had no future.

Piper looked away from Tanya and studied her boss. She knew what her heart was starting to tell her, but no matter how well things were going, Dal had continued to pull back every time they seemed to be growing closer. And Piper didn't want another dead-end romance. She took a gulp of air, then released it.

Dal had been sitting politely through Tanya's fawning, but Dal's eyes turned to her as Piper let out that long slow breath. Finally getting a moment to speak up, Dal turned back to Tanya. "Piper is the one who's organizing our fundraiser, not me."

Tanya frowned, not looking happy at that response.

"And I'm positive the time she has remaining at her job with us is already way overbooked." Dal concluded the discussion, and Piper almost laughed out loud at how Dal had politely cut Tanya off at the knees regarding her not-so-subtle efforts to insert herself into Dal's life using the CritterLove fundraiser as an excuse. Piper had to give Tanya credit for trying.

As servers continued to deliver entrées to the tables, Piper tasted her vegetarian dinner as she listened to the ebb and flow of fork clanking, talk, and laughter that filled the room. Tanya continued to spend the entire meal directing her attention at Dal, her plate only partially empty when the servers started clearing the tables and delivering dessert and coffee. Piper watched Dal take a few bites of the torte that was in front of her, ignoring the coffee. Then she turned to Piper and slightly raised an eyebrow, nodding at the door.

Saints be praised. Piper'd had a decent day, but she was done with her former girlfriend and the organized events until tomorrow.

Dal addressed Tanya. "It's been so nice to share some time with you. Maybe we'll see you tomorrow." Then she stood up and waited for Piper.

As they left the room and headed to the hotel lobby, Dal silently stood for a moment, unmistakably debating with herself before coming to a decision. She'd been nothing but controlled since this morning, with no hint of the person Piper had bantered with over a paper cup of coffee, cream, and sugar earlier. So when Dal finally spoke, Piper's spirits rose.

"Do you want to get a bit of fresh air and walk down to a bar I noticed as we drove in last night, a few blocks away?"

Piper looked at Dal, thrilled that she was making the offer. Dal might have her convictions, but Piper acknowledged again that she sensed Dal was conflicted about their relationship. Based on all she'd heard and observed, she wouldn't be surprised if there was more to Dal's issues than just their professional roles of boss and employee.

Piper responded to the invitation. "I would. Although I think I'll only have some soda tonight."

"Lightweight, huh?" Dal turned, leading them out of the hotel, Piper at her side. "Probably a good thing. This bar is a few blocks away, a longer way home than last night. Not that I wouldn't see that you got back."

"Thanks. I'd hate to make you have to hold my hand to get me to my room again. I know you probably didn't want to last night."

Dal sighed, then reached over and linked her pinkie finger around Piper's as they walked down the sidewalk. "This didn't happen," she growled in that seductive alto tone—as she didn't let go and it did happen.

"Nothing happened. Pinkie swear." Piper grinned, raising their pinkie-locked hands a few inches and savoring the minimal connection between them. There was a wild bird trapped within Piper's thoracic cage, fluttering crazily in place of her heart. She suspected it was a lovebird.

They spent an hour in the crowded bar. Piper thought of it as two people insulated by the noisy buzz of the world, that buzz encasing them in their own isolated bubble created by the sheer pleasure of each other's company. At least Piper knew that she was loving Dal's company. Dal had a glass of white wine again, and Piper stuck with soda. They talked about the conference and what they'd learned.

Piper decided it was time to shift the conversation to the personal. Now or never. "Are you going to bring me a chaser for soda pop in the morning?" Piper raised an eyebrow.

"Are you going to oversleep and require a wake-up call?" Dal raised one in return, a finely sculpted eyebrow that was just part of her beauty—best in show if she was being judged on her gorgeous grooming, Piper thought.

"Hmm." Piper pretended to give the question a great deal of consideration. "If you're delivering, I'm not setting my alarm," Piper finally replied.

"You know that was a one-time, get your butt out of bed special notification because while I wouldn't do that for most anybody else, I have my limits." Dal's eyes danced with suppressed humor.

"Dal's butt out of bed notification service to special customers. One per Piper, huh?" Piper couldn't take her eyes off this Dal, the entertaining one with the hidden levity that emerged from where she confined it, carefully contained beneath the surface.

"You might fall in love with me if I kept it up." Dal watched Piper right back.

Piper wanted to confirm that she just might, but she needed to keep it light, not give Dal a reason to withdraw. This was the unguarded Dal that she wanted to know better, but it was tricky territory. Maybe the wine was relaxing Dal.

"Oh yeah, you keep bringing me coffee, cream, and sugar—there's no telling what I'd be willing to do."

"I don't go for easy girls. Learned my lesson." Dal muttered something about not doing relationships.

"Me either, Dal. My type's not easy." Piper was afraid the conversation might be heading toward serious topics and she didn't want to shut Dal down, so she decided to keep it light. "Now if you're talking complicated, moody, a bit bossy, lovely lips…"

"Well then, I guess it's a good thing I don't have lovely lips." Dal slowly licked those lovely lips.

Piper grinned. "Whew. Saved by those less-than-attractive pinched and chapped ones adhered to your face."

Dal chuckled. "Enough about lips. It's not boss-employee appropriate."

"Not in the handbook, huh?" Piper was thoroughly enjoying the exchange.

"Nope. And the handbook says it's time to get back. Another full morning tomorrow, plus the drive home."

"I'm glad you came," Piper told her.

Dal didn't reply. She took Piper's hand and led her through the crowd and out the door before letting go. Piper missed the contact but was grateful for the hour she'd just spent with Dal.

As they headed back to the hotel, they strolled in comfortable silence, their hands brushing several times as they walked side by side. Piper would have loved to just take Dal's hand, but she knew she couldn't, if only because that wasn't what Dal wanted. Dal had held her hand last night in order to assist her back to her room. And the fingerhold this evening was something she hadn't figured out. As they walked back, every light skin connection simmered with a heat that ran straight up Piper's arm. Barely a touch, but sensual in a different way than the full-body presses they'd accidentally shared.

It was only half past eight when they reached the hotel lobby. As they waited for the elevator, people swarmed into the space, exiting the dining hall en masse after time spent over dessert and a speaker at the end of the evening. The time alone with Dal had been so much better than another hour of the conference crowd.

They moved to the far back of the elevator, followed by as many other people as would fit. With Dal against the back wall, Piper found herself facing the door, her entire backside pushed tightly against Dal's front. While she couldn't see Dal's face, there was no missing that alluring fragrance of jasmine and personal scent that floated forward in their close proximity, triggering olfactory memories of prior close encounters. If hand brushing elevated her heart rate and created pressure in her chest, this was a heart attack.

Dal's mouth was within inches of the back of Piper's neck, her warm breath hitting the sensitized skin, a teasing invisible bond. Piper tried to relax and just enjoy the serendipity of it all. Simply an accident, and unavoidable with regard to the guidelines of whatever rulebook they were trying to follow. Piper wondered what Dal was feeling.

Then a hint of the moment poured into her ear as Dal raised her mouth a fraction of an inch, her respiration controlled but accelerated. "Sorry, Piper. I can't move."

Piper didn't think she sounded sorry. "No complaints from me."

Just then, the bell rang as the ride jerked to a halt at the second floor, swaying the entire elevator full of people against each other. Piper lost her balance, not that there was any space to fall, and Dal's arms went around her waist and held her.

"Prisoners of circumstance." Dal chuckled into Piper's hair. "Lucky for you I'm not that guy over there."

Piper felt Dal's head nod to the left, and she looked over to see an older man who appeared irate at the indignity of the crowded ride.

"Guess what," Piper threw back over her shoulder.

The responding flow of a breathy "What?" floated the inch between Dal's mouth and Piper's ear, teasing Piper's treacherous libido.

"Packed in here tight like this, I think I won the sardine lottery," Piper said.

"Are you insulting me with a comparison to stinky little fish?" There was fake indignation injected into Dal's tone.

"The piranha lottery." Piper amended her statement. She couldn't help herself. "They'll eat you alive, you know." Piper pushed her backside against Dal's pelvic region, and Dal tightened her hold.

Dal choked down her amusement before whispering, "What would your granny say?"

"Sorry, Granny," Piper offered, not feeling very repentant.

The ride started again, Dal's warm breath continuing to tickle Piper's earlobe until they jerked to another stop at the third floor where people shuffled around each other as they exited. Nobody tried to get on—prospective passengers were probably willing to wait for the descent. Even as the tightness of the crowd loosened with people exiting, Dal continued to hold Piper around the waist, keeping her stable at every stop. More people exited at the fourth, fifth, and sixth floors, and the remaining two couples left the elevator at the seventh floor, but Dal didn't let go of Piper.

"We're here, Dal."

"I know."

"What do you want to do?" Piper could hear the yearning in her own voice, the need that could not be fulfilled in this business relationship.

"Don't ask me that." Dal sighed and moved her hands to Piper's shoulders, guiding her out the door and into the hallway, back out into the real world.

Dal walked beside Piper to her room. Fishing her key card out of her back pocket and remembering the key card connection the night before, she quickly unlocked her door. Piper turned to face Dal. When Dal's eyes darkened and she didn't move, Piper leaned in and skimmed her mouth across Dal's cheek.

"That one's on me. My fault. Rule breaker," Piper said.

Dal bit her lower lip as she softly feathered Piper's jawline with her fingertips. "Thanks for the wonderful evening, Piper. I'll see you tomorrow." Then Dal quickly spun around and left.

❖

Piper had washed her face and was reading in her sleepwear when her phone rang. It was an unknown number but it wasn't quite ten o'clock yet, so she decided to answer it.

"Hello? This is Piper."

"This is Viola. I can't reach Dal." Viola sounded flustered. "Ruby was at a sleepover and cut her chin. She needed some stitches. Dal's wife, Chantal, gave permission when we couldn't reach Dal."

"Dal's wife?" The world stopped for a moment. *Dal's wife!* Piper blinked back the tears that had suddenly blinded her, fought the emotions that scaled her throat and captured her tongue. Her head told her that this was about Ruby. She'd face her own hurt later. Piper collected herself. "I'll have Dal call you."

"Thanks so much, Piper. Tell her it's all taken care of."

Quickly shedding her shorts for her jeans, Piper decided her sleep T-shirt was okay for running down to Dal's room. She pulled on her pink sneakers and left her room.

Dal's wife. Dal's wife. Dal's wife. Piper couldn't get that out of her head as she hurried to Dal's door.

She knocked, and Dal answered in shorts and a T-shirt, barefoot. Her hair was down and her face scrubbed clean. Piper couldn't believe how naturally stunning she was, then cursed herself.

"What's wrong? You look upset." Dal tilted her head, inviting Piper inside her room.

Piper remained in the hallway. "Viola called me when she couldn't reach you. Ruby fell. She cut her chin, but she's all sewn up and doing fine."

"Ruby's okay except for some stitches?" Dal ran her hand through her hair.

"That's what Viola assured me. I promised you'd call her."

"Okay. I will. I had my phone on silent mode all day, during the sessions and dinner. I'd watched for texts and calls, but forgot to turn it back on. I was just brushing my teeth when you knocked and must have missed Viola. Thanks for telling me." Dal nodded, obviously digesting the news.

"If you need to leave tonight, let me know. I can be ready in a few minutes." Piper fought to remain calm and focus on the important issues of the moment. She felt gut-punched and knew she wanted time to process the information that Viola had imparted before she tried to confront Dal without completely falling apart. Besides, Dal needed to make Ruby a priority tonight.

"It sounds like it's under control. I'll go call, and I'll plan to see you in the morning. Good night, Piper."

Dal shut the door, and Piper stumbled back to her room in a daze. Now that she'd delivered the message to Dal about Ruby, Piper needed to deal with the shocking revelation—Dal was married. The information Bryce had shared about an ex was either about another wife or wrong about this one. Either way, Piper knew that she was an idiot.

When she reached her room, Piper pulled off her clothes and took a long, hot shower, trying to wash the entire goddamn fucking world down the drain. She vacillated between anguish and anger, and she didn't even apologize for her swearing. How could she be so stupid?

Dal had never promised her anything, but Piper was positive there had been a connection, some romance, as hard as they had been trying to stay inside the rules of working together. But a totally inappropriate connection if Dal had a wife—at least from Piper's perspective. After crying for a while, Piper decided that she needed to calm down and process things, so she pulled out her laptop and did a little writing. It helped her organize her thoughts, but she was still disconcerted and confused when she finished.

Maybe the rule book was an excuse if Dal didn't want things to go too far. But why play the game at all? Dal hadn't struck Piper as the game-playing type who would pull someone in only to hurt them. Piper thought she knew Dal's issues, and *player* wasn't one of them. Bryce had said Dal was a player, but she thought Bryce meant a consensual no-attachments player as a single woman who wasn't in a relationship. Not a break-someone's-heart-on-purpose player.

DANCING IN THE WEEDS WITH PIPES THE UNPLUGGED

"The Distance Between Two People"

The distance between two people has nothing to do with anatomy. Nothing to do with the four small spans between one's five fingers, where another's delicate fingers fit so perfectly. Nothing to do with the shared topography of knuckles and tendons mapped out so flawlessly in the link of two people's laced hands, nothing to do with the silk and heat landscape of the skin of one's palm pressed softly against the palm of another. Nothing to do with the cardiac thrum of two touching wrists, no air between them, beating in companion cadence. The distance between two people has nothing to do with the simplest link of that smallest digit locked in a pinkie hold with that smallest digit of another person. The distance between two people has nothing to do with the space that was closed when caring hands held someone steady against the solid beat of a heart, against the warm, sweet flow of another's breath. The distance between two people has everything to do with an abyss filled with what has gone unsaid.

CHAPTER THIRTEEN

Dal had called Viola the night before, and on Friday morning she decided to check in again on Ruby's condition. Viola reassured her that it was just one of those kid accidents—Ruby would be fine. The phone call had taken more time than she'd planned, so Dal was running late. But they could check out when the conference ended at noon. Dal hated to admit it, but she'd really been looking forward to spending time with Piper this morning. She hurried downstairs to grab some coffee and a roll.

When looking around the morning buffet area didn't provide any results, Dal headed to the presentation she thought Piper would attend. She was surprised when she didn't see Piper there in the conference room either. Sitting down and watching the door produced no results as she waited. Dal frowned at the fact that she felt a profound emptiness, an absence in the place where the happy expectation of sharing the morning with Piper had been. She didn't want to admit how much she'd enjoyed their time together last evening. Hell, she enjoyed most of the time she spent with Piper. Of course, it was perfectly legitimate to enjoy Piper's company here at the conference events—this was business. However, Piper didn't appear to be where Dal expected to find her. Where the hell was she?

When the hour was up and people stood to leave for the next presentation, Dal grabbed her purse and headed back upstairs to their rooms. She went to Piper's door and knocked several times with no success, then decided to head back down to the conference area to look. Dal was becoming more concerned as she acknowledged that Piper seemed to be missing. Concerned for the welfare of her employee, she told herself.

"Hey, Dal. How are you today?" Tanya beelined across the lobby toward Dal when she saw her exit the elevator. "I was hoping I'd see you before the conference was over. I'd love to chat with you sometime soon. Maybe dinner in the Bay Area."

Dal had no interest in spending time with Piper's former girlfriend, and getting together was the clear message she was receiving from Tanya. Dal didn't want to deal with Tanya's advances.

"Have you seen Piper this morning?" she asked, cutting Tanya off. She could hear the impatience in her voice, but she didn't care. She needed to find Piper.

"I saw her going into the area where they were doing mini-presentations during the first session." Tanya looked a bit aggravated that Dal hadn't addressed her offer for a future date. Dal didn't care.

She frowned. Dal was almost certain they hadn't planned to attend any of the mini-presentations—how to throw a successful bar crawl, board game night, croquet championship, or athonathon—whatever that was.

There were four scheduled conference options this hour, so Dal walked from room to room, sticking to the back of each and scanning for Piper. She finally spotted her seated off to the far side in a presentation on setting up a website. Dal paid a professional to do that, and she liked the result. What the hell was Piper doing here?

Dal took a closer look across the room, noticing that Piper was slumped in her seat, her head down, not looking at the speaker. Dal's heart rose into her throat. She'd never seen Piper looking upset like this. Had holding her little finger been a total misreading on Dal's part? Even if it had been bad judgment, she'd been positive it had been consensual. Piper was no good at hiding her feelings, and Dal was positive that the hour they'd spent together in the bar afterward talking about the conference and chatting had been enjoyable for both of them. There had been no indication that Piper had been upset about the tight elevator ride either—she'd even pushed the boundaries and kissed Dal on the cheek afterward. Dal considered the rest of last evening and had a hard time believing that Ruby's accident would upset Piper this much. Piper was the one to tell her that Ruby was okay.

Dal stood at the back of the room and waited for the hour to end. As the audience shuffled out, Piper finally stood and slowly headed toward the door. When her eyes connected with Dal's, they widened, and then Piper looked away. Dal swallowed. Piper was just as transparent as any canine Dal had encountered.

As Piper tried to ignore her and walk past, Dal followed her. They crossed the lobby with Dal a few feet behind, then ended up in the elevator together with several other people. Dal wanted to fix whatever the problem was. To take Piper in her arms and hold her. To close this giant gap that seemed to be separating them, but she couldn't. Piper didn't say a word, just cast her eyes down, so friggin' sad—that kicked-puppy look.

Dal shifted her gaze down also and saw that Piper was wearing the pink sneakers. How could pink sneakers connect so effortlessly with her heart? She knew the answer—they belonged to Piper. Shit, she was getting in way too deep, but she at least had to settle whatever was going on between them.

When they arrived at the seventh floor, they both exited along with a few others, Dal trailing Piper to her door. If nothing else, she was Piper's ride back to Oakland.

"Can I come in?" Dal stood behind Piper as she fumbled with her key card.

"I guess," Piper murmured. "It's not like I can easily get home without you."

"Why would you want to get home without me?" Dal's stomach clenched. This was definitely about something she'd done.

Piper pushed on the hotel room door and headed inside, leaving it wide open for Dal to follow. She turned and sat on the edge of the bed. Piper's tired features suggested that she hadn't slept much last night. Exhaustion painted across her face and settled in her unhappy liquid eyes. Her suitcase was packed and sitting in the middle of the bed.

Dal frowned. "Again, why would you want to do that? Need to get home without me?"

"Because I'm an idiot." Piper's eyes welled with tears, and she wiped them with her forearm.

"Because?" Dal pressed her lips together, still confused by Piper's distress.

"Because you're fucking married, Dal. And I was stupid enough to think maybe you felt a little something for me, besides just playing me. Because I've felt something for you." Piper was looking at the ceiling. Anywhere except at Dal.

Dal's heart flipped and then her throat constricted. She didn't know where to start with the whole saga of Chantal.

"Viola said when they couldn't reach you, they called your wife. You have a fucking wife, Dal."

"Fuck." Dal decided it was her turn to swear. She took a breath and held it for a moment. She had known her growing feelings for Piper were a bad idea.

"I know we haven't done anything, but I'm falling for you. I thought you kind of knew that," Piper said.

"There are so many reasons I can't get involved with anyone." Dal needed to focus on addressing the goddamn facts, not on taking Piper into her arms and trying to fix this.

"A *wife*, Dal?" Piper's tone was a mix of pain and disbelief. "Is she waiting at home for you?"

"Okay. You deserve to hear this." Dal paced back and forth in front of Piper. "She's my ex. I've had nothing to do with Chantal for three years, except trying to get her signature on divorce papers. We both have lawyers. She walked out—left me and Ruby three years ago. She's never wanted anything to do with Ruby, but she won't give me custody without a ransom."

"A ransom?" Piper repeated the words, glancing at Dal, then away again.

"Well, probably not technically, but she wanted two million to give me full custody of Ruby after the divorce, on top of a generous alimony."

Piper repeated Dal's words again, like an echo. "Two million." Then she added, "Dollars?"

"Yes. Two million dollars." Dal didn't even try to hide the bitterness in her voice. "Then recently it was lowered to one million. Then Wednesday night as I was leaving work—"

"Like, the night before last? The night we drove here?" Piper's eyes were wide.

"That's the one."

"Sorry, go on," Piper said, finally holding Dal's gaze.

"She called me just as I was ready to leave the office. We're supposed to go through our attorneys. She said she was willing to settle for half a million. Then one hundred thousand. She wants the divorce—

she's got some other sucker scoped out." Dal gave herself a moment, acknowledging her disgust with Chantal and with herself for ever getting involved with her. "She's an ex in every way except for the piece of paper she won't sign. She wants money for Ruby. I've wanted to avoid court, hoping I was dealing with a reasonable person, but court may be the last resort. It's been hell." Dal closed her eyes briefly and inhaled.

Piper sat on the bed, not moving as she absorbed what Dal was telling her. "No wonder you've got so many rules, so many boxes." She massaged her forehead, talking to herself. "Money for Ruby," she said. "I'm sorry I jumped to conclusions. Viola only said that your wife had given permission for the stitches."

"So, you thought I was playing pinkies with you while I had a wife at home?" Dal tried to keep her tone neutral, even though she was upset that Piper thought she would do such a thing. Then a wave of self-recrimination hit her because she'd let this attraction to Piper elevate things to the level of Piper's perception of cheating. She fought to simply focus on Piper's dismay.

Piper nodded, looking chagrined. "I had no idea. I'm sorry for what I assumed. I would have talked to you, but I needed a little time."

"I can't blame you." Dal touched Piper's shoulder. "I'm sorry you found out this way, that I didn't tell you, but deciding to marry Chantal was a failure on my part." All the weight of that failure pressed on Dal too. "My life's a mess. I'm a mess. I never intended to get involved with you. You need to take your heart and walk away. There are no promises left in me." She wished there were, but she honestly didn't think so. Dal knew she'd been an emotional mess much of her life.

"I get that you're still married." Piper straightened, clearly processing all that she had just learned. "I don't want to be involved with a married woman."

Dal suddenly felt a tsunami of sadness wash over her, and she was furious with herself. She'd had her pledge for a reason. For multiple reasons, and her heart was just one of them. She was grateful she hadn't let herself get in any deeper with Piper.

Piper held up her hand. "But that doesn't mean I'm just walking away. I'm not ready to walk away from you. Or Ruby. Not yet."

"What does that mean?" Dal didn't know what to think or how to feel. What did Piper want? What did she want? Dal wasn't sure.

"It means I believe there's something between us. Something that could grow if given a chance. Bloom with the right amount of care and light." Piper frowned. "Why am I so good with plants and so bad with people?"

"You're good with people. Exceptional. This is on me."

"I need to know that you have Chantal's signed agreement—that there will be a divorce. I know even uncontested divorces take time, that dissolution is just a matter of the waiting period, but I need to see that a divorce is coming." Piper closed her eyes and gulped. "Not years down the road. Or never—I can't stay with no prospect of a future."

Piper shifted on the bed, looking over to where the sun was entering the room through partially closed curtains gracing the window. Then she finished what she had to say. "I'm willing to wait for a while. To see if we just need the right season for that bloom. As long as I can manage, and I don't know how long that will be."

"Look at me, Piper." Piper shifted her gaze from the window to Dal. "Don't bet on me. I'm not a good bet. I have my rules for a reason, and I don't know that I can change. That I'm willing to change."

Piper stood up. "I'm sorry. I know exes can be hell. But instead of carrying all of the bad that Chantal's done to you, maybe look at the good."

"The good?" Dal was incredulous. She studied Piper…not naive, but optimistic when given the opportunity, even in her pain.

"I know that the involvement of Ruby has put your experience in a whole different place from mine, but my exes have changed me. I've grown." Piper took a deep breath, and Dal watched her attempt a smile. "I've learned what I want and what I don't want. That's the good." Piper pulled her suitcase off the bed and headed past Dal toward the door.

Dal stood there, struggling to digest Piper's positive spin on Chantal.

"We don't want to be late for checkout. There are rules, you know," Piper said, injecting some teasing into her tone. It lightened the mood.

Dal couldn't help it—she chuckled.

❖

"What do you mean she's married?" Bryce and Piper were out running around Lake Merritt on Saturday afternoon. The ride back to the Bay Area with Dal the day before had been companionable, surprising Piper somewhat, but their earlier conversation had seemed to clear the air, even if it did add another layer to the obstacles to a future with Dal. Piper didn't want to make a rash decision, but she knew the clock was ticking for her. If she couldn't bear the pain...

She'd taken BART to Cate's office that morning to check the plants and messages, even though it was the weekend. She'd left her plants unattended for too long. Then she'd spent some time with Sunny while she'd done some writing. Posted a blog. Bryce had phoned her midafternoon, and now they were sharing a bit of exercise and catching up on each other's lives.

Piper explained the circumstances of Dal's marriage, or rather her lack of an agreement for a divorce.

Bryce glanced at Piper as they jogged along. "Jeez. You sure know how to pick 'em. So, what are you going to do? You really like her, don't you?"

"I'm going to try to not do anything I'll regret. There are two weeks left in this working relationship before Cate gets back, so I've told myself I don't have to think about her marriage until after that. I know it's still there, but I don't have to deal with it because for now, she's my boss and off-limits. After that, if we don't just walk away from each other, I'll have to deal with the fact that there is a wife who is holding Dal's daughter hostage for a lot of money before she'll agree to a divorce." Piper looked over at Bryce. "She has so much baggage. I don't know that I'll have any decisions to make. She keeps sending messages that she doesn't want to give us a chance, but we have a connection."

"Holy crap, Pipes. Why can't you just enjoy her for the moment? Take her to bed and move on?"

Piper scowled at Bryce. She thought about how tempted she'd been to go to bed with Dal in her drunken haze at the hotel. "Because I know that I want more. I'm tired of dead-end girlfriends. I'm not saying that I know how this will end with Dal, but I know I don't want a relationship that has no chance at love. I don't want to settle for less—I want what you've found. Lasting love. And Dal is talking to my heart like no other woman ever has."

"Well, if you put it that way. I know I couldn't be happier with Hannah. Hannah knows it too. She's a fuckin' miracle in my life. So, you just let me know what I can do to help—maybe arrest her for being a fool." Bryce poked her in the ribs.

Piper had to laugh. "Yeah, that'll win her over."

Bryce picked up her pace, pulling away from Piper. She looked back over her shoulder. "Just say the word, and I'll get the warrant. Stolen hearts come with a life sentence."

Piper thought about that. Dal wasn't like her other exes. She knew that Dal was stealing her heart. She wanted to get out of this without it being broken. But she also wanted a chance with Dal, and a broken heart was the risk. She'd wait until it hurt too much.

"Thanks so much, guys." A beaming Jeremy and Nick posed with Fred as Piper took several snapshots of the trio. The shepherd mix looked so happy. It was her normal Sunday volunteer time at Wee Critter Haven, and she'd spent the morning taking pictures of adopted animals and their families for a story wall—an idea she'd gotten from the conference. Fred's family had brought him in, and the moments she captured radiated with both dog and boy joy. Several families had shown up, so Piper had collected multiple images of real-life adoptions.

After the families had left, Piper downloaded the intake-day photos of those adopted animals onto a thumb drive, planning to juxtapose the day of an animal's arrival with the current image on posters for the wall. She took some additional photos of Boris, the resident cat, and some adorable puppies and kittens, and by the time she finished, Piper thought she had the potential for a terrific wall display at the fundraiser.

On Sunday evening Piper went to the FedEx website and placed an order for twelve posters for the story wall at the gala. She decided she'd put together a short narrative about the Fred Fund to place next to that poster, demonstrating how donations changed lives. What Dal had done for Fred and his family, even if she wouldn't take credit, only made Piper more aware of why she was attracted to Dal, even with all her issues.

Heading into her NAS office on Monday, Piper was determined to focus on finding a celebrity for the gala. It was her top priority now, and she was having no success. At a loss as to where to look next, she refused to give up. She was back in her office, combing the internet for ideas of people to contact that she hadn't already tried.

Piper focused on her task, plowing ahead with planning the gala and finalizing one aspect after another. Dal remained secluded in her office all morning, and Piper missed the spontaneous chitchat sessions that Dal seemed so hell-bent on avoiding.

It was midafternoon when Piper looked up from her computer after she'd heard someone in the hallway. Dal stood in her doorway. "Just making sure you don't need anything before I take off to meet with Alex at one of the clinics," Dal told her.

Piper hadn't heard from Dal since she'd dropped her off at her apartment on Friday afternoon after the conference. Piper could feel that invisible bond between them, the invisible threads of caring and desire, but now woven into what had already been that complicated cord of connection was Dal's divorce, and Chantal.

"I'm good. Just going to spend this week making sure everything is in order, as best I can, and leave the fundraiser notes with a decent spreadsheet that's up to date on where everything stands and what else needs to be done. I have a reply from the mayor's office saying she'll be attending. I didn't commit her to a speech or anything because I'm still working on a different type of entertainment—celebrity entertainment."

"Well, I'll leave you to it, then," Dal said. "Have a nice evening."

"See you later." Taking the hint that Dal wanted no further discussion, Piper turned her attention back to her computer screen. Dal had indicated that she was in no mindset for anything but minimal interaction. But Dal didn't leave immediately. She stood there silently looking at Piper long after she'd returned her focus to her computer.

Piper didn't like the distance between them, but at least they'd talked, and she'd stepped back from the edge of the abyss where she'd stood on Friday. There was no solution except to allow time, but she couldn't wait forever. Piper thought of the *Agave americana*, an aloe succulent native to Mexico. Also called the century plant, its story was that it only bloomed once every one hundred years and then died. Piper shook her head. She wasn't that crazy. She wouldn't be here in a hundred years. But she could certainly wait for a little while. Until she decided that caring for Dal was something her heart couldn't take any longer. And she could hope.

DANCING IN THE WEEDS WITH PIPES THE UNPLUGGED

"Exes"

Maybe some of us need to take the long way home. There's no map, no driver's manual, and maybe there isn't even the fantasized home at the end of the plot-twisty road with the exits *that you didn't* take, at least not the *expected* destination *exactly* like the one you exalted *in your head when you were in the* express *lane, hell-bent on holing up in what turned out to be the* expensive *(of course it cost you something) Nothing to See Here Town with the real estate where you just stuffed the closet full of* extraneous experiences, *some* excruciating, *that weren't really* extrinsic *at all because if you're honest and examine them closely, you will find that if you* expunge *them,* excise *those exes from your* existence, extract *them from that journey that is your life, then you will not pass the* exam *at the end of the* exploration, *the one where you receive an* exemplary *score for growing into the person you were meant to be, the unique and mind-boggling being that knows what you really want, what you really need, who knows what true love is. Because some of us need to take the long way home.*

CHAPTER FOURTEEN

On Wednesday morning, Piper detoured by the San Francisco FedEx store and collected the large packaged bundle of posters before taking a rideshare to get to the NAS office.

With her arms filled with the dozen-poster bundle, she struggled to make it through the door. Nettie didn't get up to help, leaving Piper to conclude that Nettie must think that an ex-relationship precluded her from common manners.

Piper wedged herself into the minimally open door, then butt-pushed the door wide open. The door soundly smacked Piper on the backside as it swung closed, but she was protecting her package at all costs.

Apparently hearing the commotion, Dal came from her office. Shaking her head at Nettie, Dal rushed to help. Piper carried the package back to her office and set it on her side table, Dal following.

"Quite the moves there, Piper. I hope you didn't bruise anything."

Piper thought she detected a playful undertone to Dal's comment. If she wasn't going to walk away from Dal, she was going to maintain some personal connection. Maybe pushing the line a bit, but she knew Dal wouldn't let her cross that line. "Nettie is useless, but you could examine the damage for me." Piper couldn't suppress a cheeky grin.

"Sure. I could look at your shoulder." Dal sounded like she was toying with Piper, but wore the neutral expression she was so good at maintaining.

"That's not what got whacked, but the rule book probably doesn't include a boss review of my backside." Piper let her gaze linger on Dal.

Dal's color flushed a bit before she plastered a stern look on her face.

Piper didn't want to let Dal ignore their connection. "Isn't this how we met? Bruised derriere." Piper couldn't suppress the pleasure she felt in bantering with Dal. "Maybe it's our thing. Like some people have a song or a movie." Piper paused, wondering what the hell she was doing. There was a line she shouldn't cross. Then she decided that waiting for a married Dal to at least obtain an agreement after three years of negotiating a divorce offered some leeway in the interaction department—even if Dal threw roadblocks up at every turn. Dal didn't have a wife sitting at home loving her. That moved the line a bit for Piper, but she noted that she still worked for Dal too. She just couldn't completely ignore her heart.

Dal cleared her throat and pointed at the package. "We better stick to the task at hand."

Unwrapping the paper holding the stacked posters together, Piper flipped through them until she found the one that she was searching for. It was a poster with two side-by-side photos: a depressed, lost Fred on his arrival day, and a picture of Fred and the two boys radiating love. She pulled it out, holding it up for Dal to see.

"For the story wall at the fundraiser. A tangible visual of what the nonprofit does. This one is Fred's story in two simple photos. Pretty cool, huh?"

Dal nodded, still not saying anything.

Piper studied Dal's face, stopping at her contemplative steel-blue eyes. "You made all the difference in the world to this dog and these boys. Changed some lives." Piper reached over and touched Dal's arm, not thinking about what it might mean beyond just wanting Dal to know that she knew the impact Dal had made with the anonymous donation, the fake Fred Fund. Dal's eyes darkened as Piper felt the jolt of the contact sweep up her arm and wash her body with warmth. Not lust, but emotion. Piper pulled her hand away, breaking the connection.

"Well, I'd better get back to work. I've still got a lot to do to hand this gala project off to someone else."

"I guess you'd better." Dal exhaled, then turned and walked out of the room, taking all of the emotional energy with her.

❖

The aroma of the spaghetti they'd all just enjoyed hung in the air as Dal came back into the kitchen to join Viola after tucking Ruby into bed. Still resting on the far end of the table was the multicolored abacus Dal and Ruby had been using to practice counting before dinner. Dal had laughed when Ruby had insisted on going from nineteen to twenty-teen and declared that *teen* belonged on everything after twelve. As she sat watching Viola, Dal wondered what the kid was going to be like as a teenager. She decided maybe there were a few advantages to being someone who'd been taking on challenges her entire life.

"What can I do to help?" Dal leaned down to pat Einstein who was stretched out on the kitchen floor next to the table, his tail thumping when he saw Dal approach.

"You can sit down and chat with me while I finish up. I don't need you in my way," Viola said, her dark eyes sparkling. She nodded at the empty chairs around the table.

"You're the boss. That spaghetti's the best. Thanks."

"How's the fundraiser coming together?" Viola turned her head toward Dal so she could see her better as she scrubbed the sink.

"Fine." Dal took a seat. She knew where Viola was going with this conversation, and she didn't want to discuss Piper.

"So did the conference give you and Piper any ideas for ways to improve it?"

"A few."

Viola grunted at Dal's minimalist answers. "Piper still working out okay?"

"Mm-hmm." Damn. Viola always had a purpose.

"You still falling for her?" Viola shifted to wiping the countertops.

Dal frowned, powerless to stop Viola without giving too much away if she put substantial effort into a diversion. Viola was too astute.

"Just checking in after you two spent a little time together." Viola was using her practiced innocent tone. It didn't fool Dal.

Dal finally gave up—Viola would get it out of her eventually anyway. She always did. "She knows about Chantal. That I'm still married. When you called about Ruby's accident and told her my wife had been the contact for the stitches."

Viola stopped wiping the countertop and turned to face Dal. "Was it bad?" Her brow was furrowed.

"It was. Piper thought I had a loving wife I neglected to mention. Sort of revealed that she liked me." It still didn't settle well with Dal that Piper had thought she was a cheater. That she had let their connection escalate to the point that she had clearly hurt Piper. But that wasn't going to be part of this exchange if she could help it.

"And that's bad?" Viola pressed her.

Dal blew a raspberry, filling the conversation with the buzz of her frustration. "That she likes me? Yes. That she knows I'm still married? No. It's a good thing because now she knows I'm unavailable. That this can't go anywhere."

Viola chuckled. "I'm glad to hear that there is a *this* that can't go anywhere."

Dal glared at her. "There is no *this*. I don't want a *this*."

"Well, the *this* that doesn't exist. The *this* you don't want. It sounds like maybe you don't get to control it."

"I don't go places that I have no control over. Besides, she put the brakes on things as long as I'm married, or at least don't have a final divorce agreement in sight." Dal pressed her mouth tightly shut. No more raspberries. She sounded too much like Ruby.

"Well then, I guess you'd better get things settled with your ex so you can get on with the *this*—on with Piper." Viola added, "Dahlia Noble, you're too smart to not know that you can't control love."

"Don't go there." Dal wasn't going to have this discussion. Not even with Viola.

"What's the problem? That you can't control it? Or that it's got the potential for love?"

Dal knew she was scowling. "Either one."

"You need to accept both." Viola turned to head downstairs to her apartment. "And you can thank me later. It's past my bedtime."

"It's barely eight o'clock." Dal rolled her eyes at Viola's retreating form.

"Good night. Sleep well." Viola disappeared into the stairwell.

"Shit," Dal muttered.

"I heard that, Dahlia." Viola's voice drifted back up into the kitchen. "And you're welcome."

❖

Piper was back at Cate's law practice on Thursday, and the emails from the honeymooners contained pictures of them in Spain. Piper was anxious for their return at the end of next week. Her mom was out of town too, so she was feeling the lack of available maternal company and advice, and she wanted some advice about the situation with Dal. Or at least one of them to let her talk.

On Friday, Dal flew to Southern California to tour some of the NAS clinics. She was returning on an early evening flight, so Piper didn't see her all day. After work, Piper decided she wanted to take a run at Lake Merritt. Maybe it would help her sleep better. The uncertainty around whether a relationship would ever be possible with Dal, the worry about not finding a celebrity guest who would attract the big donors next week before she went back full-time to her paralegal job—those things were keeping her awake at night.

After feeding Sunny and changing into her running clothes, Piper drove over to a street near the lake path while there was still enough light to enjoy one lap around the water. She needed to decompress.

Piper finished her lap and was walking back to her parked car in a nearby neighborhood when she heard yelling and a scuffle up ahead. Moving forward, she saw a young man with a fawn-colored French bulldog on a leash and a bigger person with a ski cap pulled down over their face. She watched the larger individual shove the young man down and kick him, attempting to wrench the dog's leash from his hand. Piper realized that she was witnessing a dognapping in progress.

Without stopping to consider the consequences, Piper reacted. She ran, shouting as she approached. "Stop! Thief! Help!"

Piper grabbed the person who was stealing the dog and held on. From their size, she concluded it was most likely a man. As she fought with him, other people started to approach her to help, but they were not close enough for her to back off. She clung to the thief so he couldn't take off with the animal. Panicking and swinging his fist at her, he connected with Piper's chest and knocked the air out of her, and then as she stumbled, he shoved her. Piper felt herself falling backward. She hit her head as she connected with the ground.

In no time at all, several strangers were standing around Piper. An older woman was bent down next to her, telling her to relax. Piper sat up. The woman asked her name, and Piper told her. All Piper could think about was the canine.

"The dog." She groaned and waved at the woman to go save the stolen animal.

The woman assured her that the Frenchie was fine and back with the young man, who was his walker. However, the dognapper had gotten away.

A police officer showed up and took down the information but advised the crowd that the chances of catching the thief were low. The woman who had stopped to help insisted on taking Piper to the hospital to get checked out because Piper had a significant bump on the back of her head.

Piper was finally brought into an exam room. The nurse asked for her emergency contact, and Piper took a moment to consider the request. The back of her head hurt, and the area on her chest where she'd been punched was sore when she put pressure on it, but Piper managed to pull her phone from her pocket and gave the nurse Pete's name and number. Most everyone else she knew was out of town, including Bryce and Hannah, who had headed down to LA to visit family. The nurse left Piper stretched out on the table, then returned and took Piper's vitals. She told Piper that she'd reached Pete. Just as the nurse finished, a young woman in a white lab coat with a stethoscope around her neck knocked and then entered the room.

"I'm Dr. Enlow. I hear you stopped a dognapping and ended up here with a significant swelling on the back of your head." The physician talked while she looked over Piper's vitals on her chart. "Hopefully, it's just soft tissue, external, and your brain wasn't involved."

Piper nodded.

Dr. Enlow did a physical exam before focusing on the head injury and the chest contusion. Then she said, "I'm going to put you through some tests and questions to check for signs of a concussion, and we'll decide if there's any need to do any imaging. You have a bruise on your chest, but your vitals are all fine. Any notable chest pain?"

After Piper told her that her chest felt okay, the doctor took a penlight and observed Piper's pupils for comparative size and reaction to the light followed by having her track her moving finger. She continued the physical assessment before asking Piper a series of questions.

"You aren't showing signs of a concussion at this point. I'll release you, but only if you have somewhere to go where someone can monitor you for forty-eight hours. It's a precaution to ensure you don't develop head injury symptoms that might require emergency intervention. Do you understand all that?" The doctor waited for Piper's affirmation.

"Okay." Piper was relieved that she didn't have an obvious concussion. She wasn't sure how it would work out with Pete, and she felt guilty that he might have to watch her for two days. She was also worried about Sunny. She closed her eyes and waited for the doctor to finish and leave.

The nurse returned and told her that she'd be released when someone came to collect her, repeating the requirement that she'd be observed for the next two days and agreed to return if there were any further problems. Piper was wheeled from the exam room to a bed behind a curtain in a line of similar recovery spaces where she could be watched while she waited. She was dozing on the bed, half listening for Pete to show up, when she heard a familiar voice, and then the curtain was pulled back.

Looking over, Piper couldn't believe it was Dal who had shown up. "I thought Pete was coming. What are you doing here?" She was so happy to see Dal.

"*Shhh.* Pete has the flu, and so he managed to track down my number. I'd made it back from my day of clinics in Southern California, so I was home without any plans tonight." Dal came over to the side of the bed and gently placed her hand under Piper's chin while studying her eyes like the doctor had done—probably for signs of a concussion, Piper thought. "They told me when I came in that you're a hero. You saved the dog." Then Dal shook her head. "Of course, you and dogs on walks don't mix. You ended up flat on the ground again, but you stopped the bad guy. At least this guy deserved to be bushwhacked." Dal paused and then growled, "He deserves to have the crap beat out of him for hurting you."

Piper tried to smile. "That's me, flattened hero. Now if you'll just take this hero to her apartment..."

"No way. They've been very clear. You need observation. This could still develop into a concussion, and they want to make sure it doesn't develop into something worse. You're coming home with me. Who better than your own personal veterinarian?" Dal chuckled.

"What about Sunny? He's home alone."

"Did you feed him his dinner? If not, I'll go do it after I get you to my place and sic Viola on you." Then Dal quietly added, "It'll be nice to have someone else for her to pick on."

"I fed him before I left."

"He should be okay tonight, then. I'll go tomorrow morning and check on him. Do you have a neighbor who can look in on him and feed him over the next two days?"

"Yes. Luella Jones is a widow who lives two doors down from me," Piper replied. "She'd probably be willing. He'll get lonely, but I guess he'll survive. Bryce and Hannah are out of town, and so's my mom."

Dal nodded. "Okay then. Let's get you a wheelchair to get to the car, and I'll take you home. Ruby is going to be ecstatic when she wakes up in the morning."

❖

All Piper wanted to do when they arrived at Dal's house was crawl into a bed. They'd driven up into the Oakland hills, the headlights of Dal's car cutting a bright, white tunnel that lit the way through the trees, around the curves of the narrow road as they climbed from the city up above the East Bay into a completely different world, far more nature than urban.

Piper couldn't tell much about Dal's house in the dark except that it was on a hillside and surrounded by trees. Pulling into the carport, Viola emerged to assist Dal in escorting Piper inside. Piper was still feeling shaky from the ordeal. Once in the door, Viola stepped back, letting Dal hold Piper's arm and lead her into an open living room. Piper looked around. There was a pile of stuffed animals in the middle of the floor. The space fed into an area with a dining room table that was adjacent to a kitchen. She could see the refrigerator door covered in colorful kid art, all held in place by magnets. Dal led her on through the living room and down a hallway into a large bedroom with a king-sized bed, the open door to an en suite bathroom at the far end of the room.

"I'll help you take a shower, then get you into bed. I'm going to spend the night next to you so I can monitor you for any problems." Dal disclosed her plans to Piper, not waiting for a response.

Piper gulped. She didn't know if she would rather have it be Pete helping her. At least with Pete, she wouldn't have to deal with considering that she was falling in love with someone who was off-limits. Where the heck was Viola?

Dancing in the Weeds with Pipes the unPlugged

"What Happens Between One Moment and Another"

Photo—a moment frozen in time. A single moment with so many moments stacked one next to the other on either side of that snapshot. Maybe you appreciate that one specific milli-moment in the infinite opportunity of moments, but it's not about taking the picture. It's about all that went into making the picture. About all that's gone into creating the hero of the frame. To arrive at that exact hard-copy snapshot capture of lights and darks, hues of existing—bearing still-life witness to so much more.

Fred, the poor sad rescue canine in run number seven. Failed and failed and failed in so many moments of the before. Such a sorrowful portrait. But now, this new milli-moment click in time represents the convergence of the Fred Fund, the adoration of a family, the commitment of other caring individuals, and Fred's ability to forgive. A dog with a future. A loving and loved soul.

But Fred is also the bigger life lesson. What happens between one snapshot moment and another in this world? The answer—more moments in life that could make all the difference to someone. A difference that you can make. Consider what a kind and caring you could mean to someone else.

CHAPTER FIFTEEN

Dal headed into the en suite to prepare to help Piper shower. She stayed there, alone, longer than she needed to. Her nipples were on full alert, the heat between her thighs was in danger of spontaneous combustion, and her heart was pounding out in rapid cardiac code a clear message that she had unwelcome feelings for this woman. Dal lectured herself and took a few deep calming breaths. She could do this. She had to focus on the fact that Piper was injured, a patient in need of care.

When she reentered the bedroom, Piper was still sitting on the bed. She took Piper's hand and led her into the bathroom. "I'm going to help you get out of these running clothes and get washed up." Dal employed her most clinical voice, the one she'd used with pet owners when she hadn't wanted to show any emotion.

She knew that her feelings were a mess of caring and desire and red alerts. Thoughts of helping Piper undress carried a mix of thrill and conflict, but Dal swore to herself that she'd remain stoic and accomplish whatever was needed. Piper had been injured, and Dal didn't need to be a lustful jerk. Although if it was just lust, dammit, she could take care of that with a visit to a bar and a stranger. However, that wasn't working for her anymore. Dal suppressed a cynical laugh, frustrated with herself.

Standing behind Piper, Dal saw the grime and blood on her head. The bump was hidden under that mass of ringlets, rich red hair woven with hints of chestnut and amber. Taking the hem of Piper's T-shirt from behind, Dal carefully helped Piper remove it. She tried not to look at Piper's reflection in the mirror because that would reveal more than Dal wanted to deal with.

Piper took a deep breath and exclaimed, "No wonder it hurts."

Dal couldn't help herself. She turned her head and looked over Piper's shoulder at the woman in the glass. God, Piper was alluring. Silky-smooth pale skin, some definition to her abs with the perfect amount of accompanying softness, two very adequate breasts under that violet bra...Dal admonished herself for where her thoughts had gone as she took in the contusion, red turning bluish purple the size of a closed fist over Piper's sternum, the top edge concealed by the bottom edge of her bra.

Dal wanted to kill the bastard who had put it there. She wanted to put her arms around Piper and cradle her. She wanted to kiss the pain away. But instead, she calmly helped Piper free those perfect breasts from their final cover and lower her faded running shorts to reveal tight violet-hued boy shorts with a single small unicorn emblem printed on the right leg. *So* Piper. Dal's mind flashed to the pair of ivory silk bikini briefs she'd donned this morning, and just like the pink sneakers and black flats she'd stared at while she and Piper had sat on the park wall, Dal could honestly picture the two pieces of underclothing lying side by side, hurriedly discarded on a bedroom floor. *Fuck.*

Ignoring the blended wash of emotional and physical feelings flooding her body and mind, Dal helped Piper lower those boy shorts down to her ankles and then reached down to take the underwear as Piper stepped out of them, holding on to Dal's bent upper back for balance. When Dal stood up, she locked eyes with the honey sage ones in the mirror. They stared at each other for a long moment, their pupils dilating, their eyes darkening before Piper broke the silence.

"I'm sorry, Dal. I think I've pushed you way outside the boss zone. Hell, I've never been nude with a married woman before either. Let's just blame it on the head injury." Dal didn't want that reminder of Chantal.

Struggling to keep her voice normal, Dal replied, "No apologies allowed from the woman who saved the dog."

"I'm just glad the thief didn't get him. I'd do it again in a minute." Piper stepped into the warm water Dal had turned on and moaned softly with pleasure as she turned her head up to let the cleansing flow wash over her face.

"Let me help you shampoo your hair, then get you toweled off and into bed." Dal leaned into the shower stall, taking the handheld showerhead from its holder and guiding the hose over so the spray continued to fall on Piper. Spray and mist were soaking Dal's clothes too, but she ignored the moisture. She needed to focus on helping her patient.

"I bet you say that to all the girls." Piper closed her eyes as Dal squeezed shampoo into her hair.

Dal focused on the *hair* part of her declaration, not willing to address the rest of the statement. Especially the *into bed* part. "I think the only head of hair besides my own that I've ever washed is Ruby's. Forget the boss zone for the moment. You're getting the hero treatment."

Dal wanted to keep the conversation light as she worked her hands carefully through Piper's hair and watched the soap run off her, tiny bubbles trailing from her cheeks and chin down across the rose pink of her nipples to finally swirl and disappear down the drain. Dal turned Piper around to make sure they had cleaned the scrape on the back of Piper's head, as well as to take her mind off Piper's nude front, but that didn't help. Piper's perfect ass was no easier to ignore than her bust.

This was a test of her willpower, and Dal swore she would not fail the test. Hell, she was an overachiever. After rinsing Piper's hair, she stepped back out of the stall and grabbed a large white towel that she'd set on the countertop. Unfolding it and placing it over her shoulder, she reached back into the stall for Piper.

"How're you doing?"

Piper's eyes were still closed as the warm water enveloped her. "If this is the aftercare I get, I'm stopping a dognapping every day."

Dal couldn't help but appreciate the touch of humor in Piper's tired voice. "Let's dry you and get you into bed." She concentrated on keeping her tone blasé as she turned off the shower and took Piper's arm. Dal steadied her as Piper stepped onto the bathroom rug, and then Dal took the towel from her shoulder and wrapped it around Piper, patting the towel over Piper's nude skin. Dal closed her eyes and took a deep breath—she could ignore Piper's beautiful body and do this. Dal left it wrapped around Piper like a closed cape, grabbing a smaller towel that she gingerly rubbed over Piper's hair, trying to avoid the sore area at the back of her head.

"Do you want me to comb your hair out?"

"If we don't, someone will report it to the authorities in the morning. Rebel rascal on the loose," Piper told her. They both chuckled.

Once that chore was accomplished, Dal led the still towel-caped Piper out to the bed, then pulled back the covers and assisted Piper between the bedsheets as Dal took the towel. Dal did not want to even think about the fact that she had a naked woman in her bed. A naked Piper. At least she wouldn't have to struggle to keep herself awake to observe the patient. There were plenty of reasons Dal wasn't going to get a good night's sleep.

❖

When Piper woke up in the morning, she smelled coffee. She remembered Dal waking her up intermittently during the night and checking on her. She remembered the shower too—she'd have to have been comatose to forget that. Dal's actions had been so caring underneath that effort at a clinical presentation. Piper was no fool. She'd seen the deep desire in Dal's eyes, and heard the anger and worry because she'd been hurt. That was what she wanted from Dal—the emotional connection as well as the physical one she'd glimpsed last night. Dal had been there when Piper had needed her most. Maybe there was hope. But there was no sign of Dal now. As Piper looked around the bedroom, Viola came through the door.

"There you are. How are you feeling? Up for a little coffee and toast?" Viola was like Meg, a natural when it came to the mothering department. "Avocado toast—one of my specialties. I've got your breakfast ready out in the kitchen."

Piper cleared her throat. "I'm probably better than I have a right to be. Feeling pretty good in fact. Just sore. And I'm hungry—I missed dinner last night." She listened and didn't hear any noise in the house. "Where are Dal and Ruby?"

"Dal took your keys and headed with Ruby over to feed your cat. Sunny, is it? And to see if your neighbor can check in on him and feed him until tomorrow evening. She also said something about watering plants. Then she was going to take a rideshare over to where you parked, collect your car, and bring it back to your apartment." Viola paused, then added, "I think she called Pete to update him and verify the exact description of your car. Outback is what she remembered. She didn't want to get arrested for trying to get into the wrong one." The older woman laughed.

Piper nodded. "I was way more worried about Sunny than that old car. I wouldn't want any arrests, but it sounds like Dal has it covered."

"Dahlia is efficient, no matter her faults." Viola gave Piper a prolonged appraisal. "You look good in that bed."

Piper raised the top sheet a few inches and peered underneath. "Well, I'm au naturel in here, and hungry. Any idea where my clothes are?"

"Dal washed them last night, so I'll go collect them from the dryer for you." Viola turned to leave. "Your shoes are out by the front door, and I'll put your clean socks there, so you can just go barefoot around here like Ruby and Dal mostly do. I'm old and partial to my slippers. I'll be back in a minute."

Piper felt a bit overwhelmed by the kindness everyone was showing her. She could get used to it, and yet she knew it wasn't hers to have. She didn't want to think about those things today, though. Piper wanted to enjoy the moment. She would focus on her bruised body and not her heart.

"Here you go. I'll see you in the kitchen as soon as you're ready." Viola set the folded clothing on the nightstand next to the bed. "Do you take anything with your coffee?"

Piper thought of the conference, the bantering with Dal. "Cream and sugar would be great."

"A girl with good taste." Viola gave her a long look before she headed back to the kitchen. Piper wondered if she was just referring to how she liked her coffee.

Piper swung her legs over the side of the bed and planted her bare feet on the large area rug that covered much of the wooden floor. In her state last evening, Piper hadn't paid any attention to the rug, but this morning she appreciated that it agreed with her flamboyant style—stripes in the primary colors interspersed with varied-width lines of black. Ignoring the aches and pains, she'd just finished dressing when she heard the front door swing open, followed by a symphony of kid laughter drifting down the hallway. Little feet pounded the floor, and then Ruby charged into the room.

"Piper, we fed your cat. I liked Sunny, but he ignored me for his food bowl."

"No surprise there." Piper smiled. "Thank you so much for looking out for my little lion."

Ruby's eyes widened. "He's a lion? I thought he was just a regular old cat."

"He's a lion at heart. But you're right. He's stuck in a regular old cat body."

Ruby nodded. "It's a good thing he doesn't roar or they might kick you out of your home."

Dal came into the room, chuckling at the two of them. "We saved the little lion. We watered the plants. We found the car. Your neighbor is going to take care of Sunny until you get home tomorrow. Plus, I brought you your laptop so you can check emails or whatever. How is your head? And the rest of you?"

"My head is good. I hurt a bit, but not bad. I'm hungry, though. Viola said she has avocado toast and coffee ready." Piper stood up and headed over toward Dal. "With cream and sugar." She raised her eyebrows and placed her hand over her heart, ignoring the slight soreness of the bruise.

"And I thought you were the flower bouquet type," Dal said. "But now I know that I'd just need to buy a pound of sugar and a pint of cream if we ever had a falling-out."

Piper loved this version of the relaxed, bantering Dal who wasn't on guard. "I'm not that easy. I'd need the coffee too. And speaking of coffee, can we?"

They all headed out to the kitchen to eat what was now a brunch that Viola had prepared, a fun, noisy, brunch full of comradery and family and love. Piper could only soak it in and appreciate it.

❖

Dal was exhausted after spending much of the night awake on Piper watch. When she was ready to head in for a nap in the early afternoon, Piper and Ruby were sitting on the living room couch, cueing up the movie *Puss in Boots*. Her gaze locked on Piper's as they both acknowledged it would be a participatory experience for Piper, Ruby already narrating dialogue and forewarning major plot points. Viola made popcorn and filled glasses of orange juice before she headed downstairs to read. Dal hoped it would be the perfect recovery afternoon.

"Okay, you two. Behave yourselves while I get a little sleep. No wild antics," Dal cautioned them, directing her warning at Ruby.

"What's a wild antic, Mom?"

"It's you two robbing a bank while I'm getting a little rest," Dal replied.

"I heard Viola on the phone talking about someone who was trying to rob your bank. She sounded mad." Ruby reported this in all innocence, but it was like a silent bomb had been detonated in the room, Ruby oblivious.

Dal watched Piper's expression shift from relaxed joy to sad reality. She'd thought the weekend was going okay, that she had everything under control, and then Ruby had so innocently kicked Piper in the gut. Maybe she should just let it go—better to grow the great divide with Piper now than try to explain to Piper later why she couldn't bring her into her life. Let it be all Chantal's fault.

Dal would have loved to do that, but it wasn't her nature to just walk away and leave any animal in pain. And Piper wasn't some rescue. The problem was that Dal wasn't sure what she was. She knew that Piper was kind and funny and willing to be injured to stop a dognapping. She could go down the list of her attributes. It was a mile long, but that was just a list. It was being with Piper, talking to her, laughing with her, watching her with Ruby—those things connected with Dal. And that was exactly the problem. Piper was growing on her, and she was afraid, full-blown petrified because she had no room in her life for that kind of threatening love. Shatter your heart kind of love. Ruin your life kind of love if things went wrong. Way more than anything she'd ever felt for Chantal.

Dal got up and went to the top of the stairs that led to Viola's apartment. She knocked on the open door that led down the stairwell before proceeding to descend into Viola's space.

"Can you come up and stay with Ruby for a while? I need to talk to Piper."

"Sure. Is Piper okay?" Viola put her book aside and stood up.

"She's fine. At least physically. Ruby and I just sort of upset her, with Chantal. By accident. I can't just not say anything."

"Of course. And Dahlia, you're a smart woman. I raised you to be that way. Smart." Viola gave Dal one of her looks. The one between *I love you* and *Don't do something stupid.*

Dal pressed her eyes closed, but that didn't shut out what was going on inside...inside her head, her heart. "There's a right way and a wrong way for me to let her go. I just don't want to do it the wrong way." This whole Chantal blowup had just brought Dal back to reality.

Viola made a show of saying nothing and looking everywhere but at Dal, a sign Dal knew meant that she had other things to say but was holding her tongue. She followed Dal upstairs to the living room where Ruby was deeply engaged in giving a play-by-play of the movie while Piper sat in reserved silence.

"I have an intense hankering to watch this movie with you, Ruby." Viola sat down on the couch. "Just what is it that we're watching?"

Dal didn't miss the look Piper gave them as it registered with Piper that Viola had no real interest in the movie. Ruby didn't look away from the TV, totally absorbed in the animated show as she answered Viola.

"Can I talk to you?" Dal asked Piper.

Piper nodded. Dal noted that her eyes were moist before she turned and walked down the hallway with Piper trailing behind. When they entered the bedroom, Dal indicated that Piper should sit on the bed. Piper stretched out her legs and leaned her back against a pillow that Dal had propped against the headboard for her. Dal couldn't help but take her in, the muscular legs that ran down to her bare feet, the loose T-shirt that hid those high, firm breasts, the lean arms, and finally, those guileless liquid eyes that waited for whatever blows Dal was going to land.

Dal sat on the edge of the bed, her back to Piper because she wanted to talk without the distraction of actually seeing Piper. Dal just couldn't watch the damage she was doing. But it was for both their benefits, she told herself, the conviction always weaker when she was in Piper's presence.

"I'm sorry." Dal studied her hands, clasped in her lap.

"For what? It was just Ruby telling the truth and reminding us that you're married. Maybe locked in an ugly fight with your wife, but the truth."

Dal nodded. "I am still married—if only on paper. But Chantal will be history at some point in time." Dal paused, gathering her thoughts. Then she continued, hearing the pain in her own voice, no matter how hard she tried to keep it out. "That's not all of it. My childhood—a father who loved alcohol, but not me. He didn't want me. He encouraged me to love him and then hurt me every time I did—on purpose. I protect my heart for a reason. You need a whole person, Piper. You deserve a whole person. Not someone like me. Flawed."

Dal felt all the pieces of herself converge in the pit of her stomach— the war of the past and the present battling over the future, a future she had worked so hard to keep in her sights for years. To maintain control, after her terrible younger years. To maintain control, until she'd made that one disastrous misstep that had taught her that seeking passion or even a long-term partner wasn't worth the chaos to her life.

"What is a *whole* person?" Piper asked.

"It's not me. I've been through too much." Dal still wasn't looking at Piper.

"I've said it before," Piper replied. "Maybe that's the point, becoming our best person if we can learn from the journey."

"I'm sorry." Dal repeated the apology. She wanted to send Piper away, but she wanted to be near her a little longer. She was only so strong, and she was going to have to be at her Herculean best when she said good-bye to Piper at the end of the temp job next week.

Dal felt Piper's hand on her shoulder. "Will you sit here next to me, Dal? I'm not asking anything else of you. I'd just like a few minutes with you before you get some sleep."

Dal couldn't say no. She didn't want to leave this memory with a giant chasm between them today. Dal knew that she'd need to widen that chasm this next week so that she could walk away. She might need this memory to make it through the future.

Dal stood up and turned around as Piper scooted over. Dal leaned up against the headboard with a pillow behind her next to Piper, their flanks separated by about eighteen inches. Her resolve couldn't survive being any closer. Piper reached across the space and took Dal's hand, set it on the bed, and hooked her pinkie with Dal's smallest finger. It was the slightest of links, but it closed the chasm for the moment.

❖

When Piper returned to the living room, Ruby and Viola had just finished the movie.

"Dal's asleep. I need to make a call, let Wee Critter Haven know I won't be there tomorrow."

Ruby looked between Piper and Viola. "Maybe Mom and I could go with you. I want to see Boris."

Piper decided to wait and see if Dal was willing to do that. As the afternoon passed, Piper did some writing on her computer, and when she'd finished, Ruby brought out a deck of cards and they played several hands of Slapjack. They declared Ruby the final winner, and Ruby stood up and cheered while prancing in circles with Einstein right behind her. Piper made an effort to join in and laugh, trying to mask how torn she was between wanting to stay forever and wishing she was at her apartment, where she wasn't growing more and more attached to these people.

Dinner was another gathering around the kitchen table, although Piper and Dal were both more subdued. Dal agreed that she would accompany Piper and Ruby to the rescue the next day, clarifying it was because she had promised to be the one to observe Piper. She told Piper that they could probably return her to the apartment afterward, as long as Dal could text her during the afternoon and evening to make sure there were no indications of additional issues from her head injury.

That night, Dal slept in the spare room, coming in every few hours to check on her. Piper knew it was for the best, but there was a piece of her heart that didn't concur. It was probably the devil be damned piece that would get the rest of her heart broken to bits in the inevitable final crash. The piece that would have thrown out all the caution about a woman with a hurt-filled past, the rules, the lines, the boxes, the still married issue—the piece that would have just made love to Dal. Because Piper knew. She loved Dahlia Noble.

Dancing in the Weeds with Pipes the unPlugged

"A Whole Person"

She told me I don't need her because I need a whole person in my life. But she doesn't seem to recognize that most journeys require baggage. Or that a person usually didn't arrive at whole via the shortcut or the easy road. They navigated those sinkholes, those hairpin curves, those dead-end roads that offered a firsthand view of the rough passage that leads to empathy and understanding. They fought their way up those steep, steep hills, those killer inclines with the high vista views that include a perspective beyond oneself. They traveled through a fog so thick they were lost until they discovered the personal joys that lit their way and guaranteed they would find themselves. They sailed some stormy seas, took on water to the brink of sinking, but learned to bail with perseverance. They stood on the edge of the world with a wounding wind at their back and found the strength to not go over. They learned the value of caring and loving and mapping their own brand of good in the world. No, the easy road without baggage didn't get them there. Whole was never a destination—it was a journey that forged the whole person. And whether she knows it or not, she has made her own pilgrimage to whole.

CHAPTER SIXTEEN

It was Piper's last week at NAS with three workdays left as a temp. Joining the Monday morning BART crowd, Piper settled back into an empty seat as the train pulled out of the station, thinking about the day before.

After taking a slow morning at the rescue yesterday, at Dal's insistence, mostly reading books with Ruby to the animals, Dal and her daughter had driven Piper back to her apartment where Ruby had hugged Piper. She'd told her mom that she wanted to have another sleepover soon, maybe next time at Piper's house with Sunny. Dal had tossed an indirect look in Piper's direction, avoiding looking her in the eye while pinching those pink lips firmly closed—a clear communication to Piper, and maybe a memo to herself, that their weekend connection was not coming to work the next day.

Then Dal had opened her mouth and informed Ruby that it was time to return home. They'd quickly departed with Piper thanking Dal for her care. When they'd slipped out the door, they'd taken all of the weekend's happiness with them, only its shadow remaining, casting shade on the walls of Piper's heart. As soon as they'd gone, Piper had felt the gaping emptiness their presence had filled, a missing piece carved out so much larger than the one that usually resided there. The biggest bruise of all.

Now moving toward work in the transit car, Piper tried to focus on being grateful for what they'd offered her, even if it had only been for a few days under the doctor's orders. Despite the pain of the injuries and the ache of the present, it had been a glorious weekend. But as Piper had tried to settle back into her apartment last evening, the texts from Dal had been short and void of warmth, just a quick inquiry to verify Piper was okay. Sunny had fluctuated between happiness that his human was finally home and extreme annoyance that she had abandoned him. Piper had gone to bed early last night, determined to focus on how lucky she was to have a comfortable life. Determined to focus on all the things she still had to do regarding the fundraiser during this last week at Noble Animal Services. Determined to keep her mind off the fact that there would be no further reason for Dal and her to spend time together.

As the train entered the tunnel under the bay, Piper took a deep breath and sat back to listen to the transit hum along the tracks as everything exterior to the car went mostly dark, the train buried beneath the depths of the water. She wondered which Dal she would encounter today at the office, the warmer one or the guarded one she was expecting. If Dal interacted with her on a strictly professional level, there would be no chitchat or banter or any of the other interactions she was growing to love with Dal, the ones she viewed as the real Dal. There was no avoiding the fact that Dal was working hard to create distance between them—she'd experienced it yesterday. As the BART car reentered the land of the living on the San Francisco side of the bay, Piper made herself a promise that no matter what happened, she would finish the job to the best of her ability before walking away.

Coastal mist was still enveloping the city, and it hung moist and gray around the tall buildings in San Francisco. Piper reached her fog-shrouded destination and looked up, thinking of all that had happened in the time she'd been working here—thinking of that first day when she'd looked up at this building before she'd entered the NAS office, expecting Dal Noble to be male. Remembering when instead, she'd encountered the rude woman from the Lake Merritt jogging trail.

The elevator doors were open as Piper entered the ground floor, so she ran across the lobby and jumped in. The door was just sliding closed for the ascent when a striking woman called out to Piper to hold it for her, which she did.

"Which floor do you need?" Piper asked, her hand over the buttons.

"The fourth," the woman said, quickly glancing over at Piper. Piper knew what she saw—her top of untamable red hair, khaki slacks, a yellow button-down shirt, and chunky black boots today. Then the woman ignored her. Piper took a closer look at her elevator companion.

Her emerald-green dress was tightly fitted to a curvy form and low-cut in front to expose ample cleavage. Not a coiffed hair was out of place on her frosted blond head. While she wore a heavy layer of makeup, her skin appeared unblemished and her facial features perfectly proportioned—she didn't need all of the product to look gorgeous. As Piper watched her on the ride up, there was both self-absorption and anger in the woman's expression. She completely ignored Piper in the enclosed space, having blatantly written Piper off as inconsequential, which was fine with Piper. When the doors opened on the fourth floor, the woman charged out past Piper, who took a moment to assess her from behind. If not for her attitude, she was a stunning woman who made moving rapidly in four-inch heels look like a stroll in the park. The woman was undeniably practiced in a way Piper knew she could never achieve, even if she strapped on four-inch Louboutins for the next ten years and took private balancing lessons. This woman was a package that Piper could never compete with.

Trailing behind, Piper watched her elevator companion enter the NAS office. Standing in the open doorway, Piper took in the visitor waiting impatiently at the receptionist's desk where Nettie was seated with her eyes radiating interest as the woman introduced herself and made her demands.

"I'm Chantal. Dal's wife. I need to see her. Now."

Nettie's shocked expression had to mirror Piper's own. The feeling of being inconsequential in the elevator morphed into feelings of total inadequacy as the identity of the woman registered. If this was the type of woman Dal chose to marry, Piper knew she didn't stand a chance with Dal. This woman was so much more manicured, put-together, not a hair out of place picture-perfect than Piper could ever dream of being. She oozed the confidence of a woman who had orchestrated her appearance and knew how to use it. This woman wouldn't be caught dead in a pair of pink Converse.

A wave of nausea hit Piper, and she fought it off. Slipping past Chantal and lurching to her office down the hallway, Piper closed the door, collapsed into her desk chair, and put her head in her hands. Who the hell had she been kidding?

❖

The warm Monday morning rays streaming into Piper's office glinted off the clear glass vase of yellow daisies sitting on the table next to the window, where Piper had placed them late last week. Sitting in her office alone with the door closed, Piper studied them. Flowers always helped to calm her. With the glass restraint, green stems intertwined in a chaotic weave of botanical threads, but once free of their container at the top, they fanned out into flower heads.

Piper considered that the floral presentation was even more meaningful to her than when she'd had the urge to buy them from the street vendor on Friday. She'd purchased these little beauties, similar to the closely related sunflower, for their message, and as she sat taking in their offerings, the ache that was making it hard to breathe began to recede into the cage where it belonged.

She'd started to hope that she'd tamed it, but the ferocity with which the ache had attacked made Piper realize that it wasn't simply the old loneliness gnawing at her heart anymore. It was larger and more defined because she'd touched what she knew she wanted, if only momentarily. But for now, if she was going to get through her last week at NAS, Piper needed to focus on the daisies' silent message of joy and optimism.

Taking a breath, Piper swore that she'd be damned before she'd let the gorgeous Chantal stop her from doing the best job she could for the fundraiser and the animals. "Screw Chantal—and please forgive me, Granny," Piper said to herself. She'd face her angst later. She had the mayor's office to contact. There was no big celebrity responding to her pleas, so Piper knew it was time to go for one of those greedy politicians who would be climbing over the top of every other anxious elected official for a chance at the limelight in the presence of puppy popularity.

Piper was considering just how cynical that was when her cell phone rang with a number that she didn't recognize. She didn't answer it. A minute later, the dark screen lit up again with a voicemail alert. She listened to the message.

"Hi. This is Fiorra Firebrand calling for Piper Fernley. Could you please call me back? I'd like to talk with you. Thanks."

Ensuing disbelief and then irritation flooded what remained of Piper's patience after her encounter with Chantal. Fiorra Firebrand was one of the hottest stars in the pop music scene right now. She was top in the pop charts, had been all over music streaming platforms, and featured on entertainment shows and social media. She was so sizzling hot that Piper had never dreamed of contacting her agent as an option for celebrity entertainment at the gala. No way in hell would the real Fiorra Firebrand be calling her in person. The prank call was just another bad event in a day that had gotten off to a terrible start. Not in the mood to be toyed with, she turned her ringtone off.

Considering a politician as the guest speaker a defeat, Piper took her time looking up the mayor's office's phone number. The spreadsheet for the person who took over the planning, likely Nettie, needed a few updates, so she made those. She decided she'd write a blog that evening about rescues, to focus on the positives in her world. Then she made a personal call to Pete, who had left a message earlier asking for a status report on Piper's condition. Assuring him that she was back at work, they touched base on Cate and Meg's return home from Europe on Thursday evening. Maybe the four of them could do coffee this coming weekend if the two honeymooners were up for it.

❖

Chantal was back at it again, creating havoc in Dal's life, in person too, and Dal was furious. She escorted Chantal out of her office and called her lawyer, asking him to contact Chantal's lawyer to see what it would take to resolve this, or at least threaten a restraining order.

Nettie mentioned that Chantal had arrived at the same time as Piper, and Dal realized that Piper had encountered Chantal and was now shut in her office with the door closed. She had planned to avoid Piper as much as possible this week, to put some distance between them as Piper finished off her temp job, and then they could both get on with their separate lives.

She'd told herself that she'd helped Piper this weekend because Piper had been injured and needed help, that it was the right thing to do. But here Dal was today, hating that she was such an emotional wreck, worrying that Chantal had done something to hurt Piper. Something worse than still being her legal wife. Dal just wanted control of her life back, but first, she needed to check on Piper.

Einstein was at work with Dal because Viola was out with a friend all day. The dog followed her down to Piper's office.

"Piper?" she asked as she knocked on the closed door. Piper never shut her door. Dal stood there impatiently in the hallway, waiting for an answer, and then the door opened. Piper turned her back as she returned to her chair, waving Dal in.

"I'm sorry if Chantal did something to you," Dal told her. "I know she can be an ass."

"She didn't do anything to me," Piper replied. "And I don't want to talk about your marriage." Piper focused on Einstein, reaching down and petting him as he settled on the floor near her office chair.

Dal watched Piper look at the vase of daisies by the window. Dal had no clue what else she could say about her marriage. It would be a fact of her life until it wasn't. Even after that, she had too many issues. Too much past. She would need to tell Piper how much she'd appreciated her help these six weeks and then wish her luck before telling her good-bye. Taking a deep breath, Dal decided to at least see if she couldn't engage Piper for the moment in a bit of...chitchat. She owed Piper that after whatever Chantal had done.

"So, do you have the fundraiser under control? Nettie and I probably need to meet with you so we'll know the details of the planning." Dal's voice caught in her throat. Piper was so attractive in the morning light that was streaming through the window, that gorgeous vase of background daisies almost accessorizing her in her yellow shirt. She was genuine, so real and unpretentious. Dal expelled a disconcerted sigh—it had to be the contrast with Chantal, who couldn't be more artificial, all the way to her self-centered heart.

"You shouldn't have any major problems. I've got a spreadsheet that'll be totally up to date before I leave, and you can always call me at Cate's." Piper turned her computer screen around so that Dal could see the organized summary of her efforts.

Dal studied it and realized all that Piper had accomplished.

"The only big piece left is the celebrity guest. I was just getting ready to contact the mayor's office. She's coming, and I have no doubt that she or one of the other politicians will be happy to speak." Piper frowned, then added, "I had a prank call this morning that claimed it was Fiorra Firebrand, the famous pop singer. It couldn't be her because I never contacted her—she's so far out of our league for this event.

Besides, she'd never contact me in person, she'd have a representative do it."

Dal put her hand on Piper's shoulder, enjoying the connection and not wanting to think about the week after this one when Piper would be gone. One week at a time, and she had to get through the one they were in.

"Been slacking in here, huh?" Dal asked Piper in a tone that she hoped would lighten both of their moods. "So now you've got one of the world's top pop stars calling you?" Dal thought about that. "Do you have the message?"

Piper unlocked and handed Dal her phone. "It's the most recent voicemail."

Dal tapped it and listened. "I'm in the mood to take on a scammer or a prankster." When Piper nodded, Dal hit the number that had called Piper, giving her a grin.

Dal listened to someone who claimed that she had reached Fiorra Firebrand. She needed a little entertainment after the morning she'd had so far. "So, Fiorra, this is Dal Noble, Piper's boss. She's doing all the work around here this morning, and I've got nothing to do, so I thought maybe you could sing me a few stanzas of your number one song." Dal put it on speakerphone so Piper could hear.

Dal wasn't sure which of Firebrand's songs was currently number one, but it didn't matter. She winked at Piper, then she listened to the woman on the phone say, "Sure," and break into a perfect rendition of Fiorra's song, "I'm Going to Lust You into Forever."

The lyrics were so captivating, about lust turning into love. Locking eyes with Piper, Dal saw no disagreement in those dilated green-sienna ones looking back at her. Piper seemed to concur that it was a great impersonation, if not the real Firebrand.

The woman on the phone laughed. "So, do I get the job?"

"What job?" Dal asked.

"My services in any way Piper needs them." The woman chuckled.

"Are you propositioning her?" Dal put some threat in her tone. This was a prank call. Either that or Firebrand was way out of line.

"Whoa. From what I understand from my dogwalker, Piper saved Louie from a dognapper on Friday night. Louie is my Frenchie. My baby. And I can't thank her enough." The woman was sniffling over her dog. "I got Piper's name from the police report, and I was able to find out that no one by that name was admitted into the hospital, so I'm hoping she's okay. I want to thank her and see if I can give her tickets as my special guest to a concert, or something else."

Dal tilted her head and cocked an eyebrow at Piper. "Let me hand Piper the phone." Dal did that, snapped her fingers for Einstein to follow her, and then turned and headed back toward her office, suddenly thinking that Chantal and Piper couldn't be two more different women. Chantal would never put herself in harm's way to save a dog. Chastising herself for thinking about either of them, she went into her office and shut the door. She had work to do.

❖

Fifteen minutes later, there was a knock at Dal's door.

"Who is it?" Dal demanded. She was just finally getting her mind back to business.

"It's Piper. Can I come in?"

Dal sat back and picked up her pen. Tapped it a few times. "Might as well." She remembered that she'd read somewhere that Firebrand was single, and a lesbian. Yeah, might as well hear how the Firebrand conversation had gone. Might as well hear how Firebrand was going to thank Piper—make her a special concert guest or spend time with her in some other way. Dal fought the wave of fucking jealousy that steamrolled her...dammit, now every time she swore, she'd think of Piper and her granny.

As Piper entered, Dal warned Einstein to stay in his bed, then returned her eyes to her computer screen, waiting for Piper to take a seat, which she did. But she didn't sit still. She friggin' bounced.

Something big had transpired—Piper could never hide her feelings.

"So, what is she going to provide in thanks?" Dal could hear the jealousy in her own voice. She looked at Piper and cleared her throat, sitting back in her chair as she struggled to appear relaxed.

Piper rolled her eyes. Then she grinned, and Dal pursed her lips.

"Do you two have a date?" Dal tried to sound casual. Disinterested. But she didn't pull it off.

As Dal watched, she noted that Piper was looking a whole lot better than she'd looked after her encounter with Chantal earlier this morning.

"We do have a date. It's not what you seem to be thinking, although I kind of like the jealous you." Piper's tone was teasing.

"Out with it, bushwhacker," Dal demanded. She would not tolerate being tortured, even if it was self-imposed torture.

Piper leaned forward in her seat and gushed. "Forget the stuffed suits, the no-name politicians, all the people who turned me down. Fiorra Firebrand is going to be our celebrity guest at the fundraiser."

Piper stood up and did a happy dance, and Dal couldn't help but burst into laughter at her antics as Einstein barked. Dal wanted to join her, kiss her, so she clasped the arms of her chair and held tight. She knew that she didn't want those things simply because of the coup for the fundraiser, although that was great news. Piper wasn't going on a date with Firebrand.

Dal let Piper celebrate a bit. It was so much nicer to see her happy than sad like she'd been this morning. Sad just wasn't Piper's nature. Dal was dreading saying good-bye to her—it would be so difficult. She remembered that feeling of hurting an innocent when she'd had to explain to Piper that she was still married.

Dal sat and took in the contagious laughter, Piper's animated hands communicating perfectly the thrill of success as they waved wildly in the air, celebrating the joy of being alive, expressed so easily by this rare woman she had feelings for, feelings she didn't want to acknowledge. Piper didn't know how to stay sad for long. It wasn't in her makeup. Piper was honesty and kindness and sunshine—and so easy to care about.

Dal acknowledged that it wasn't just Piper who was going to feel terrible after Friday. But life was way too complex not to stick to her pledge and get things back under control. Protect her heart, because it was clearly at risk, dammit. She wouldn't be worried about anyone's feelings, including her own if she just hadn't opened the door in the first place. Dal just needed to get past Friday. It was time to slam that door shut.

"So, is saving a dog and getting the crap knocked out of you the new standard for landing the entertainment for a fundraiser?" she asked, wanting to send Piper away to where Dal wouldn't have to feel any of this. "I think you need to get back to work and add that to your spreadsheet."

Piper nodded. "I know I can't compete with Chantal, but getting Fiorra Firebrand for the rescues feels like I've done something right. I'll get back to work." Piper squatted down and kissed Einstein on the forehead, then turned to leave.

Dal didn't say anything. She'd compared Piper and Chantal all right, but it was like comparing altruistic and narcissistic, genuine and phony, heaven and hell. Dal didn't know what to say. She was caught in a quagmire of emotions she'd spent her adult life avoiding, and they weren't welcome now.

DANCING IN THE WEEDS WITH PIPES THE UNPLUGGED

"You Can't Buy Love, but You Can Rescue It"

Every single one of them started as a puppy. A tiny wonder descended from a community of wild wolves. And if that canine was lucky, someone said, "I'll rescue this one." But really, who rescued whom?

That is how it is with a dog I know named Einstein. If you look on the internet, there's discussion about a statement Einstein made about not blaming gravity for falling in love. That shows you how brilliant Einstein really is. He doesn't care about energy equals mass times the speed of light squared blah, blah, blah. Oh, he cares about energy, but it's equal to how far you can throw a tennis ball, or how many laps is the right number to loop the park, hell-bent on the pure joy of running in circles, or the inverse of how warm the bed is on a cold morning. And he certainly knows all about love. How to accept it. How to give it, waving his feelings with that appendage, his tail. Kissing you sweetly with the same lips that kissed what's best not identified. Missing your presence with a fierceness you'll not find elsewhere in your life, waiting, watching, yearning patiently for your return with no other reward expected except simply being with you.

So, if you have a chance to help out a rescue, do it. And better yet, if you are privileged with the opportunity of being rescued by a pooch, take it. Dog bless you.

CHAPTER SEVENTEEN

Piper could have kissed Fiorra Firebrand. Not like she wanted to kiss Dal, but with a friendly, grateful peck that would let Fiorra know how much she appreciated the megastar bringing her talent and popularity to the gala fundraiser in thanks for what any decent person would have done witnessing a dognapping in progress. Riding that Firebrand high got Piper through the rest of the day at NAS, Tuesday at the law practice, and even Wednesday working at NAS, finalizing all she could for the fundraiser with Dal conspicuously absent.

Thursday was Piper's last day at the law office without Cate, and she hummed to her plants as she put in another solitary day. Realizing how pleased she would be to see Cate and Meg home again, she knew the flip side was her anxiety about what the end of her temp job with Noble Animal Services was going to do to her relationship with Dal... and Ruby and Viola and even Einstein. She didn't want their relationship to be just an unplanned encounter around town, a possible passing each other on the jogging trail, a chance meeting at her Sunday volunteer rescue shift. She was willing to try to give Dal some time to sort out her divorce settlement and her other issues if that was what Dal needed, but Piper wasn't sure time would be the answer. Dal claimed there was no place for someone like Piper in her life, in her heart. And Piper had now witnessed that when there had been room for someone, it had been Chantal. How could she ever compete with someone as gorgeous and polished as Chantal?

Trying to be optimistic, Piper focused on the positives. The next time she'd be in this law office, Cate would be here too. Piper missed Cate. In addition, her time at NAS and seeing more of the business side of the nonprofit and all that it took to get a rescue animal to a forever home convinced Piper more than ever that she wanted to get a law degree—she wanted to influence animal welfare. While *animal welfare* might sound like a broad, rather generic term, she knew the reality of such work would be the impact it had on individual animals like Fred and Boris and Einstein and her own cat, Sunny—and even the elephants of the world, like Osh. If only she had the time and money to pursue that dream.

Having locked up the law office Thursday evening after making sure all of her plants would be happy until Monday, Piper was heading home to spend some time with her book and cat when her cell phone rang. Bryce's name flashed on the screen, and Piper hit the answer button.

"Hey, Pipes. Where are you?"

"Just waiting at BART."

"Ah, yes. Aren't you glad you don't live in the Fresno area instead of the Bay Area?"

Piper smiled. *F-A-R-T*. "Been thinking of moving to the Central Valley and waiting fifty years for the tracks to be laid, just so that when you called, I could tell you the name of my ride." They both laughed at the dumb joke. It was good to have Bryce in her life, if just so they could both leave the adult world behind on occasion. "So, what's up?"

"I wanted to see if you'd like to stop at the bar for a beer on your way home," Bryce said. "I'm free tonight."

Piper wondered if this was just for a bit of friendly comradery and alcohol consumption, or if Bryce had an agenda.

"Cate and Meg are due in late tonight from their honeymoon, right?" Bryce asked.

"Yup."

"And tomorrow's your last day at Dal's, right?"

"It is." Piper's head ached. Her heart too, if she was being honest.

"So, I thought you might like to talk about it. You haven't told me what's up in your life lately, and as your very best friend for years and years and years…"

Bryce had confirmed her agenda.

"Can I take a rain check? I want to just spend the evening with Sunny and do some reading. Tomorrow is my last day at NAS. I'm hoping for more with Dal when she's at least got an agreement on her divorce, but I don't know if other issues will ever be resolved—from her past." Piper swallowed hard as she finished that last sentence, thinking of all that Dal had endured in her life and wondering if she was enough for Dal to get past it all. Thinking of their banter, their chitchat, their connection. What Dal was doing to her heart.

"I'm sorry, Pipes. Sorry that she's not your younger, blond, Piper-worshipping dream woman," Bryce said. "But I guess we both knew that when she flattened you during that first encounter on the lake trail—although she looked like a pretty good fit, lying there on top of you." Bryce chuckled before continuing in a more serious tone. "I've had hopes she'd be something more. She's flawed if she lets you walk out that door tomorrow. Is there anything I can do?"

"I have to confess that I'm falling for her. Love." Piper whispered the last word, as the truth and the pain of saying it out loud hit her. Loving someone shouldn't hurt the way this hurt.

"Well, shit. If you're not going to go get drunk with me, maybe the alternative is telling her how you feel."

"I haven't even kissed her. How could I feel this way?" Piper was asking herself as much as asking Bryce.

"Yeah, I bet she's an awful kisser. Absolutely fucking terrible." Bryce was trying to cheer her up.

Piper had to laugh, Bryce's words making her picture the wet sloppy dog kisses she occasionally received at the rescue. "Maybe that's what's saving me, not knowing what a great kisser she is. If she's the kisser of my imagination, the kisser in my dreams, I won't survive her rejection. You have to pinkie swear that you'll adopt Sunny if my heart breaks."

"Oh no. I might be that little lion's godmother, but you're going to have to go through a lot more hell than this before he's mine. Remember all the bullshit Hannah and I put ourselves through before she got her head out of her ass and realized what an absolute catch I'd be?"

Piper had to laugh again. "You're right. If there are miracles big enough to blind Hannah to your myriad of faults, maybe there is hope. I don't think it was *her* head in *her* ass." Piper remembered it as Bryce fighting love as it smacked her in the face.

Bryce snorted. "Are you sure you don't want to discuss my love life? Because I've got a six-pack I could bring over while I enlighten you. We could get Sunny drunk while we're at it."

"Not tonight, but you save it for Sunny and me, just in case a lurid tale of your love life is the best offer I get for the rest of my life."

"You've got it. I'm on duty tomorrow, but I'll check in with you this weekend. Good night, Pipes."

"Night, Blaze."

❖

Dal wasn't in the office on Friday morning when Piper arrived. It was Piper's last morning at NAS, and she felt it in the turmoil of her stomach. She'd initially thought she might not survive the eighteen days working for Dal, and while Piper considered that might still be true, it was for a very different reason. She hadn't wanted breakfast.

Nettie sat out front and only offered Piper a nod when Piper did her best to offer Nettie a friendly hello. She went back to her office and focused on making preparations to sit down with Nettie so she could pass off all the information on the fundraiser to her before noon. It was still early when Piper received a text from Cate, who probably didn't call because she didn't want to disturb her at work if she was busy.

Cate: *We're home. I'm looking forward to getting back to work.*

Piper: *I'm looking forward to seeing you and Meg. BTW the law practice is still in one piece.*

Cate: *Good to know. You up for a relaxed coffee with Meg and me and maybe Pete this weekend—before we get back to the grind? Tomorrow morning?*

Piper: *Whoo-hoo. Affirmative.*

Cate: *Ok. We'll set it up. Got to go. The wife is waiting.*

Piper: *Wife—you're a very lucky woman.*

Cate: *I know. And thanks again.*

Piper: *For?*

Cate: *Being you. I'll get back to you about tomorrow morning. Meet maybe 10ish.*

Piper put her phone away. She went out and asked Nettie to come into her office so they could sit down and familiarize Nettie with the fundraiser spreadsheet and notebook. Dal still hadn't come in, and Piper felt her absence as a hollow dread in her chest. Her stomach hurt. Was Dal avoiding her?

A few hours with Nettie only emphasized the world of difference between what had once been an unsatisfactory relationship with an immature person who floated through a self-absorbed life, and what a relationship might be with a complex person shackled by a past that defined her and a marriage that handcuffed her, but who honestly knew how to give and love and share life when she allowed herself to do so. Piper hoped that Dal would at least show up before she left the office for good this evening. She'd probably cry if Dal did, but she'd cry harder if she didn't.

The wall clock read four forty-eight, Nettie had left at noon, and Piper was feeling empty as she prepared to leave Noble Animal Services for the last time without even a sendoff. As she continued to gather the last of her personal belongings into the big cloth bag she'd brought for that purpose, Piper heard the front office door open, and she was sure that her heart did a cartwheel or two. As she finalized her packing, Dal appeared in Piper's office doorway. It was four fifty-three.

"Going somewhere without saying good-bye?" Dal leaned against the doorframe as she faced Piper.

"Back to the legal world." Piper tried to swallow the lump in her throat. "I wanted to see you."

"I'm sorry I was gone all day. Ruby had a field trip and they were suddenly one parent chaperone short. Didn't Nettie let you know?"

Piper shook her head. She didn't know if Nettie forgot to tell her or if it had been on purpose, but she was willing to be magnanimous. "We were busy for much of the morning going over the fundraiser notebook and spreadsheet, so she probably forgot."

Dal frowned, then looked at the clock on Piper's office wall. Piper saw that a minute had passed since she'd last checked the time.

"I'm glad you came in. I want you to know what being here has meant to me."

The hint of a smile graced Dal's mouth. "Yeah. A lot of work, a grumpy boss…"

"The Fred Fund, an elephant at the zoo, the conference. And the time at your house—it was everything." Piper didn't want to cry as she thought of how Dal had changed her, so she teased Dal. "The no chitchat ban was a little harsh. I do my best work after a little chitchat."

"Your *best* work, huh?" Dal glanced at the clock again, then back at Piper, who didn't miss the smoldering heat in Dal's eyes.

"I'm trying to be a professional here." It was four fifty-five. "Five minutes and you're not my boss." Clearing her throat, she refocused on *professional.* She could do that for five more minutes. "Being here has made me realize how much I'd like to go back to school so I can get that law degree and make a bigger impact on animals' lives. And get involved in some of the political LGBTQIA+ issues too, but I'd love to make a big difference for animals."

Dal played along, staying professional too. "That's admirable. I'd like to hope that will happen. The nonprofit could use a good animal rights attorney on retainer."

"For you, if I get there, pro bono," Piper replied.

"Don't sell yourself short. Save the pro bono for the truly needy with no access to funds and charge those of us who can afford it. You can always use your profits for good."

"Like you do with the rescues."

"Yeah. The rescues. Those and Ruby are the best of me, make me look a lot better than I am. You don't need any image rehabilitation. Me, I've got my issues." Dal looked at her with wistful eyes, unable to conceal the regret that Piper could detect before Dal let the conversation wander from professional. "You are so bloody attractive. I'm not talking just looks. Sincere, honest, authentic…" Dal's voice dropped as she cleared her throat. "Stay who you are, Piper." Then amusement ghosted Dal's face, reaching her eyes too. "No complaints from me. Except for maybe that black-and-blue vest—the one that matched our first encounter." Dal chuckled.

"I'm just glad you didn't diss my pink sneakers. That would have wounded me." Piper put her hand on her chest, struggling to keep the conversation light.

Dal harrumphed. "I have nothing against pink sneakers. I like your pink sneakers." She paused, then added in a teasing tone, "But I prefer my backsides unbruised." Piper felt her face flush, and the corners of Dal's mouth tugged up before she took a breath and blew it out. "Damn, I wish things were different."

"I'll wait, Dal." Piper wanted Dal to know that she wasn't just walking away. That she wanted more.

"It's not just Chantal—the divorce—and you know it. I can't ask you to wait. I've had enough pain to know that I don't want any more heartache in my life, and the only way to avoid that is to keep control and not set myself up." Dal wouldn't give in. Piper knew that maintaining control over her life and heart was Dal's North Star.

"I think there's more potential here between us than heartache. Is avoiding passionate love going to spare you heartache? Because I think there's a *Titanic*-load of heartache that comes with avoiding passionate love. Enough to sink you. Maybe you need to let the icebergs melt." Piper wasn't going to let Dal off the hook without saying what she needed to say. "At least enough to sink me." Piper quietly spoke those last words, wondering if they were more for herself than for Dal.

Dal stood and looked at Piper, then broke their visual connection as they both glanced at the clock. It was five p.m.

"I would never hurt you on purpose. I love you, Dal." Piper's heart swelled with emotion as she admitted that to this woman who was no longer her boss.

Dal's eyes widened and her brows rose.

"Those lines, that working relationship—gone as of five o'clock," Piper said.

Dal shook her head, returning her expression to a stoic mask. So practiced at shielding whatever she was feeling, Piper thought. Dal simply said, "I'm not divorced."

"I know. I said I'd wait because that's a matter of a signature from Chantal and time. But if it's not just the divorce"—Piper took a deep breath—"I don't know what I'll do." The thought of walking away was crushing her.

"I can't tell you to wait."

"What can you tell me?" Piper heard her own voice shake.

Dal stood there, obviously carrying on an internal war. She frowned before closing her eyes for a long moment. Then Dal turned to the side, reached over, and flipped off the light switch. The room was bathed only in the soft diffuse light filtering through the partial slits in the window shade that Piper had lowered earlier in the day. Piper could only focus on how beautiful Dal was in this low light, the glow of the evening sun gently bathing her perfect features. God, she couldn't fathom how much she wanted this woman, but she didn't move. This was Dal's call.

Dal stepped directly into Piper's personal space, pulling Piper against her body, close enough for Piper to lose herself in Dal's fragrance—floral, fresh, and so sensual. Dal held her with one hand on the back of her neck and tilted Piper's face up with her other hand beneath her chin, leaning back so she was looking at Piper's mouth with her dilated eyes. Dark hungry eyes, approaching more indigo than steel blue. Then Dal moaned and leaned into Piper's mouth, not quite connecting, but exhaling her need across Piper's waiting lips in warm sensual puffs.

"I've spent six weeks not kissing the hell out of you." Dal's voice had taken on a low, throaty timbre.

"Six weeks as my boss. That's done. Do you want to kiss me? Because I want you to." Piper studied Dal's face, and her gaze snagged on Dal's enticing mouth. The proximity of Dal made it hard to breathe, stoking the smoldering sparks of desire.

Dal captured Piper's bottom lip, holding it gently with her teeth, pushing the entire length of her front against Piper. Lighting Piper—who wanted it all—on fire.

❖

Dal wanted so much more than this kiss, but she couldn't do that to Piper. Couldn't do that to herself. She was strong enough not to push Piper onto the desk and make love to her, something she knew had crossed both their minds that one evening when she'd accidentally pinned Piper against the front office door, and it had crossed her mind so many more times since then, but she wasn't that much of an ass.

Her resistance wasn't because she didn't care for Piper. Hell, she'd had sex with plenty of women she didn't have feelings for. In fact, the issue was just the opposite. She was resisting making love to Piper because she did care for her. Making love to Piper and then walking away because she knew she had to walk away, that would be so much worse for Piper.

Her own heart wasn't going to get out of this unscathed either. She just needed to limit the damage. She was strong enough to resist an all-out display of her feelings, but she wasn't strong enough to stop the kiss.

Dal traced the soft fullness of Piper's lips with her tongue before she captured and devoured them. Piper opened her mouth and welcomed Dal inside, the two of them exploring each other, tasting each other, losing themselves in a moment as intimate as any lovemaking Dal could imagine. It was that realization that this wasn't just a sweet first kiss, but that she was losing control, making love to Piper in her mind, feeling Piper embedded in her heart—those things forced her to pull back and hug Piper, turn, and softly whisper, "Good-bye." Then she left, while she still could.

DANCING IN THE WEEDS WITH PIPES THE UNPLUGGED

"The Kiss"

There was the kiss I imagined so many times, that flirty mirage of me leaning in to her and her leaning in to me—one small patch of skin meeting another small patch of skin in a two-soul touch. There was the kiss that floated through my dreams, night after night, a piece of me, a piece of her. It was always a slow languid lip-lock, a magic caress, a glorious taste of us in the recipe of everything unspoken.

And then there was that first real kiss. Celebration. Addiction with no cure. The best in the 4,500-year-old recorded history of kissing. I could claim her mouth captured mine like prey, but I fell into her grasp with wild willingness. My heart had been there for a while. The intimate inferno of her passion left me wanting to be hers for all time. A branding bond. It was more than I imagined. It was more than I dreamed. It was me screaming love—while she tried to convince me it was just a final good-bye.

CHAPTER EIGHTEEN

Saturday morning came with a light drizzle that couldn't dampen Piper's mood any more than it already clung to her, wet from her tears and devoid of even the tiniest spark of sunshine that she always tried to find in her life. She rolled over in bed, pulling Sunny close. He swatted his paw against her cheek, not putting any claw into it—almost gently—before jumping down and heading to the kitchen. Piper figured he could chow down on his always-present dry food until she cheered herself up enough to crawl out of bed.

Piper reached for her phone over on the nightstand in its charger—no more butt-dialing Pete if she could help it. There was a text message from Meg asking if she could meet them at the Blissful Bean at ten o'clock for coffee and pastries. Piper replied that she could, knowing that Meg's mothering and her boss's no-nonsense conversation were probably what she needed in order to begin to deal with her feelings for Dal.

After a quick shower and a rush to dress and feed Sunny, Piper headed out to join Cate and Meg, and hopefully Pete. As she entered the coffee shop, the joy of seeing Cate and Meg for the first time in six weeks lifted her mood. Pete was sitting there too, cups of coffee in front of all three of them at their table. They all welcomed Piper, then Meg stood up and took Piper's rainbow travel mug out of her hand and asked what she wanted. Taking her order for a cream-and-sugar coffee and a blueberry muffin, Meg set the mug down for a moment on the table and wrapped Piper into a tight hug.

"I've missed you so much, honey." Meg stepped back and held

Piper at arm's length. "There's something different about you." Looking her over, Meg settled on Piper's eyes.

"Maybe it's love," Pete said. Piper remained silent because she couldn't deny it. "She has that look Cate had when she was falling for you, Meg." Pete looked over at Cate and raised his eyebrows before he asked Piper, "How's it going? Besides landing in the emergency room saving a Frenchie from a dognapping?" Then he added, "I did my best to steer you into Dal's arms. Even caught the flu for you."

Even with her pain, Piper couldn't prevent the pleasure she felt in being here. She loved these people. "I'm glad you recovered," she told Pete. "I guess you're offering a little Piper and Pete Matchmaking Service—with me as the star attraction. It's a rocky road." Piper felt her chest constrict just thinking of Dal's good-bye last evening.

Pete offered a fake cough. "The Pete and Piper Matchmaking Service did its best, you know—fever, stuffy nose, terrible cough—to get the hospital to call Dal to save you. What I sacrificed for you. I—"

Cate interrupted. "You and Dal?" She stopped to reflect on the idea. "Yeah, I can see that working. You'd be good for her." Cate nodded, looking closely at Piper. Piper wondered if Cate had ever met Chantal, seen what a mismatch she was when compared to Dal's wife.

Meg inserted herself into the conversation. "You take it at your own speed. Don't let these two bulldoze you. And speaking of speed, I'm a little slow—let me go get your order and I'll be right back. Coffee with cream and sugar, and a blueberry muffin coming right up." Meg headed to the counter.

Cate stood up as Meg left and pulled Piper into an embrace too. "Thanks for all you did while I was gone. I couldn't have had that European honeymoon without you."

"Hey, boss. I could get used to this." Piper hugged her back. She couldn't remember Cate ever hugging her. "I think marriage is agreeing with you. Going a little soft and all."

"Harrumph," Cate said, but her eyes lit up. "Don't insult me. I'm the same hard-ass boss you know and love."

"Well, that's a relief," Piper told her. "You had me scared there for a moment. I was wondering what six weeks in bed with Meg had done to you." Piper couldn't help but waggle her eyebrows.

"Holy crap, Cate," Pete said. "She's worth keeping. I suspected she helped keep you in line, but I'm seeing it in action."

Cate put on a bogus air of indignation and gave Piper a stern look. "Don't tell me I'm going to have to fire you before we even get back to the office."

Just then Meg returned with Piper's order and looked at Cate. "Oh no you don't, darling." Then Meg turned to Piper. "I heard that, and of course six weeks in bed with me brings you a changed woman." Meg winked at Cate, and as Pete guffawed his approval, Piper couldn't help but watch them interact. They were so good for each other. Meg and Cate had found everything she wanted.

"It's a good thing you've got me wrapped around your little finger, Meg Mullins." Cate smiled at her wife.

"More than my little finger, Cate Colson." Meg's tone was full of love, and her eyes danced with amusement. "But we aren't going to talk about how I made you a changed woman."

Piper couldn't remember when she'd last seen Cate blush, but it was a good look on her because through the pink flush, Cate radiated a happiness that she'd always wanted for Cate.

"Okay. It's time to save the boss so she hires me back," Piper declared with a chuckle. "I also saved the dog from the dognapping. The dog that happened to belong to the one and only superstar Fiorra Firebrand. The celebrity who has offered to come and perform at the CritterLove fundraising gala."

"You've got to be kidding us. Dal must love you," Pete said.

Piper took a deep breath. These were her friends. She needed them today. "I think the good-bye she gave me before I left yesterday was her letting me know that she can't make us work." Piper blinked her eyes as they welled. Stating this out loud made her chest ache even more.

Cate studied Piper. "Dal's a hell of a woman. I've known her since Berkeley. She's pulled herself up by the bootstraps, with some guidance and support from Viola. She's been let down by important people in her life, and she's always been guarded. That's why she loves animals more than most humans."

Piper nodded. "I told her that I love her." Piper gulped as she told them of her admission to Dal the night before. "But she's still married—working on a divorce, but no agreement yet. And a lot of scar tissue. I said I'd wait for a while, but she advised me against it, said good-bye, and walked away last night." The tears in Piper's eyes spilled over, and she used a napkin to wipe her face. "Plus, there's no way in Hades she could want someone like me. Did you ever meet Chantal, her wife? I'm not even close." Piper sniffed some more.

Meg, who was sitting next to her, touched her shoulder. "Piper. I can't promise you anything because I don't know the woman, but maybe not being like Chantal is to your advantage. After all, Dal is divorcing this Chantal."

"Did you sleep with her?" Pete asked. Good ol' Pete, Piper thought as Cate kicked him under the table.

"No, Pete. She kissed me last night before she walked out—we'd never even kissed before that." Heat rose up Piper's neck and spread to her cheeks. She wasn't usually the kiss-and-tell type, but she needed the support of these people to work through her anguish.

"She kissed you? It wasn't you kissing her?" Pete asked.

Piper considered the question. "No. I needed the next move to be hers after I told her that I loved her. She kissed me…not that I didn't participate." Piper knew her face must be crimson.

Pete raised his brows. "Glad to hear that you offered her a little hope. Maybe she needed to test the waters. Think about it—it was pretty brave of her to put herself out there like that. My expert advice as the lead counsel in the Pete and Piper Matchmaking Service is to give her some time."

"That's what I had to do with Cate. Step back, not push her. Be a Cate whisperer." Meg laughed.

Cate looked at Meg. "Hey, I'm sitting right here, babe."

"I know you are, love. I'm just telling Piper what worked. I walked away, and you showed up on my porch. I tried to take it very slowly, and Oscar did the rest." Humor played across Meg's expression as she retold the story. "He jumped down while we were both petting him, and we ended up holding hands. It only got better from there." Meg gave Cate a teasing grin. "Then I showed her my etchings." Cate nodded in agreement and they all laughed.

"I remember hearing about Oscar's smooth moves," Piper said. "Cate said she'd thought you'd trained him. Called him a conniving cat, as I remember. Sunny isn't quite as helpful as Oscar." Piper paused. "I've decided it's up to Dal now. I'm just sad. She's told herself she needs certain things in her life, and I don't fit. She needs independence—I think that's financial, which she has. But she needs control of her life.

And she can't take any more heartache. Any partner would be a threat to those, and the more she loves someone, the bigger the threat."

"So, the level of threat is proportional to the degree of love she feels for someone. And it seems that she's terrified of you. Do the math, kid," Pete said to Piper. "She loves you."

Meg looked at Piper. "Pete's got a point. Now this is your other mom speaking—that's her head talking about control and vulnerability to heartache. Either Dal loves you enough or she doesn't—either her heart is going to win out over what she's telling herself or it isn't. Give her time for that battle."

Piper wiped her eyes again and smiled at Meg. "Thanks...*Mom.*"

The four of them turned the conversation to other things. Meg told Piper it was time for them to get back to Piper joining her for weekend watercolor sessions, and she promised to call Piper and set the next date for that. They teased, they laughed, and by the time Piper left, she realized how perfect these friends were, how they'd made her feel so much better.

❖

Dal moped around the house on Saturday while Ruby watched one movie after another. She hadn't cried in ages. Maybe a few happy tears when Ruby was born. Certainly no tears of deep heartache when Chantal had left—her response had been anger at who Chantal turned out to be and at herself for being duped. She'd left her office last night struggling not to cry, fighting tears of misery as she'd walked away from Piper. And now, she was still telling herself she would not fucking cry.

That was the whole point of walking away. If she cared enough about Piper to need to cry, then she was in way too deep. Okay, maybe it was even love. But that thought was even more terrifying—she'd never felt this way before about any other woman. Had she learned nothing from her childhood about protecting her heart? From Chantal about losing control of her life when she'd been in a position to control it but hadn't? Neither her father nor Chantal had chosen her, and they'd left their scars. Taught their lessons. Dal was sad about the situation, furious for allowing herself to get in so deep with Piper.

Dal was spending the weekend alone with Ruby. She was grateful that Viola was out of town. She knew that she couldn't take her scrutiny. Dal couldn't visit the zoo with Ruby because that had too many memories. When Ruby begged to go to the rescue to see Piper on Sunday morning, Dal was gruffer than she meant to be when she told her daughter that was not going to happen.

Finally, on Sunday afternoon, Dal packed a picnic, Ruby, and Einstein, and they went and sat on a dog-friendly beach. She watched the waves kiss the shore, then pull back—flirting with Ruby and Einstein the way she'd flirted with Piper. Connecting, then fleeing. Enticed, then withdrawing. It had left her nowhere except with a sunburn. But it was Dal's heart that felt like it had been torched. She went home and put Ruby to bed early, hiding from Viola in her bedroom.

Walking into NAS on a Monday morning hurt because Piper wasn't there. She went through the fundraiser status with Nettie, which only hurt worse because it emphasized that Piper was permanently gone.

The gala was exactly three weeks from this past Saturday, and Dal made sure that Nettie knew to be tracking the RSVPs as they arrived. Piper had mailed the invitations over a week ago. Save-the-date emails had been sent by Piper to all past donors and several prospective ones several weeks ago. While she and Nettie had it on their computers, Piper had also left a hard copy list of who had been mailed an invitation in Dal's office. Dal looked through it. Piper had sent one to Cate and Meg because Cate was her lawyer and had attended in the past. But Piper hadn't sent one to herself. That meant she wouldn't be attending. Good to know, Dal assured herself. She didn't have to worry about seeing Piper there, having her heart battered and pummeled any more than it already was. And yet her battered and pummeled heart wasn't ecstatic at the news.

Tuesday, Dal drove to Wee Critter Haven to confer with her contractor, Joanne, about the expansion at the shelter. She walked inside, and knowing that Piper had probably been there on Sunday made it hard to breathe. And when Elsie greeted her and told her how Piper had worked miracles on Sunday with a traumatized dog, she'd thanked Elsie and headed next door to see Joanne, not returning to the rescue when she was done.

Wednesday hadn't gone much better at the office, and then on Thursday morning, her lawyer called her about the divorce agreement.

"Hey, Dal. It's Nora Lowry. Chantal's attorney called me and it sounds to me like she wants out, so waiting has paid off. My take in reading between the lines is that she has someone else she's interested in."

"So, what's her bottom line?" Dal was so sick of her wife. Ex, in her mind.

"She wants the alimony payments. She's agreed to a five-year sunset on those or her remarriage—whichever comes first. So, that's part of my take on her having someone in her sights—the five years is just insurance in case it falls through. And she'll settle for a twenty-five-thousand-dollar lump sum...a little less than the two million she started with," Nora wryly noted.

"Do it," Dal replied. "I need to end this charade. As long as all the legal paperwork has Chantal walking away from Ruby, who she hasn't even bothered to ask about since she left."

"I think that's an excellent move. I'm not sure that holding out any longer will achieve much, and if you're lucky, she'll remarry as soon as the divorce is finalized, and then the alimony will end."

"I'm not worried about the alimony," Dal said. "It's just time to end this whole nightmare."

"I get it, Dal. To be honest, I've had some bad divorces, but this has been the biggest roller coaster. Getting a two million demand down to twenty-five thousand makes you the biggest winner in my record book."

"I'm not exactly feeling like a winner in terms of the idiotic move I made in marrying her, but getting her signature is a relief."

"I'll have the settlement paperwork sent over to you this afternoon. Look it over tonight, sign it when you're ready, and we'll file it. In six months you'll get the final decree, but you're virtually there. I know how this has weighed on you."

"I'll have it to you by tomorrow. Thanks, Nora." Dal expelled a sigh. She was finally so close to having Chantal completely out of her life and no longer a threat to Ruby.

"You're welcome. I'm happy for you. You enjoy Ruby. She's a lucky girl with a mom who has her best interests at heart."

They hung up. An hour later, the paperwork came through, and it was the first time in days Dal had felt even the least bit optimistic. She gave herself a pep talk—she was rid of Chantal and would soon be running her life again, regaining control. And yet, she still wasn't ecstatic.

❖

Viola finally cornered Dal on Friday night. Ruby had already gone to sleep, and Dal was in her bedroom unsuccessfully trying to read her most recent veterinary medical journal when she heard the tap on her door. She took a deep breath and let it out. She had known this was coming.

"It's time we had a talk, Dahlia." Viola tapped again on the partially open door hard enough for it to swing open.

Dal nodded for her to come in and sit on her bed as she remained with her back against the headboard, her journal set aside on the mattress. Viola sat near the foot of the bed with her head turned so she could look at Dal.

"Piper should have been done at NAS last Friday. A week ago. Have you seen her since?" Viola didn't waste time getting to the topic she wanted to discuss.

"No." Dal didn't want to discuss Piper. She remained too front and center in Dal's head and heart.

"That's because…?"

"Because she finished the job. She was a temp, remember? She's back at Cate's." Dal knew Viola was aware of this. Damn if Viola didn't have an agenda.

"So now you can date her without all the rules about being her boss getting in the way. Right?" Viola pushed.

"I'm not going to date her."

"Because the divorce isn't done?"

"It was done today. At least we've reached an agreement and the paperwork is filed. It will be six months until final dissolution, but essentially done." Dal was still absorbing that information, after three long years of legal battle.

Viola frowned. "No boss-employee rules. No contested divorce in the way—so many years of your life wasted there. So, what's the issue?"

"It's me. No more anguish over romantic relationships." Dal didn't want to argue with Viola.

"I'd say you've got plenty of anguish, trying to deny that you love the woman. And heartache, trying to ignore what the heart knows. More anguish than if you'd just admit it and bring her into your life. You've been lonely for a long time. You can fix that, and Piper seems perfect. What's wrong with her?" Viola studied Dal.

Dal pressed her lips together and stared back at Viola before she finally broke the silence. "I love her—that's what's wrong with her," she blurted out before turning from Viola and focusing on the ceiling. "I never thought I could love any woman like I love her. I'm setting myself up for all kinds of hurt that I swore I wouldn't let happen. I'm not controlling my life." Dal wasn't going to let herself forget the wounds that her father and Chantal had inflicted. When they'd both used her. She should have learned from her father, but she'd failed again when she'd let Chantal into her life. She wasn't going to take that risk again. The stakes with Piper were way too high.

"Oh, Dahlia." Viola shook her head. "Don't you think that maybe it's the opposite—is your pledge giving you control of your life or is it controlling your life? What is control? If you think it's rigid personal dictates that are going to give you a perfect life, I've failed you. There are always trade-offs. You'll never have complete control, so are you going to insist on never having to deal with another person who loves you, and instead live with the heartache that loving her back but walking away is causing you? Is that control?"

Viola paused a moment as Dal shook her head, not able to say anything without crying until she regained control of her emotions.

"Is protecting your heart worth breaking your heart?" Viola continued. "You love her and it's a risk. How does that stack up to the heartache of walking away and always knowing that you'd finally found passionate love and didn't pursue it?" Viola gave Dal her wise-mother look, holding Dal's gaze and just throwing the questions Dal did not want to consider right out there onto the mattress between them where Dal couldn't avoid them.

"What if I love her, give her everything, and she's the one to walk away? What if she doesn't choose me? Like my father, who never put me first. Like Chantal, although I know that I didn't love her. Not like I love Piper, and that love will only grow. I don't need any more rejection in my life. Ruby doesn't need it either." Dal thought about the pain. She'd spent so much of her life in pain or preventing it as best she could.

Viola reached for Dal's hand. "Oh, baby girl. Piper is not your father, and Piper is as far from being another Chantal as a person could be. I could kick Chantal's phony butt all the way to the South Pole. She's ice, Dal. Piper is fire if you give her a chance. And yes, this old lady is talking passion and love and someone who will walk with you into the sunset. I can't promise that something won't happen that's out of everyone's control, but Piper is not the type to leave. She loves you. She loves Ruby too. But only you can decide if you trust that love, trust her with your heart. Has she ever given you a reason to believe you can't? She's *not* Chantal."

"Not a Chantal fan, huh?" Dal felt a bit less defensive, despite her distress. At least she could agree with Viola on that assessment.

"Never was. Never will be. But I am a Piper fan. You'll have to think about things, consider what I've said, and make your own decision, but since your pledge includes control and heartache, you need to decide what those words mean and where you'll end up." Viola stood up to leave Dal to consider what she'd just imparted. She'd never refrained from offering her opinion, but she'd usually left it to Dal to make her final decisions.

"Thanks." Dal swallowed. "I'm petrified." That wasn't easy to say, and Viola was probably the only person in the world she would admit it to.

"You've been through hell. It's time for a little taste of heaven. Give her a chance and see where it goes when you aren't trying to stop your feelings. Let it grow." Viola searched Dal's face, obviously wanting Dal to seriously consider her advice. "Nobody's asking you to marry Piper." Then Viola laughed before she added, "Yet."

Dal tutted at Viola. "The ink's still wet on the divorce agreement."

"Your marriage ended three years ago when Chantel walked out— the rest is just official legal hoop jumping. Chantal has wasted enough of your life. That six months will fly by and shouldn't stop you and Piper from sharing time together, getting to know each other better.

You just told me that you love her. You married the wrong girl. I'm with Ruby. Piper!" Viola headed out the bedroom door, calling back, "I love you, Dahlia."

Dal couldn't help but smile as tears filled her eyes. She would not cry—she controlled her life so she wouldn't need to cry. Dal wiped her eyes with the bedsheet. Now she'd have to think about what Viola had said.

DANCING IN THE WEEDS WITH PIPES THE UNPLUGGED

"Advice on How to Cry"

First, you need to arm yourself. A hankie or tissue or a napkin will do. Probably a pile of them, just in case. Or you could say you forgot your umbrella and it was the rain that soaked your face. Then go to a place with a cool name, like the Blissful Bean, although anywhere with friends will work. Think of it as therapy, but with caring people who offer it for free. As you struggle with the tears, accept the hugs, the coffee, the blueberry muffin. Even a glass of water or a doughnut will work because the food is just an excuse for letting them pull you up when you're down. You might have done your worst ugly crying before you ever arrived, maybe at home with your cat, or in bed with the covers pulled up over your head, but your cat and your covers didn't quite convince you that everything would be okay. You might need to just let the waterworks flow right there in public, among these supportive friends, because it isn't really about passing judgment or navigating the morass, or even what you should do. This is about them sharing the moment with you. Seeing you through the pain. Leading you through the blubbering with patience and love and humor. And as your spirits rise, as the subtle glow of good-hearted companionship helps tip the world upright on its axis again, you'll know the crying is done when you can't help but smile and laugh with this chosen family who is there for you.

CHAPTER NINETEEN

It had been a week since Piper had met with Cate, Meg, and Pete at the Blissful Bean. A week and a day since Dal had kissed her, not that she was keeping track. Today, she was going to share Saturday watercolor time in Trinity Hills with Meg, who had taught her so much, not only about watercolor. And Piper was hoping that time with Meg would take her mind off Dal.

Painting with Meg always lifted Piper's spirits. Right now, she needed that.

Piper showed up at noon, and of course, Meg had soup and sandwiches ready to share. They talked about Sunny and Oscar, Meg's kids, ramping up Cate's law practice after a six-week hiatus—they talked about everything but Dal. After lunch, they headed to Meg's studio, a back room that she'd converted to her dedicated art space after she was widowed.

"You've been exploring watercolor so you could paint flowers. Right?" Meg asked as they set up.

Piper nodded her affirmation, picturing the flower she wanted to portray.

"I love your style," Meg enthused. "Watercolor just might be your perfect medium. I'm such a controlled, conservative watercolorist compared to you. I love your ability to paint so freely—when done well, that's the beauty of watercolor. Wet into wet, vibrant colors, and let the paint loose in the water to do its own thing. It's you on the paper."

When they had started these shared sessions, Meg had told Piper that she needed to explore techniques and become her own artist. *Soul on the paper*, Meg had called it. Piper had told Meg that maybe art was similar to attire—an empty canvas was like a nude body, and everything you put on it was just your style. Self-expression. Like clothing, everyone had to make their own choices of what worked for them.

"Yeah. I'm loving this. Not just the art. Thanks for sharing time with me." Piper loved the way Meg nurtured her and made her feel like there were still bright spots in her life.

Meg reached over and touched Piper's arm. "This is what friends do. Spend time together. Now what do you have in mind today, flower-wise?"

Piper paused and took a deep breath. "I've been wanting to paint a dahlia. My favorite flower."

Meg nodded, understanding Piper's choice. "Have you heard from her this past week?" she asked, compassion in her tone.

"Not a thing. I think she's just going to move on." Piper tried to keep her voice even, not let the sadness creep in.

"Cate and I are going to the CritterLove fundraiser in two weeks, since Cate's their attorney. I just want you to know that you're welcome to join us."

"I appreciate your willingness to include me. But if Dal doesn't want me to be a part of her life, I'm not crashing her event." Piper's breath hitched. "I'll never get over her that way, if I ever will."

"I get it, sweetheart. Let me say one thing before we get to painting. I think the big beast that is love is easier than the complexities of love. It's critical to have the big beast—I knew I was falling in love with Cate fairly early on. But then we had to wade through all the things that made it possible for that beast to work for us." Meg reached over and touched Piper's hand. "Dal probably has a lot more of those complexities to sort out than you, if she can. I can't promise she can, but my advice is to let her try because it seems to me that she's not fighting the big beast—it already bit her."

Piper offered Meg an eye roll at her characterization of love, but she agreed. It was a beast. And Meg was right about the complexities. She thought again about the hope she was trying to hang on to—until that hurt too much.

"Dal seems to be drowning in her past, protecting herself from similar pain. Her childhood, her marriage, and even her self-image of too much baggage for me to deal with—they're all obstacles. I know I might not be as complex as many people, but I'm not naive either. And I'm good at dealing with complex. I work for your wife."

Meg laughed. "That you do, and you make it look easy. We both appreciate you for that. It's why we both think you and Dal could work. If you look at what Dal's done in life, she's an amazing person. Cate and I are pulling for you." Meg studied Piper. "And it's not that you're not complex. Like all of us, you are. You're also refreshing and unpretentious and honest, Piper. A beautiful person."

Meg's kind words triggered a blush that Piper felt heat her face. "Thanks. Now that you've been so good at offering Meg therapy, shall we try some art therapy?"

"That's what we're here for. Do you have an image or a sketch of the dahlia you want to paint?"

Piper pulled out her Arches watercolor pad and flipped it open, showing Meg the light sketch that she'd planned out on the page, and a photo she'd taken of a dahlia that she'd chosen because it was kissed by the sun, the exact lighting she'd been aiming for. So multifaceted and beautiful, like Dal. "I love the hues and the intricacy of the bloom. Love, devotion, beauty, dignity—the floriography of the flower."

Meg grabbed Oscar and set him in his cat bed, so he wasn't in the middle of her painting area where he'd decided to settle. "I love that you love plants. I hear that you hum and sing to them."

"Bryce calls me Pipes because I've been singing to plants since I was a kid. That's where I got my blog name. The Royal Horticultural Society in the UK reported plants that are talked to grew more than plants that aren't, and other studies show they respond to sound waves, like singing." Piper considered for a moment. "There are also studies that say it doesn't make a difference, but it makes me happy. Plus, when you talk or sing to them, you expel carbon dioxide that is used in photosynthesis, and they give you back oxygen. Now there's a working relationship."

"Now I'm going to have to start singing to that one indoor ficus that I have. Although my singing voice just might kill it." Meg chuckled and Piper joined her. "So, let's get some water and get to it. I'm using a landscape photo with goats in it that I took in England for today's picture. There was more to that honeymoon than Cate would have you believe."

"Well, a painting of the sheets in a hotel room would be rather boring, and a nude of Cate might be too exciting." Piper fought to suppress a snort. A portrait of a nude Cate—*so* not her carefully cultivated professional image.

"Aside from the fact that a nude of Cate would get me banished from those sheets." Meg's eyes danced.

"I'm not going there, and I agree you shouldn't either. You're such a great artist that there would be no doubt it was Cate. With my loose style, nobody would know it was the boss. Might not even know it was a person instead of a goat." Piper grinned, unable to suppress her mirth. "Maybe there's an advantage to being wild with a paintbrush—I won't get fired."

"Wild." Meg repeated the word. "Ever heard of Fauvism? Fauve means *wild beast*. French artists in the early 1900s used bright colors right out of the tube, applied to create a bit of explosion on the page, movement of color."

Piper smiled, amused that there was a *wild beast* label for a style of painting. Meg laid the brushes she had selected down next to her paper and then turned back to Piper. "Maybe that's what describes your art. A wild beast soul on the paper." She picked up a brush and pointed it toward Piper. "Like your clothing. I love that it reflects who you are. Like your heart—you give it all. Brightens my day."

Meg always made Piper feel so much better. "I'm glad I'm here with you today. I needed some time with you."

"You know, charting your own path in painting, if done well, can be liberating. Same with life. You just keep being you," Meg said.

Piper knew what she wanted to write about next, and she decided that she couldn't have been luckier in landing Meg as another mother, especially as she navigated her way through her heartache regarding Dal.

"I know why Cate and I call it The Meg Effect. I'd almost forgotten my love life woes for the moment." If she lost Dal, Piper wondered how it would impact her. She knew she would not be the same person. Would she follow her own advice and learn from the experience, or would the pain significantly change her in a negative way? She hadn't dealt with this kind of pain with former girlfriends, and Dal hadn't ever even been her official girlfriend. Just a woman she'd grown to love.

❖

Struggling to keep her mind off Piper, Dal worked long hours the next week. On Thursday afternoon, with just over a week until the big event, Dal realized that the photos that Piper had created into posters for a story wall were still sitting on the table in Piper's old office, not having been touched since Piper left. There was no place planned yet for the display at the venue, at least no place that would do them justice. Just setting the posters on a table wasn't acceptable. Not that Dal was doing it for Piper, but the posters deserved the most attractive presentation she could manage, one that would tell the story they were created to tell, the rescue story. Dal knew that Meg showed at Legends Art Gallery in San Francisco. She called the owner.

"Hi, Olivia. This is Dal Noble at Noble Animal Services. Meg's wife, Cate, is our attorney and so I'm familiar with your gallery. I oversee a nonprofit for animal shelters, CritterLove Rescues, and our big charity fundraiser is a week from Saturday."

"Yes, Dal. I know your rescue shelters. How can I be of assistance?"

Dal went on to explain that the display would tell the story of several rescue animals in images that Piper had used to create twelve posters. Fred would have a separate small written presentation of his story as well. "I'd like to contract for you to create the story wall if you have time."

"I'd love to take the job. I remember Piper from Meg's art opening and their wedding reception here. Refreshing woman," Olivia said. "I think it's a terrific idea. I can order folding art-display walls through contacts I know who will get them to us on time."

"Terrific. You're hired." Dal struggled to ignore the undercurrent of despondency as she dealt with the completion of the story wall—Piper's story wall. She had a job to do.

"Do you want the posters matted and framed?" Olivia asked. "We've done similar before, and then the pictures become part of a silent auction at the event for the charity."

"That sounds perfect. They can be part of the silent auction that's already planned. Animal lovers will be interested, and I can see them as captivating art in some of our various donors' businesses." Dal decided she was paying for the display wall out of pocket. She could afford to cover the cost of the matting and framing as well.

Dal took several deep breaths as she collected herself and buried her turmoil about Piper. She needed to support Piper's vision of a fabulous story wall, but it had nothing to do with Piper. It would benefit the fundraiser.

"Can I bring the posters to you when I'm done here? On my way home?" Dal was pleased that if Piper's story wall was going to happen, it would be given professional treatment. She wanted to get the posters into Olivia's hands as soon as possible.

"Perfect. I'll contact my source for the folding art-display walls when we hang up, and give my framer a heads-up. We should have it all set for you by the end of next week before the event. I'll see you in a while for the poster drop-off."

Dal headed into Piper's office to retrieve the posters. They were stacked and wrapped on the table where Piper had placed them before she'd left almost two weeks ago. Dal hadn't been in the office since Piper's last day. She'd been doing her best not to think about their kiss.

Removing the packaging, Dal examined them again before she headed to the gallery. As she moved through the stack, she saw one poster after another, each sharing split images—dejected animals looking so sad at the time of their initial rescue and filled with such joy afterward.

Dal didn't know what was constricting the blood flow to her head, suffocating her breathing, until she came to the poster of Fred. It was another split image—an earlier picture of Fred in such emotional pain because the world had failed him, and then the recent photo of an ecstatic Fred with people who loved him. With a family he loved. That poster revealed the entire transformation. The success of the rescues.

Without warning, tears flooded Dal's eyes and spilled over. She cursed. Friggin' crybaby. Then she let out a small hysterical laugh of appreciation that she was the only one left in the office because, as she stood there, she knew that she was creating a miserable mess of her face that needed no witnesses. The racking sobs that caught in her throat were the auditory accompaniment to her visual catastrophe. But it was the sudden epiphany as Dal looked at Fred that slammed her heart and made her collapse into Piper's office chair.

Viola had brought her a long way from where she had been as a kid and had loved her as a mother would, but Dal had always been wary of romantic passionate love. Chantal had never been about that kind of love, but she'd still chalked Chantal up as a failure in achieving it.

Viola was right that she had lost control of her life. Her pledge had taken control away from her, not preserved it. It was running her life and she wasn't—Dal had already started to come to that conclusion. But the pledge issue wasn't what had hit her so hard. It was this poster of Fred, and remembering Piper's words when they were talking after the zoo trip that had just flattened her.

Piper had pointed out the wisdom and beauty of dogs, the very thing that Dal had devoted her life to because she'd recognized that most rescues, even the ones with horrendous pasts and piles of baggage, could usually accept love into their lives and move forward when properly nurtured. They could let themselves be happy. They could offer love back. Piper had pointed that out about Fred. And here was his poster, photographic proof of Fred's journey.

Dal sat there wondering how she hadn't been willing to see what Fred could see: That her past didn't have to define the rest of her life—the entire rescue premise she believed in. That living in the pain of the past only prevented what she saw in Fred's eyes now. Joy and love. That was what rescuing was all about. Healing and turning a life around. Taking a chance on a fulfilling future. Being willing to try to live one's best life. She had made this the center of her professional life for all those animals, for all these years, and yet she had missed it for herself.

There weren't very many people that Dal genuinely liked. She much preferred the authenticity of animals, and yet here she was, wanting Piper. The kid-loving, animal-loving redhead with the unruly hair, distinctive fashion style, and pink sneakers, willing to be who she was without pretense. She didn't want anything from Dal except her love. And she loved Dal—she'd told her so.

Dal acknowledged that she wanted to try to live her best life, like Fred. She was ready for passionate love. She was ready to take a chance on a future with Piper because Dal trusted her. Because Dal loved her. But she didn't know if Piper still wanted her. If Piper would still choose her. Dal was afraid that she'd blown it. She wiped her eyes. She hadn't really cried in decades.

DANCING IN THE WEEDS WITH PIPES THE UNPLUGGED

"The Art of Being a Dahliaphile"

Maybe I'm a Fauve—a wild beast artist, like Matisse. Brushing passion into my renderings, the colors of my soul. Although this one holds my heart as well—love on paper, vibrant and sensual, rising to the full height of hope. But as my favorite professional artist once wrote on her blog, "Things never come out the way you plan." I thought that was a reference to her watercolor painting. But maybe she was speaking to me.

So, for now, without a plan, it's my heart on the page. I have an initial sketch, a beautiful flower I want to know better, to savor and study forever. Caressing the image with water, I consider the breathtaking complexity in bloom. A petalsome presentation—graceful and undulating, light at the surface, dark in depressions. I drop pigment to show gold at the center—that hidden hotbed of goodness. Soften the shadows of pain if I can, but note that the underpainting creates value and depth.

I want to glaze it with hues of happy, spatters of whimsy, drop-ins of joy, streaks of unrestrained laughter. In whites and pinks and lavenders and yellows the shade of sunshine. I want to paint this flower cherished, adored, treasured, and loved. To share her essence on the paper. To hold her in my heart. If only she'll let me.

CHAPTER TWENTY

It had been over two weeks since Piper had left NAS. She was doing her best to keep a positive outlook, but she knew that she was struggling. This past weekend, she'd simply holed up at her apartment with Sunny close by. She'd even passed on her volunteer shift at the rescue the day before—she'd needed a break from reminders of Dal.

Wrapped in the mellow shades of twilight that embraced her Oakland apartment living room, Piper sat on the couch with her legs crossed and flipped through the mail on Monday evening. The ivory-tinted envelope sent her heart into her throat.

"What the heck?" Piper asked Sunny as he headbutted her for some dinner. She knew she was holding an invitation to the CritterLove gala fundraiser, an invitation she hadn't been the one to address because there had been so much uncertainty about her future with Dal. She hadn't wanted the additional angst of an invitation to decline. She'd known that if she and Dal had resolved their issues, there would be no need for a formal invitation for her to be there with Dal.

So this invitation confused her. Dal had offered no indication that her good-bye kiss hadn't been final, and her silence had spoken volumes. Maybe Nettie had mailed more invitations if the gala wasn't sold out. Piper needed to ignore it because her heart needed her to ignore it. She needed to move on while her heart still had a chance of not shattering to pieces.

Over these past two weeks, Piper had grieved the loss of Dal, the loss of that future. There had been some good moments with friends. They'd done what they could to help, but now Piper understood all of the songs, the movies, the poetry produced in the name of love. She knew that she'd never been in love before, nothing like this consuming ache with the power to ruin her. She understood the bouquets and flowers dedicated to the language of love. The problem was, every time she looked out at the dahlia plants growing on her patio, they only reminded her of what wasn't to be. She wasn't sure how she was going to survive their beautiful blooms. She poured her heart out into her blog.

❖

Piper had just finished watering the office plants after arriving at work on Tuesday when Cate called Piper into her office. Cate sat at her desk, the San Francisco skyline shrouded in fog out the third-story window behind her.

"How's that jungle of yours doing? I think that ivy plant is planning to take over. What kind of ivy is it?" Cate asked, cocking an eyebrow.

"*Epipremnum aureum.* Commonly known as devil's ivy." Piper looked at her, wondering where Cate was going with this.

Cate's mouth barely twitched, but she couldn't keep her obvious good mood from reaching her eyes as she leaned back in her chair and nodded for Piper to take the seat across from her.

"So, when it confiscates that office space of yours down the hall, do I have to put another plaque on the front door to this place, one under my name, declaring devil's ivy is practicing law as my partner?" Cate chuckled. "Or heaven forbid, *epic prune orifice*, or whatever you said."

The humor in Cate's butchery of the plant's scientific name overtook Piper. She couldn't help but grin. "*Epipremnum aureum.* Stick with the lawyering, boss, because I don't think you'd make it as a botanist." Piper sobered. "I'm sorry. I'll trim it back."

"Good call because I have other plans for that office space of yours," Cate replied.

Piper's heart leapt into her throat. Could Cate be considering firing her after all they'd been through together? She focused on Cate, trying to read her. The smile on Cate's face matched the one in her eyes.

"Meg and I have been having some discussions about what's important to us, and we've come to some decisions." Cate's expression shifted and became stern. "I'm not being soft, but we both agreed that the law profession can always use an elevation of image. Just trying to do my part to make lawyers look good."

Piper sat up straight. What was Cate talking about?

"Cheer up. Hell, I'm not firing you." Cate's tone softened. "I have other plans for that second plaque, the one that will go under mine. The one that says *Piper Fernley—Attorney at Law*."

Piper still didn't understand what Cate was trying to tell her. She had as much chance of finding the money and time for a law degree as that potted plant did.

"Meg and I have plenty of money, and we're going to invest in your law degree. I don't know how I'll manage without your constant singing and humming to that greenery out there, but I'll pay you for the time you're busy polishing your legal skills—that will only benefit the practice. Not that I don't expect you to work your tail off while you're in the office, and we'll get extra help as we need it." Then Cate added, "Don't get the wrong idea. Let me repeat, I'm not going soft. Just expanding the income around here, elevating the profession." Cate cleared her throat and flushed a light shade of pink.

Piper looked at her boss. At her friend. Such a marshmallow under all that huff. This was the bright spot in Piper's past few weeks. She was so overwhelmed she couldn't say a word.

"You'll be a good addition." Cate's swallow was pronounced before she added, "And we expect you to focus on animal welfare and human rights if that's what you want."

It took Piper five minutes to get her emotions under control. Cate kept pushing tissues at her until she had to drag the trash can over next to Piper. "I didn't think you'd take the news like someone had died." Cate's tone didn't hide her amusement at Piper's reaction.

"I don't know how to thank you and Meg. You know I love you both." Piper sniffed several times. "Can I hug you?" Piper asked as she rounded the desk.

"Can I stop you?" Cate groused, but her eyes communicated how pleased she was as she put her arms around Piper. "Just so you know, I'm only doing this so I don't need to have that damn devil's ivy plaque associated with mine out there on the front door."

"Best boss ever," Piper enthused before Cate announced that they'd loafed long enough. There was work waiting.

❖

Viola came into the living room "So, have you heard from Piper? You told me that you sent her an invitation."

It was Wednesday and Dal had heard nothing from Piper. She was so unsure of herself, and she hated that, but she decided she deserved it. She'd let Piper go. Maybe she didn't deserve to get her back.

Dal looked over at Viola. "Just because I love her doesn't mean she loves me. I'd been telling her there was no place for her in my life. I was pretty clear when I said good-bye—I left as soon as the word was out of my mouth, practically ran away." Dal didn't go into detail with Viola about the kiss. "If she thought she cared about me, I probably crushed it right out of her." Dal was afraid to hope that Piper still wanted her.

"Don't be so hard on yourself. You're a little slow, but you're catching up."

"Hell. If I'm the rescue, then I'm also the dog that bit her." The declaration caused Dal to wish her armor was thicker. How could she even hope that Piper might still be considering that Dal was someone she cared about?

Viola gave Dal her *listen to me* look. "I've never known you to just roll over, even when you should—and this isn't one of those times. You need to do the work to prove to Piper that you love her." She kissed Dal on the forehead before heading downstairs to her apartment.

After tucking Ruby into bed, Dal headed to her bedroom to stretch out on her bed and consider Viola's advice and what she should do about it. When Dal had realized she was falling for Piper, she'd run away. On the other hand, Piper had processed her own feelings and been willing to take a chance. Dal just hoped Piper wasn't finished with her yet, that love would prevail.

Dal decided the first thing she would do was contact Cate. She hoped Cate would help her fix this if that was even possible. She'd call Cate first thing tomorrow morning.

❖

After Piper came into work on Thursday morning, watered her plants, and checked the computer for messages, Cate called out to her. "Can you come in here for a minute, please?"

"Sure." Piper still couldn't believe that she now had a way to achieve a law degree, thanks to Cate and Meg. One of her dreams was within reach, and while there was still a gaping hole in her heart that Dal occupied, she felt like she might survive.

"You need another hug? Heck, I might even offer you a chaste kiss," Piper told Cate.

Cate studied Piper, drummed her fingers on her desktop, and then nodded for her to have a seat. "Hell no to hugs and kisses. What kind of professional decorum are we maintaining around here?" Cate's tone might be chastising, but a smile tugged at the corners of her mouth. "Now that you're heading toward a plaque on the door, I have a request to make." Cate grew serious.

"Sure, Cate. Anything."

"Glad to hear it." Cate took a deep breath. "Meg and I are going to the CritterLove gala this weekend, supporting our client. You need to go too, as a future partner in the law firm. The seat's all set."

Piper's heart raced and she tried to breathe. "Really, Cate?" She barely managed a choked whisper. "Nettie or someone sent me an invitation, and I'd already decided I don't want to go. It still hurts too much." Piper brushed away the tears that overtook her.

Cate took another deep breath. "Dal's a client. You're going to have to face her sometime." She softened her tone. "Trust me, Piper."

DANCING IN THE WEEDS WITH PIPES THE UNPLUGGED

"Help Wanted"

Love walked in off the street right behind me on that first day on the job. Looking back, I wondered if maybe I'd been followed all the way from the jogging path. Love didn't fit any job description in that noble establishment where I worked, but there Love was, with all of her prior experience, shadowing me like she actually belonged. I'd never seen this version of Love before, all dressed up in that stunning haute-couture-for-the-heart attire, hinting at forever with her audacious air and seductive soft drawl. Love had her great days, working her magic, warming my heart, doing her job before finally flinging off any display of head-over-high-heels, saying good-bye with crumpled-note memories scrawled on my soul.

Love has moved on, into my past. All I can do is try to move on too. Post a help-wanted ad. Temps need not apply.

CHAPTER TWENTY-ONE

Meg had her right arm hooked around Piper's left arm as they walked in unity toward the gala venue on Saturday evening, Cate flanking closely on Piper's other side. Piper had taken care to put on attractive, but not too flamboyant attire—a pale pink button-down shirt under a soft gray vest with matching slacks and blazer, opting to skip a tie and instead leave her shirt with a relaxed three-button opening. She'd debated donning her pink sneakers as a statement of rebellion against this entire calamity Cate had pushed her into, but she usually tried to wear those pink sneakers to brighten the world and didn't want to taint them with dread of seeing Dal and reslashing still weeping wounds. She'd opted for her best pair of black boots instead.

Piper had worked hard to tame her hair too, donned makeup, and added gold hoop earrings to both piercings in each ear, a larger one at the front with a smaller one behind. If she was going to die tonight of a cardiac fracture, she'd at least go out looking good and presenting like she didn't give a damn about Dahlia Noble. If she could only pull it off. If she could just not look like she was wearing her heart on her sleeve.

As they entered the expansive high-ceilinged room, it was all of the round, white-cloth-covered tables that Piper noticed first, followed by the steady buzz of chatter broken by the occasional loud burst of laughter. There must have been at least forty tables evenly dotting the space, with eight chairs each, most with guests sitting or standing around with drinks in hand, the men in suits and tuxedos, and the women in dressy evening wear. Piper didn't see Dal in the crowd, and she was grateful—she didn't need a reminder of what she'd lost.

After Cate gave her name, a hostess escorted them toward their seats. The three of them switched up formation into single file as they wove their way through the maze following their usher, Cate in front of Piper and Meg behind. As she continued to look for Dal and hoped she wouldn't see her, Piper felt as if she was drowning, the weight of an ocean of dread pressing on her thorax, her head pounding, and her sight and hearing shifted to a subdued state of narrowed clarity. This was her overwhelmed body in full self-preservation mode.

When Piper stopped to shake her head to clear it, Meg put both hands on her shoulders and whispered in her ear, "You're going to be fine, Piper. I promise."

When they finally reached their targeted destination, Piper saw that they were at the table closest to the stage with only a dance floor separating them from the planned entertainment, which would be Fiorra Firebrand. Meg guided Piper to a seat.

Piper removed her blazer and hung it over the back of her chair. Meg took the seat to the left of Piper while Cate took the empty place on Meg's other side. Viola sat across the table, and her welcoming words with the offering that Ruby was at a friend's house for a sleepover floated across to Piper.

Three other chairs at the table were taken by additional well-dressed guests over the next few minutes, leaving a vacant one on Piper's right side. Piper tried to ignore it. Surely Dal was busy running the event.

Heading to the open bar to collect beverages, Cate took Meg's drink order before turning to Piper to inquire what she might want. Piper asked for sparkling water because she figured if she started drinking anything alcoholic she wouldn't stop, and then she'd make a fool of herself.

As the other guests introduced themselves, Piper noticed the floral arrangement at the center of their table, different from all the other centerpieces in the room. Absolutely stunning. It wasn't anything she had contracted for when she was planning the event. She had arranged for a bouquet of daffodils at each table in a small clear glass vase, representing care and goodwill. She'd noticed that was the case at all of the other tables she'd passed as she'd walked in. But this table had a large, elegant white Lenox vase filled with dahlias in a mix of white, pink, lavender, and yellow hues intermixed with the greenery of ferns.

Piper was shocked at what the unique floral arrangement at their table represented. Dahlias for the love, devotion, dignity, and beauty of Dal sharing a vase with small lacy fronds of maidenhair fern, symbolizing a secret bond of love and also her, Piper Fernley.

As Piper sat in surprise, taking it all in, trying to process what it meant, Dal suddenly appeared and sat in the empty seat next to her, looking a combination of ravishing, repentant, and hopeful in a sapphire-blue designer dress that perfectly accentuated the hints of sapphire in her bluish-gray eyes, eyes that were showcased with makeup befitting the evening event. Her light brown hair was loose tonight, a style that played to her golden highlights. It swept below her shoulders, full and thick, with a touch of curl on the ends.

Dal looked sideways at Piper. Then she touched Piper's hand, and a jolt of sensation that tapped directly into all of the pent-up emotion of the past weeks gripped Piper, an electric shock of need and want and love. Piper thought she saw the same emotion in Dal's expression. Oh God, she hoped so.

"My turn to be the bushwhacker." A chuckle seemed to catch in Dal's throat before she swallowed. "I'm so glad you came. It took some orchestrating to be sure you would, but we've got some good people on our side." Dal looked over at Cate and Meg.

Piper locked eyes with Dal, studying the mosaics of blues and grays, willing herself not to cry. She didn't say anything, afraid she'd misconstrued the meaning of what was directly in front of her. What had changed Dal's mind? Was she finally off the roller coaster ride that always ended up with Dal shutting down?

As Piper looked at Dal, a hush began to fall around them as somebody tapped the microphone on the stage. Gazing up, Piper recognized the one and only Fiorra Firebrand—pretty, with a head of spiked, bleached hair with pale purple tinting the front. A draped black dress, tight at the bust and hips, covered the essentials, with wisps of frayed cloth hanging down below the main bodice of the costume. Fiorra stood on gold-toned platform shoes that added three inches to her height as she carried herself like the star she was, at ease and in charge.

"In case you don't know, I'm Fiorra Firebrand," she joked while the crowd laughed. "I'm here for the entire evening," Fiorra promised. "But while they bring out dinner and before this party gets started, I'd like to welcome you all on behalf of Dal Noble and CritterLove

Rescues, and I have a few choice words to impart." The room was now quiet, watching and listening to the celebrity on the stage.

Fiorra continued. "I'm honored to be here to help raise funds for all the rescue animals, and I'm also honored because I wouldn't have known that I wanted to be here if Piper Fernley hadn't risked her life to save my dog, Louie, from a dognapper. She's my hero. Please come up here, Piper."

The room broke out into a roar of clapping and cheering and whistles as Meg and Dal nudged Piper from both sides to stand up and go onstage. She climbed the steps and approached Fiorra. The singer took her hand and twirled her around before letting Piper loose to return to her seat.

"Now eat your dinners, and then I'll be back and we'll start the entertainment and dancing." Fiorra left the stage, and a few minutes later, plates of food appeared and were set in front of each person, the specific cuisine matched to what each guest had ordered.

Returning to her seat, Piper was embarrassed by all the attention. She was feeling overwhelmed, both hopeful and afraid. What was Dal thinking? She hadn't contacted Piper for three long weeks.

Meg leaned in to Piper and whispered in her ear, "Don't overthink this, sweetie. If there's one thing that allowed Cate and me to be together, it was talking to each other. You know that. You told Cate to be an adult, to talk to me."

Piper had to smile through the anxiety of her uncertainty. Then she whispered back, "It's a lot easier to give advice than follow it. But I hear you, Meg."

Dal was concentrating on her food, either not overhearing the whispered conversation or giving it time to play out.

As they finished their dinners, Dal turned to Piper. "Will you come with me to look at the story wall? The one that you made the posters for?" Dal held out her hand for Piper to take.

Piper nodded, but she wasn't ready to take Dal's hand yet. She didn't want that connection if what she was hoping for wasn't real, so Piper stood up but shook her head at the outstretched hand and simply followed while Dal led.

They ended up over on the far side of the large room where tables displayed items for the silent auction. The bidding included many donated entertainment offerings like dinners at nice restaurants, hotel nights, sporting events and other excursions, and there were also several actual items like bottles of wine and gift baskets. Meg even had an offer to paint someone's pet. And there in the middle of that line of tables was a portable art wall at least eight feet tall and twenty feet wide. The twelve posters had been matted and framed and were now artfully arranged on the black wall for viewing. Piper thought it looked professional, and the presentation did a wonderful job of sharing the stories of so many of the rescues.

Dal stopped back far enough from the center of the exhibit so that she and Piper could peruse the entire display.

"What do you think?" Dal maintained her gaze on the posters.

"I think you did the posters justice." Piper looked at the wall and then sideways at Dal, so elegant tonight. But she had always been beautiful, even in jogging shorts and a T-shirt that first day they'd met.

"Thanks. Legends Art Gallery did the display. I wanted them to look good and go for a high price. They're part of the silent auction," Dal said. "All but one," she added under her breath.

Piper looked at each poster, at the visual story each told. And then she came to Fred. The before and after. Where the other posters had a number on the wall next to them that correlated with the silent auction bid sheet over at a nearby table, Fred's had no number—just a small label that stated: *Not for Sale*. Next to the poster in a small frame was the typed story she'd written and left in the gala planning notebook about the Fred Fund and how donations helped.

Piper looked at Dal, tilting her head toward the poster.

"Not for sale." Dal sucked her cheeks in.

"So I see." Piper was wondering what else Dal would disclose. She appeared a bit defensive, so Piper waited.

Dal sighed. "It's mine. Going on my office wall."

"To remind you of the Fred Fund?" Piper looked back to the poster.

"No. Not to remind me of the pittance I gave to the dog. To remind me of what he gave to me."

Now Dal had Piper's full attention. She looked away from the poster and at Dal. "Care to share?"

"I'm a fool." Dal's usual self-assured demeanor seemed a bit compromised, although she'd just called herself a fool with authority. Piper decided that she'd meant it.

Piper grinned for the first time that evening. Hope surged because

Piper could tell that Fred was somehow tied to the two of them. "I'm not going to argue," she said in a teasing tone. "So what did good old Fred do to earn my undying respect? Because if he has you recognizing you're a fool for the right reasons, I'll love that dog even more."

Dal held out her hand again, and Piper took it this time. Then Dal led her over to a far corner of the room, away from everyone else.

Piper let go of Dal's hand, facing her to speak. "I'm listening."

"Fred was failed by so many people." A momentary frown settled on Dal's beautiful face.

Piper nodded as she glanced at the poster with Fred's intake photo. So crushed.

"But he didn't let that ruin the rest of his life," Dal said. "He took it slow, made sure he was reading things correctly, then he was willing to move on, doing exactly what so many rescues are willing to do—not let what happened in the past destroy the future." Dal paused and wiped the moisture that had collected in her eyes. "Willing to love and be loved. He chose to take the risk. To have the chance of a happy life. You said it that day after the zoo. In dog terminology—to fetch his forever." Dal chuckled.

Piper thought she knew what Dal was saying, but she wanted to hear it from Dal. "So how did a rescue dog make you a gorgeous fool?"

Dal compressed her lips at the words, but her eyes acknowledged amusement. "I've dedicated my life to rescues, and the whole premise is that with the right care, a life can be changed. Yet I've refused to be rescued myself."

Piper reflected that this was a day for tears as several escaped and fled down Dal's cheek.

"Fuck. Ruining my makeup," Dal growled.

"You're beautiful. Nothing's going to touch that." Piper spoke softly. She desperately wanted to kiss Dal's tears away, but they weren't at that point yet. "Dal, look at your life. You let Viola help you, and you know that you love each other. You have Ruby. Plus look at what you do every day. This room is full of people wanting to help your rescue vision."

"But I'm not complete. I suck at romantic love." Dal's declaration was followed by a gulp. "I don't want to. Not anymore."

"You tried with Chantal."

Dal waved a hand back and forth, dismissing Chantal. "I probably chose her because I knew she'd never break my heart. She didn't love me, and I knew I didn't deeply love her—my heart was safe. But I've seen my marriage, my decisions, as a failure on my part, controlling my life for these past several years."

Piper digested this—Dal had never deeply loved Chantel. If Chantel wasn't Dal's type, maybe there was hope.

"I'm essentially a divorced woman if that matters to you." Dal gently touched Piper's cheek. "Chantal signed. The final dissolution is just legal protocol, but the agreement is signed. Uncontested." Dal looked pleadingly at Piper. "Essentially divorced," she repeated.

Piper closed the space between them, offering Dal a soft kiss, then pulled back. "It matters to me. If only for you and Ruby." She studied Dal. "If I'm reading you right about us, there's always a risk when you love someone. But if you don't take it, there's no chance of"— Piper waved between the two of them—"you and me. There have been lines, boxes, a wife contesting a divorce agreement, your past, and your personal pledge. Are you saying we have a chance of trying?"

Dal nodded but didn't speak.

"Love is work. For everyone," Piper said.

"Piper. I think we have more than just a chance of trying."

"Holy shit," Piper murmured, her heart hammering with the hope that Dal was saying what Piper thought she was saying. "Sackcloth and ashes, Granny."

"Yeah, holy shit, Granny." Dal laughed. "You're such a goody-two-shoes." She looked down at Piper's black boots. Then her tone softened as she added, "Your pink ones are my favorite."

"I suspect you'd like them even more if those goody-two-shoes were all I was wearing." She offered Dal her best cheeky smirk.

"Don't tempt me. I'm behaving myself so that I don't embarrass either of us," Dal cautioned Piper.

Piper sobered. She needed to hear more. "Are you ready to be rescued, Dal? I mean willing to trust. Willing to try. Like Fred. To love and be loved." Piper looked at the poster of the rescue dog. The one Dal was planning to hang on her wall.

Dal nodded that she was. "And my pledge, it was controlling my life, not giving me control."

"Who do you want to rescue you? Who do you see with you in this love and be loved?" Piper wasn't going to say it. This answer had to come from Dal. After all, Dal had been the one to walk away. Piper needed to hear exactly what Dal believed she wanted because Piper wanted to know just what she was putting her heart on the line for.

"You," Dal whispered.

Piper felt all the hope she'd been holding dissipate into reality. Dal wanted her. The relief was exhilarating. Piper wanted to twirl Dal the way Firebrand had twirled her a few minutes ago, but she refrained. She'd save that show of emotions for later.

As Dal was sniffling, Cate found them.

"Sorry to interrupt," Cate said. "I think the after-dinner program is waiting for you." She handed Dal a napkin she'd carried over.

"Of course. Thank you. Could you tell them I'll be right there?" Dal carefully dabbed at her face, visibly attempting not to mess up her makeup any more than it already was. Then she turned to Piper.

"You look divine," Piper assured her, leaning in and capturing Dal's mouth with her own, gently putting the hunger she felt into the kiss she gave Dal. A promising kiss. Then Piper took her hand and led Dal back to where they'd been sitting.

Dal grabbed her purse and took off for the restroom. Piper took her seat, then pulled out her phone and posted a quick blog entry— maybe she'd tell Dal about the blog later. She thanked Meg and Cate for their part in the evening while they waited for Dal to fix her makeup, and then Dal appeared on the stage and took the microphone, thanking everyone for their support of CritterLove Rescues.

After Dal had spoken about what this fundraiser meant to so many animals and thanked the attendees, the donors, Fiorra, and Piper for their contributions to the gala, she turned the microphone over to the singer and made her way back to the table.

"Before we get started with the evening's entertainment, I want to make sure that you all know there's a silent auction in the back with awesome items, and there's a dance floor right here for some dancing," Fiorra informed the audience. "This first song is a request by Dal and is dedicated to Piper, *with love*." The singer drew out those last two words. "So those two need to come up here and show us a slow dance that will scorch the dance floor while I sing a special song to them."

Dal couldn't believe how fast her heart was pounding. She'd never displayed her emotions this publicly before, but she needed Piper to know that she was willing to tell the world how she felt. To go on record. She wanted a future with Piper, and she needed to finish convincing her of that.

Dal held out her hand to Piper, imploring Piper to take it in a silent request.

Piper chuckled. "You're clearly the bushwhacker tonight. How do you know I can even dance?"

Dal pulled Piper up into her arms and the audience cheered. "I don't care if you can dance. I know you can kiss." Dal placed her mouth firmly on Piper's bewitching, grinning one, held it captive for a moment, then leaned back and returned her grin. "This is serious business, Piper Fernley. We're the opening spectacle at this Fiorra Firebrand show. You know I never dance publicly. But for you..."

"But for me...Well then, let's show them how it's done." Piper took Dal's outstretched hand and followed her onto the dance floor.

Fiorra announced, "For Piper." Then she broke into one of her most famous songs, Piper's favorite: "You Are the Garden of my Life."

Dal put her hands on Piper's waist and pulled her tightly against her front before she started the slow rock of her body, side to side, bringing Piper along with her. Piper's body fit perfectly against hers, those same peaks and valleys that had melded so congruently out there on the park pavement, against the office door—those contours still merged perfectly with the sway of Dal's body.

"Good song choice," Piper breathed into her ear.

"She didn't have a song titled You Are the Thorn in My Side." Dal chuckled. "Um—that cactus you gave me."

"Modified leaves," Piper faux-huffed. "I'd never have dared to give you thorns. You were prickly enough."

"Symbolizing *enduring love* if I remember correctly," Dal replied. Then she cleared her throat, leaned back, and looked directly into Piper's eyes. "I love you, Piper. I've realized how much. Too much to not be with you. I need you in my life." Dal searched Piper's glistening eyes.

"I love you too, Dal."

"Thank God, because I was afraid that you'd given up on me," Dal said. "I didn't want to fail tonight at showing you how I feel. That I know what I want."

Piper pulled her closer and spoke into Dal's neck. "As if the overachiever could fail."

Dal struggled to keep her mind off what she wanted to do to Piper. They had the entire night. And every night after. Dal was finally comfortable thinking about their future together. She knew that she trusted Piper. Trusted Piper with her heart. She'd finally found the right woman.

Holding tightly to Piper, Dal said, "I was nervous. I've never done anything like this before, in front of everyone." Then she gave Piper another gentle, promising kiss. "But I needed you to believe me. To know that I'm ready for *us*."

"Well, you don't get your grade until we finish the night. No partial credit." Piper's tone was laced with delight as she offered the warning to Dal.

Dal laughed. "This was the hard part. The rest of the night is a surefire A."

Piper offered her best harrumph. "I'm counting on an A-plus performance, Dahlia Noble."

DANCING IN THE WEEDS WITH PIPES THE UNPLUGGED

"The Wisdom and Beauty of Dogs"

Fred's advice: Don't let your past ruin your future.
My advice: Listen to the dog.

CHAPTER TWENTY-TWO

After making sure the event was being properly closed down, Dal carried the centerpiece from their table toward the car as Viola headed out several feet in front of them and called back over her shoulder that she'd be sitting in the back seat with the flowers and Fred's poster so Piper could sit up front with Dal.

As they walked, Piper said, "I need to tell you that I write a blog... *Dancing in the Weeds* with Pipes the unPlugged. Call it therapy." She glanced at Dal. "I just wanted you to know. You can read the whole thing later if you want." Piper stopped walking and held up the phone. "But here, you can see the Fred blog that I posted this evening. 'The Wisdom and Beauty of Dogs.'"

Dal leaned in, read the post, and laughed. "Thanks for sharing with me. I'm going to love reading all of them because rumor has it that Pipes the unPlugged has a special place in my heart."

They continued to walk, the giant floral display brushing Dal's chin and cheek as she wrapped her arms around the full vase and angled it, so she could see where she was going. "To remember this night, maybe I'll press and dry these flowers for posterity."

"Sure." Piper walked close enough to help if Dal stumbled. "You'll need a ginormous place to do that—you didn't go for a small arrangement."

"I needed a statement. For you, babe."

Babe. Piper didn't even try to repress her grin. "A king-sized place. We could spend the night pressing them between the box spring and mattress of your bed."

Dal emitted a disapproving *tsk-tsk*, shaking her head. "I don't think so. I've got other ideas for what's going to occupy our time and be pressed against that mattress."

Piper looked at her sideways, not even trying to suppress how happy she was.

As they rode into the hills above Oakland, she told Dal and Viola that her dream of becoming an animal welfare and human rights lawyer was going to come true because Cate and Meg were investing in her future. She listened to their enthusiastic congratulations and supportive comments, considering that all of those missing pieces in her life were finally falling into place.

When they reached the house, they brought everything inside, the floral arrangement finding a place on a side table in the living room. Then Dal let Einstein out for a moment, and with her hands free, Piper went back and left her dress boots at the door.

Viola made a show of yawning loudly. "Leave me your apartment key on the dining table, Piper, so Ruby and I can stop in and feed Sunny his breakfast after I pick her up from her sleepover. Elsie told me if she sees you at the rescue tomorrow, you're fired." Viola cast them a tickled pink look and headed over to the top of the stairs that led down to her unit.

Retrieving her keys from the pocket of her blazer, Piper did as Viola asked in an effort to avoid scrutiny of the blush she knew she wore.

"You two can sleep in tomorrow. Just in case you don't get to sleep right away." Viola's satisfied chuckle echoed in the stairwell before she started the descent to her quarters. "Lock your door, Dahlia," was the final instruction she threw back over her shoulder.

"Well, I guess we've got Viola's blessing." Dal removed her high heels before taking a piece of chocolate from a bowl on the dining table, then poured them each a glass of wine.

When Piper set her wineglass down after a few sips, Dal did the same, letting their hands brush. Dal's hungry eyes asked permission for more, and Piper knew that her own were conveying assent. Dal got the message and gently backed Piper up against the kitchen countertop and kissed her. Not simply the short, public, promising kisses of early tonight that affirmed their love. This was the start of fulfilling that promise. This was a slow, sensual kiss. Exploring and prolonged. Sublime.

"I love kissing you." Piper looked directly into Dal's dark indigo eyes. "I thought the kiss three weeks ago was the best in the forty-five hundred years of recorded history of kissing, but this one was no runner-up."

"We're going to set some kissing records tonight." Dal closed the space and began peppering Piper's cheeks, her eyelids, her jawline. Finally shifting her mouth to Piper's ear, her breath warm and welcome, Dal spoke in a soft voice. "I want you to know that I love you...Ruby loves you too, and Viola might be your biggest cheerleader."

"And I'd been working on Einstein."

"He's a member of your fan club too." Dal stepped back, fixing her gaze on Piper. "So, before we go lock the bedroom door, there are a few things I want to discuss."

"Uh-oh. This sounds serious." Piper felt a touch of trepidation.

"Serious is exactly what I am. About you. That's why I want to talk to you." Those darkened eyes with dilated pupils, those tender upturned lips—love graced Dal's features, putting Piper at ease.

"You want a prenup?" Piper couldn't keep the tease out of her voice. "There's six months until you need that." Then Piper redirected her comments. "I want some dating, for the sheer pleasure of wooing you."

"Dating." Dal confirmed the word as if that was exactly what she had in mind too, and then she laughed. "*Wooing*, huh? Sounds like something your granny might have said."

"Hey, don't knock wooing. I'm sure my granny would never have considered wooing you the way I plan to woo you." Piper offered Dal a suggestive once-over inspection, silently acknowledging the deepening desire, her throbbing center.

Dal laughed again before she sobered. "I'm serious, only because I don't want to blow this. I think we need to go on some real dates, besides ones with a five-year-old as a chaperone. I want romantic dates for my mental scrapbook when we're old and gray together."

"What about sleepovers?" Piper asked, conjuring a cross between a pouting and pleading expression for Dal.

"Now don't you look hopeful. Hell yes. But I don't want to move in together until we've spent more time growing this love affair. I want to create the memories of getting to know you better, of falling more deeply in love." Dal waited, looking rather uncertain of what Piper's reaction might be.

Piper embraced her, knowing Dal had taken an enormous leap in the relationship, had made a commitment. "Thank you. Just tell me what you need."

"I need you, Piper. Starting with tonight." Dal swallowed hard, looking vulnerable.

"Just try to get rid of me." Gently brushing Dal's hair behind her ear, exposing her neck, Piper reassured her. "You've got me. I want you to know that you're the answer to all my wishes on stars."

Dal nodded, and Piper traced a light caressing trail of kisses right up her neck, the pulsing of Dal's beating heart palpable as Piper pressed against that silky-smooth softness before moving to Dal's jawline. When Dal responded by teasing her earlobe with her tongue, Piper turned her head and moved back to Dal's mouth for a continued tasting of the chocolate on her tongue.

Finally, Piper slowed things down enough to say, "I want to create memories too. We need to spend time together. Chitchatting, exchanging flowers or prickly plants, weekend trips, slow dancing."

"I'm glad we agree on that. One other thing." Dal cleared her throat. "I want you to know that I haven't slept with anyone since we met."

The statement pleased Piper. "Just to clarify, like *in the park* met, or *in the office* met? Just wanting to know if you were sold on me when I cushioned your fall, or whether it was my Popeye shirt and black-and-blue vest." Piper grinned again as she offered Dal some memories of their initial encounters, the beginning of her own scrapbook of memories.

"I could say it was the pink sneakers, but I was missing you before I met you. I walked out of a bar—alone—the night before Lake Merritt. I knew I needed you in my life." Dal bent forward and pulled Piper close before leaning back again so they could lock gazes. "I just wanted to tell you that I've been tested and I'm clear. I'd never do anything to hurt you."

"And you're safe with me. I don't just mean your health—I mean your heart." Piper paused to let those words sink in. "But I was tested a while ago. There's been no one since." Piper touched Dal's hand. "I'd been holding out for you a long time before the park encounter."

Dal nodded before saying with some fake indignation in her tone, "So, I guess I'm going to be girlfriend number five in your life history?"

"Just the long way home. But true love number one—one and only." Piper placed her hand over her heart.

"All those exes were just the long way home." The warmth in Dal's eyes didn't escape Piper's notice.

"Exactly. So that I could find my way to you—my heart knows it has finally found love, Dal. The completes me, contentment kind. Now about that sleepover...just to prove how compatible we are, in the interest of full disclosure. I'm checking you out, being thorough."

"As your former boss, I can verify that you always were thorough at work." Dal projected an excellent imitation of her professional boss demeanor.

"Uh-uh. Not even close to being work. But I promise to be thorough, not a single millimeter left in question." Piper ran her tongue slowly across her lower lip and tilted her head, waiting for Dal to respond.

Dal took her hand and led her down the hall to the bedroom.

❖

As Dal pushed the bedroom door closed behind them and locked it, Piper allowed all of the pent-up attraction she'd been feeling for Dal to flood her body. She'd sampled it at their first encounter when she'd cursed her libido as she'd been pinned on the ground with Dal on top of her, but now it was so much more exquisite with the love that came with the lust. Dal leveraged her body and moved Piper backward. With Piper pressed against the barrier to the rest of the world, Dal gently turned Piper's face upward before she closed her eyes and leaned in, capturing Piper's mouth in a moaning kiss.

Finally, Dal backed off enough to speak. "A sleepover, hmm?"

"I wasn't planning on sleeping. Unless you're just too tired for anything else."

Dal's mouth captured hers again in a display of unmistakable desire. Piper responded with her own weeks and weeks of delayed longing. Piper didn't want to break away to even breathe. It was too good. Too delicious.

Finally drawing Piper from the door after pushing her fingers through Piper's ringlets, Dal stepped back, her lips swollen and her eyes bright. Dal sucked her lower lip between her teeth before she released it to give Piper a sultry smile. "Sleep *never* crossed my mind."

God, Piper loved that rich seductive voice, this woman. She ignored the urge to just lift the hem of Dal's dress that was preventing her from kissing all the places she needed to kiss. Because she wanted to do this right. Because Piper wanted this first time in a future lifetime of shared lovemaking to go down in the writing of her life, in this chapter, as perfect.

Reaching across the space between them, Piper turned Dal around to face away and lifted Dal's hair so she could unzip the classy attire, giving herself permission to slowly, deliberately let her mouth worship the back of Dal's neck and then her shoulders. Dal tilted her head forward to offer Piper better access. The taste of Dal and the natural fragrance mixed with a hint of jasmine pushed Piper's slow linger to more urgent action. Piper made sure she touched skin as she encouraged Dal's dress down below her shoulders, past her hips, in its slow descent to the floor, wanting to affirm their connection. There had been little possibility of resisting Dal when the dress was on, and she stood no chance as it slipped off Dal's beautiful body.

Piper looked down at the pile of elegant cloth at her feet. "A *take me to bed tonight* dress."

"Damn right. At least I was hoping so," Dal drawled.

"There was no way I could have resisted you when I walked into that event tonight," Piper grumbled, but she knew that her expression couldn't conceal her amusement.

"Oh, babe, you didn't stand a chance from the time an air horn went off on a jogging trail and I landed on top of you. That was our call to destiny." Dal's eyes danced with her declaration.

Piper was delighted with this romantic Dal. "I love this version of you. Not that I don't love the chitchat version, the boss version, the maternal version, the rescue-animal version. But I didn't see the romantic version coming. You were so rude. And it took so long to get here."

Dal gently brushed Piper's cheek with her fingertips, studying her face. "You had to wait because I wouldn't tell you I wanted there to be an *us* unless I was sure. We both needed me to be sure." Dal didn't ease her examination of Piper, her intense gaze holding Piper's eyes captive so she couldn't look away. "I am sure, Piper." There was no doubt about the conviction in Dal's voice.

Piper nodded. "I'm sure too." Then she playfully nudged Dal. "Even with the rude."

Dal emitted a bogus huff. "You haven't seen rude, but I'm going to show you. I'm here now, for good." She planted another steamy kiss on Piper's mouth that Piper took as a sign that Dal was ready to stop the chitchat and get on with things.

"For *good*?" Piper asked in a mock incredulous tone. "Not goody-two-shoes good, I hope."

"Okay. Your granny might not approve." Dal winked. "Wicked... wicked good."

Piper decided it was both rude and wicked when Dal impeded her final removal of Dal's delicate lacy ivory bra that was barely doing its job, along with its matching silk bikini undergarment, both rude and wicked when Dal began deftly undoing the buttons that had served as tiny barricades to the opening of Piper's pale pink shirt. The barricades that had been helping divert Piper's focus from her own needs and onto Dal's.

Piper sucked in a breath, her desire for this woman escalating from the budding anticipation that she'd felt slow dancing at the gala to the current full bloom of heated arousal as her shirt fell open. She let Dal remove the top and run her fingers down Piper's front to the closure of Piper's slacks, freeing them as well. But through the sensual haze, Piper took a turn and peeled off the scant attire still concealing the last of Dal's body, recognizing that everything that either of them had experienced leading to this moment was just the precursor to bringing the two of them together.

As Piper's undergarments fell to the floor with Dal's, they both paused to linger on the ivory-hued silk bikini lingerie and the violet cotton boy shorts with a tiny unicorn looking back at them intertwined in a heap on the floor. They gazed at each other, Piper seeing the same mirth that she was feeling reflected in Dal's sparkling eyes, the glorious realization that the dichotomy of their styles worked for them. And standing there nude, without a stitch of covering, Piper knew they both recognized that all that mattered was that they were two women who had found themselves and then each other. Who loved and were loved.

❖

Dal was the first to move on from reflection to action, ready to show Piper what risking a life together meant. She was no stranger to lust, but she'd never dared love another woman like this before. To love with her entire being. To allow herself to feel whole. Or maybe it was Piper who made her whole, the missing piece. While that was as terrifying as anything she'd ever encountered, she knew that she was all-in. Dal no longer had any control over the emotions she was feeling. This wasn't about her past. It was about her future.

They never actually made it between the sheets. Dal waltzed Piper backward to the bed, naked and revealed in a presentation that sent Dal's heart into an erratic elated rhythm. This was a display of unrestrained desire on both their parts.

It wasn't simply the aesthetic impressiveness, the appeal of Piper, that put Dal into overdrive, although Piper was as enchanting and genuine in her current state of undress as she was in her pink sneakers, just as she was in personality. But what put Dal's heart in her throat was what Piper openly conveyed to Dal, the love and want that Piper held for her without reservation or calculation. Simple, beautiful love. Piper had chosen her. It allowed Dal to throw away all the constraints, the shackles, that had defined her life for so long. She trusted Piper, and she wanted to love this woman and share a life with her. Dal wanted to be the only one Piper desired to ever share a bed with again.

"The old me would have told you that I was going to fuck you senseless." Dal slid on top of Piper and peppered her eyes, her cheeks, her jaw, her throat with ravenous kisses, working hard to regulate her breathing. "But I'm not," she crooned into Piper's ear, the husk in her voice evident.

As Dal paused, Piper offered a strangled objection, and Dal chuckled. Then she grew serious. "Patience, bushwhacker. I'm going to offer you my heart, my trust, and the best show of making love until you're delirious that I possibly can."

Piper nodded. "Do your best, Dal, because I'm an overachiever too when it comes to loving you."

With that, Dal placed her mouth on Piper's and pinned her with a decisive press of skin to skin that made both of them move past any thought of further talk. Dal worked her way down Piper's body. First pausing at receptive breasts, she trailed her fingers up the enticing flesh before stopping to squeeze them with an optimal amount of pressure. Enjoying Piper's reaction, she allowed her mouth to descend on the rose-colored peaks that had haunted her dreams since she'd viewed them in the mirror after Piper's injury. She caressed and seduced those nipples, enjoying the approving movement of Piper beneath her.

"Easy, babe. We'll get there," Dal told Piper, who moaned while pressing into the curves of her body, a primal moan that represented more than just sex. This was where the long way home had led—giving love, receiving love, sharing love.

Dal traveled down Piper's body. She touched and grazed abdominal muscles taut with anticipation, then traversed her way to the soft nest of red curls between Piper's legs, enjoying every second of slowly bringing Piper to eventual ecstasy, divine torture reflected in the readiness she encountered as she mapped out Piper's arousal and the pace of the rise and fall of Piper's hips.

Dal found passage into Piper's center, her hand in harmony with the movement of the undulating dance of Piper's need, even as Piper's body sped up the tempo. Curving her fingers into a come to me beckon as she guided their lovemaking, Dal added her thumb to the symphony of stimuli directing that dance, circling the engorged place of Piper's greatest sensitivity.

Then Dal repositioned Piper onto her stomach and elevated Piper's hips back toward where she knelt behind Piper, offering the woman that she loved the very best kiss at the core of her femininity that Piper could experience—one that would be banned from any record book. But, Dal reflected, if it were made official, the record would describe Piper face down, whimpering against the mattress, her smooth back inclined up to that perfect pale rounded ass elevated above her knees, and the consummate kiss presented in prelude to parted inner thighs in nips and nibbles, then shifting to the curve of Piper's hips, until, finally, fully delivered with lips and tongue tasting and sucking and stroking—

testimony to the depth of Dal's emotions as Piper rocked and writhed at the precipice of culminated passion.

That glorious kiss would have completely dismantled Piper, carried her past that point of no return. But much to Dal's pleasure, Piper seized control and turned onto her back, pulling Dal up over the length of her body before rolling both of them to place Dal in position beneath her. Piper took the lead, delivering a slow, personal brand of erotic, teasing torment. And when Dal was ready to explode, when the rising release of her longing started to radiate out from her essence, she reached a hand to stroke Piper's core, both of them surging in synchrony over the pinnacle, to be possessed by the roar of fulfillment in this dance they shared.

Dal lay in Piper's embrace, spent in the best possible way, inhaling and exhaling in unison with Piper. She savored the moment they shared, heartbeat to heartbeat, letting this moment wash over them and cocoon them. Letting the miracle of loving and being loved sink in. Until they had rested enough to share that love all over again.

When they were both sated, Dal lay there, reflecting on the joy of finally feeling she was where she was supposed to be, at peace that she'd found the answer, deeper than flesh, that had led her out of that bar. Reflecting that maybe having control of her life actually felt like this.

If her bed was a garden, it was a spring storm and sunshine that described their lovemaking. She didn't have Piper's knowledge or vocabulary of botany. But she didn't need it. What had just happened in this bed—the life-affirming drenching of emotion and need ignited by a lightning bolt of passion that spread from her center and delivered her to a thunderous clap of completion, the sweet warm rays of tender touching and whispered wooing—all of those things did what a spring storm and sunshine did in a garden. The precious seedling of their love that had been planted over the past many weeks had sprouted and grown. Dal only wanted more, to nurture their love to its full potential, to savor the transformation to a full-bloomed permanent linking of their lives, sharing this garden bed forever. Taking the rest of the journey on the same path, to a shared future.

❖

Dal and Piper took a shower together, lingering in the moment before finally drying off. Looking in the mirror as she appreciated the reflection of their nude bodies, Piper noted that they both glowed in their new knowledge of each other and in anticipation of all that remained to be discovered.

When they arrived in the kitchen for coffee and breakfast, Piper in borrowed clothes, Viola and Ruby were at the table and back from feeding Sunny. Einstein was sitting on the floor next to Ruby's chair, watching for scraps to fall.

"Piper," Ruby squealed, jumping down from her seat to hug her. "Viola said you had a sleepover with Mom. I had one at Katie's too." Ruby crawled back up onto her chair.

Dal looked at Piper, a twinkle in her eyes as she waited for the response. They had agreed to be open with Ruby at a level that was appropriate for a five-year-old.

"We did. We had a late night at the gala, so your mom invited me over, and we slept in. Thanks so much for feeding Sunny his breakfast. How is he doing this morning?"

"He was happy to see us. He said he wanted to know where you were, so I told him." Ruby looked at the dog. "I think Sunny should have a sleepover with Einstein."

Dal smiled, watching the interaction while Viola tried to keep a straight face.

Piper told Ruby, "Maybe someday soon. Dogs and cats don't always get along, so first they have to meet each other and then spend some time getting to know each other."

"Like you and Mom."

"Yup. Getting to know someone is a good idea before you decide that you want to spend a lot more time together," Piper replied. Dal and Viola nodded their agreement.

"We already knew you for a while. And you slept over before when you were hurt," Ruby stated. "First you meet them. Then you get to know them better. Then you have a sleepover."

"If that's okay with everyone involved," Piper said. They all struggled to listen to Ruby with serious expressions.

"I'm finished eating." Ruby swallowed the last bite of her cereal. "Can I go play in the living room with my stuffed animals and Einstein?"

"Sure." Dal watched Ruby hop off her chair, dump her bowl in the sink, and head out to the living room, trailed by the dog.

Viola stood up to head downstairs. "Might do a little bungee jumping today. I'm happy you two worked things out. Like Ruby said, getting to know each other, sleepovers, and then…" Viola chuckled as she left the kitchen.

Dal leaned over, quickly brushing her lips across Piper's. "Prelude to the next sleepover," she whispered.

Piper nodded and grinned as she watched Dal eat a piece of toast. "I don't know how you beat an A-plus. Best night of my life." Then she leaned back, slowly savoring her coffee, wrapping her hands around the mug until the tips of her fingers touched. Piper finally felt complete.

Einstein came back into the room, followed by Ruby. "Just so you know, Mom, I really like Piper."

"I do too, Ruby-Doo. We're going to go on some more dates, kind of like we did to the rescue and the zoo, but just Piper and me. So that we can get to know each other even better. One step at a time."

"And have some more sleepovers. Einstein told me that he wouldn't mind meeting Sunny. He doesn't know any cats. Once they're friends, a sleepover's okay. After that, he said we can all be a family together." Ruby turned and headed back to the living room, Einstein trailing behind.

"The kid's got a plan." Dal chuckled.

"Collaborating with the dog," Piper added.

"I named him Einstein for a reason." Dal laughed, taking Piper's hand. "And I just read some advice from a brilliant blogger who I happen to love. Her advice was to listen to the dog."

"She is brilliant," Piper agreed. "Smart enough to be madly in love with you."

DANCING IN THE WEEDS WITH PIPES THE UNPLUGGED

"Dancing with Dahlia"

There were those shooting stars streaking across the sky with teasing promises. And those first stars—star light, star bright, I wished my wish all those nights. That forever kind of love...I saw it, wanted it, never gave up on hope.

But then there was reality. Me, trying to find my way home on that bumpy highway of life, some days with a little more road rash than others. At times, I was moving along at breakneck speed. Or sitting on the shoulder, no spark in the plugging. A past history of stalls and breakdowns. Stopped by another hard-ass, hard-hat detour with a Prepare to Be Delayed sign, waving individuals through the dirt and exhaust, one by one, at that slowdown to reaching true love. I was trying to enjoy the scenery, looking for love in the blooms on the side of the road. Not finding it in the weeds. Then, in a heartbeat, when least expected, because you can't plan the place or time for true love, it happened. I crashed right into it. Right into her. That beautiful flower that didn't want to be picked.

So here we are after taking the long way home. Living our way to this destination, a place where we both can blossom. And me, no longer needing to wish on stars. Madly in love. Dancing with Dahlia until the last words on the last page of this life that I am writing...happily ever after.

About the Author

Julia Underwood (https://juliaunderwood.net) grew up loving animals and pursued a degree in veterinary medicine. She's been blessed to have wonderful family members, friends, and a parade of pets to enrich her life. She's an avid writer and reader. The joy of discovering the journey to novel writing cannot be overstated. She hopes her admiration for the love, dedication, and competence women bring to the multitude of roles they fill in this complicated world comes through in her writing.

Books Available From Bold Strokes Books

Can't Buy Me Love by Georgia Beers. London and Kayla are perfect for one another, but if London reveals she's in a fake relationship with Kayla's ex, she risks not only the opportunity of her career, but Kayla's trust as well. (978-1-63679-665-9)

Chance Encounter by Renee Roman. Little did Sky Roberts know when she bought the raffle ticket for charity that she would also be taking a chance on love with the egotistical Drew Mitchell. (978-1-63679-619-2)

Comes in Waves by Ana Hartnett. For Tanya Brees, love in small-town Coral Bay comes in waves, but can she make it stay for good this time? (978-1-63679-597-3)

The Curse by Alexandra Riley. Can Diana Dillon and her daughter, Ryder, survive the cursed farm with the help of Deputy Mel Defoe? Or will the land choose them to be to the next victims? (978-1-63679-611-6)

Dancing With Dahlia by Julia Underwood. How is Piper Fernley supposed to survive six weeks with the most controlling, uptight boss on earth? Because sometimes when you stop looking, your heart finds exactly what it needs. (978-1-63679-663-5)

The Heart Wants by Krystina Rivers. Fifteen years after they first meet, Army Major Reagan Jennings realizes she has one last chance to win the heart of the woman she's always loved. If only she can make Sydney see she's worth risking everything for. (978-1-63679-595-9)

Skyscraper by Gun Brooke. Attempting to save the life of an injured boy brings Rayne and Kaelyn together. As they strive for justice against corrupt Celestial authorities, they're unable to foresee how intertwined their fates will become. (978-1-63679-657-4)

Untethered by Shelley Thrasher. Helen Rogers, in her eighties, meets much younger Grace on a lengthy cruise to Bali, and their intense relationship yields surprising insights and unexpected growth. (978-1-63679-636-9)

You Can't Go Home Again by Jeanette Bears. After their military career ends abruptly, Raegan Holcolm is forced back to their hometown to confront their past and discover where the road to recovery will lead them, or if it already led them home. (978-1-636790644-4)

A Wolf in Stone by Jane Fletcher. Though Cassilania is an experienced player in the dirty, dangerous game of imperial Kavillian politics, even she is caught out when a murderer raises the stakes. (978-1-63679-640-6)

The Devil You Know by Ali Vali. As threats come at the Casey family from both the feds and enemies set to destroy them, Cain Casey does whatever is necessary with Emma at her side to bury every single one. (978-1-63679-471-6)

The Meaning of Liberty by Sage Donnell. When TJ and Bailey get caught in the political crossfire of the ultraconservative Crusade of the Redeemer Church, escape is the only plan. On the run and fighting for their lives is not the time to be falling for each other. (978-1-63679-624-6)

One Last Summer by Kristin Keppler. Emerson Fields didn't think anything could keep her from her dream of interning at Bardot Design Studio in Paris, until an unexpected choice at a North Carolina beach has her questioning what it is she really wants. (978-1-63679-638-3)

StreamLine by Lauren Melissa Ellzey. When Lune crosses paths with the legendary girl gamer Nocht, she may have found the key that will boost her to the upper echelon of streamers and unravel all Lune thought she knew about gaming, friendship, and love. (978-1-63679-655-0)

Undercurrent by Patricia Evans. Can Tala and Wilder catch a serial killer in Salem before another body washes up on the shore? (978-1-636790669-7)